BADEN-
POWELL'S
BEADS

To Scott,
From your childhood doc

BADEN-POWELL'S
BEADS

book one
BEADS
SERIES

Paul D. Parsons

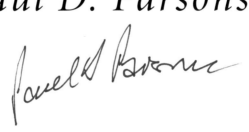

TATE PUBLISHING
AND ENTERPRISES, LLC

Published by Tate Publishing & Enterprises, LLC
127 E. Trade Center Terrace | Mustang, Oklahoma 73064 USA
1.888.361.9473 | www.tatepublishing.com

Tate Publishing is committed to excellence in the publishing industry. The company reflects the philosophy established by the founders, based on Psalm 68:11,
"The Lord gave the word and great was the company of those who published it."

Book design copyright © 2012 by Tate Publishing, LLC. All rights reserved.
Cover design by Kristen Verser
Interior design by Sarah Kirchen

Published in the United States of America

ISBN: 978-1-61862-090-3
1. Fiction / Thrillers
2. Fiction / Crime
12.12.30

To the memory of my parents,
Warren Allen Parsons and Martha Jane Parsons,
both of whom passed away just before
this book became a reality.

ACKNOWLEDGMENTS

Baden-Powell's Beads is a work of fiction. Some of the characters, places, and events are real, but their actions and dialogue are products of my imagination.

Many people provided help and encouragement in the writing of this book. I'd like to thank my writing buddies, Tim Champlin and Rick Romfh, for the hours spent editing and polishing; Diane Curtis for her expert and thorough review of the final manuscript; Drs. Star Evins and Joel Locke for their early excitement and discussions in the surgeon's lounge; Vince Flynn for his enthusiastic support and assistance with the early chapters; the staff at Gilwell Park in England; and mostly, my wife, Sue, who allowed me the time and sacrificed by my side through every emotional revision, query, meeting, rejection, pitch, acceptance, edit, and design.

The professionals at Tate Publishing have been a joy. Jessica Browning picked up details in the editing and characters I'd overlooked for years. Kristen Verser worked with me until we got the cover where I felt it should be. The feather Zulu mask pictured on the cover is by artist Virgil M. Walker and hangs in my home.

PROLOGUE

SOUTH AFRICA, 1888

Bodies of native tribesmen littered the battlefield; clouds of black flies swarmed the carcasses. Captain Baden-Powell stood amongst the dead—a stark contrast to the gory scene. Clad in a sweat-drenched British uniform of khaki waistcoat and trousers, he carefully picked his way through the carnage, his black, leather ankle boots crusted with dirt and dried blood. For days he'd commanded the small army outpost, repelling the attacking natives. Now his foes lay dead, and he hoped to learn more. What had driven them head-on into overwhelming British firepower? They'd done this before at Rorke's Drift and Blood River.

A few paces behind, camp surgeon Lieutenant D. Ernst Freeman assessed the injured, though he could do little more than wrap cloth about gaping, torn flesh wounds. The doctor tried to chase away those who wished to plunder the dying. His pleas, and those of the wounded Zulus, fell on unsympathetic ears as native tribesmen helping the British poured onto the battlefield and slaughtered those still living—the soldiers unable, perhaps unwilling, to stop them. Dr. Freeman carried a Zulu sword—more like an Arabic scimitar, really—captured in the early days of the conflict, its beveled edge finer than the sharpest Toledo blade. He'd become adept at guillotine-type amputations using the heavy, monstrous weapon.

Baden-Powell shook his head at the futile efforts of the doctor, but knew it pointless to interfere. As he watched, the doctor, with surgical precision, slashed from overhead through the mangled knee of a downed Zulu warrior, cleanly separating the ruined leg from its owner. Then with speed and strength belying his diminutive size, he wrapped the gaping stump with the loin cloth from another dead body—all accomplished before his patient had time to object or cry out. Uttering words of assurance the frightened Zulu had no way of understanding, Dr. Freeman moved on to the next.

Beneath his overgrown mustache and pith helmet, Baden-Powell grinned with pride at the stalwartness of his fellow officer, then turned his attention back to the battlefield.

Nearly naked brown bodies, still clutching spears and shields, lay atop one another, cut down by British bullets. Their faces wore the painted masks of battle. A few bodies lay torn apart, struck by Baden-Powell's lone cannon. Before him, one poor soul pulled along the ground, the lower half of his body mangled, entrails snagging on scales of parched, crusted land. Baden-Powell ended the man's misery with a merciful shot to the head, then returned his sidearm to its leather holster. At the blast, Dr. Freeman glanced up, his eyebrows pinched together and lips creased. Upon seeing the condition of the executed man, his features softened and he nodded once, then returned to his ministrations. Those scavenging the bodies skulked away from the British officers. They'd harvest plenty elsewhere on the battlefield.

A hyena bolted at the noise, then circled back, its blood-soaked snout hanging low to the ground. Baden-Powell let his hand drop away from his sidearm, resisting the urge to put a bullet through the filthy beast. Each had his job to do.

The battle had raged for days. Baden-Powell never doubted the outcome: the very idea a bunch of savages could defeat Her Majesty's forces—unthinkable. His men hadn't shared his confidence. They'd nearly exhausted their ammunition. The number of natives willing to take a British bullet seemed endless.

Convinced the leader's body lay out here somewhere, Baden-Powell continued his search. The South African sun beat down on the veldt as it had for millions of years. Shadows of vultures swept the landscape. Buzzing insects disturbed the deathly quiet. Sweat rolled down his face and neck.

Baden-Powell's mind wandered as he picked his way through the carnage. He studied the bodies and marveled at their similarity—tall and of similar build, skin color, hair, face paint, lack of fat—nearly identical.

He wasn't sure what inspired men to follow him. His soldiers had done exactly as commanded, triumphing over vastly superior enemy numbers. Some of his authority came with rank, surely not his slight stature, and he wondered about Chief Dinizulu and why the Zulus followed him to certain death. Shaka, Mzilikazi, and Dinizulu's father, Cetshwayo, had such power. What set them apart? Perhaps he might find a giant, a freak of nature, a physically awe-inspiring specimen who led through fear and brute strength. Had this chief led the charge on the first day? Probably not. His body would be among those killed last, but dead on this field it would certainly be.

Baden-Powell paused to observe a pack of jackals fifty meters away. With enough here to feed them and their cubs for weeks, they wandered—scavenging. The largest froze. His head dropped, ears and tail lowered, as he backed away from a pile of bodies. The other jackals stopped their meanderings, and they, too, retreated from this peculiar mound of dead natives.

B-P, as he was informally known, signaled to the doctor, then drew closer to learn what spooked the jackals. He approached the curiously arranged stack of bodies. Each slain warrior's hair lay in dirty, long braids to at least shoulder length, imparting a Medusa visage, unlike any Zulus he'd seen before. All lay supine with white, oval shields facing outward, creating a turtle-back in the middle of this killing field. Had they died this way, or had others stacked them after death? B-P felt it too: something different here—something sacred.

With effort, he rolled one of the bodies off the pile, then another. Neatly arranged at the bottom of this fleshy grave stretched the body of Chief Dinizulu: better fed than the rest, his headdress constructed of otter skin and ostrich-plume feathers, his body arranged as if for burial. He looked at peace, lying on his back, his shield neatly atop, arms with cow tails tied above the elbows, and legs with similar décor above the knees. The chief's closely cropped hair stood in contrast to his guards'.

B-P removed the shield, revealing the ugly, lethal chest wound. At his side, Dr. Freeman shook his head and muttered a few words of hopelessness. Around the chief's neck and body curled a string of elaborately carved beads. B-P knelt to look closer and thought there must be over a thousand. Beneath the chief's chin, two dozen beads of a darker wood stood out, set apart by a series of knots—each bead unique, about the size of a fingertip, more oblong than round. Their carvings differed and appeared old, reminding him of artwork from ancient Egypt or the Middle East—hieroglyphics, perhaps. Baden-Powell took out his clasp knife. Kneeling, he reached to cut the cord holding the beads.

Suddenly, the corpse sat upright, a long *hiss* escaping the mouth. B-P stumbled backwards over a body and into the arms of Dr. Freeman, who appeared unfazed. Fresh corpses sometimes moved, but that knowledge made it no less frightening. The chief remained sitting, his head turned toward them, eyes open and staring. The bead necklace unwound from the chief's body and tumbled to the ground at their feet.

B-P recovered his composure and glanced about, straightening his coat and thanking the doctor. With one hand steadying his pith helmet, he leaned over the chieftain's body. A gentle prod from his walking stick, and the corpse fell back. B-P gathered the necklace. The unique, darker beads felt warm to touch. He replaced the shield over the body and backed away, turning toward the outpost camp. He'd examine these twenty-four beads with his magnifying glass when he returned to headquarters. These weren't trinkets, but something unique. He felt as though Chief Dinizulu had passed them to him.

As he and the doctor approached the outpost, an aide ran to say General Smyth wanted him immediately. With one last look at the battlefield, B-P coiled the strand of beads and slipped them into the large outside pocket of his waistcoat. Taking the doctor by the arm, he hurried to the general's tent. Inspection of the beads would have to wait.

1919

Baden-Powell returned to England from the Boer War a hero, with ticker-tape parades held in his honor through the streets of London. An ordinary man would've retired and spent his remaining years with his wife and children, but not Baden-Powell. During the Boer War, he'd defended the small village of Mafeking using, at times, the boys of the village for vital support tasks. He returned to England to find the boys in his own country lacking direction and purpose.

On July 29, 1907, B-P and a friend took twenty-two boys camping on Brownsea Island in Poole Harbour off the south coast of England—the first unofficial outing of what would later become the Boy Scouts.

Now a dozen years later, B-P wrapped up his first Scoutmaster training camp at Gilwell Park, near Chingford in Essex. He rummaged through his trophies and souvenirs, trying to come up with something suitable to give the nineteen men who had become the first official Scoutmasters. Mere certificates seemed neither appropriate nor adequate. He searched through his trunk of African relics.

His time on the Dark Continent strongly influenced his work with the Scouts. He recalled how every morning during that first campout on Brownsea Island, he'd summon the boys to duty with a *Matabele koodoo* horn obtained during the Boer War. He reverently lifted the old horn from the trunk.

How long had it been? Thirty years? How he missed the South African countryside; nothing quite like it anywhere in the world—a freedom and rawness that liberated his soul. Grassy savannas punctuated with brave, widely scattered acacia trees. Herds of magnificent beasts painted against the backdrop of snow capped mountains. Populations of people eking out an existence, melting into their surroundings rather than scarring the raw land to suit their needs. Many times he talked with his wife, Olave, about returning there to live out their remaining years.

Deeper in the trunk, beneath some old uniforms, he found a cloth bag tied with a drawstring. He opened the deteriorating bag and poured its contents into his hand: the beads. He'd forgotten about these beads. Holding them brought back emotions and memories of the battlefield and the Zulus—brave, brown warriors who fought for their land with crude weapons carved from nature. He lifted the smaller strand he'd strung so long ago, the special darker beads that had hung from Chief Dinizulu's neck. Twenty-four, just as he remembered. That would do it.

After returning the other items to his trunk, he took the beads to his study. He'd never placed them about his neck, never actually worn them. He opened the strand and held it before his face, slowly bringing it closer. His heart nearly beat out of his chest, a drumbeat increasing in tempo—chanting of warriors and pounding of bare feet. Sweat trickled down his temples; his breathing rapid and shallow. He saw Chief Dinizulu's head turn toward him and mouth a warning.

Startled, he dropped the beads to his desk. Almost immediately, his head cleared. He inhaled deeply and tried to slow his heart, though the drumbeat continued. Using the neckerchief he'd designed to be worn with the Scouting uniform, he dabbed the sweat from his face.

He opened the clasp knife he'd carried since the Boer War and slit the leather thong, spilling the beads into his empty letter box. The drums silenced and the feeling of urgency dissipated. He separated nineteen of them and threaded each individually onto soft leather thongs, all the while prepared to halt this activity immediately if the auditory apparitions returned. They did not.

He studied each bead. Though similar in size, each sported different carvings, lending credence to his thought that the beads had not originated with the Zulu in the Ceza bush of South Africa. Shaking these musings aside, he placed each necklace in its own envelope labeled with a different attribute of a Scout: Trustworthy, Loyal, Helpful, Friendly, Courteous, Kind, Obedient, Cheerful, Thrifty, Brave, Clean, and Reverent. Nineteen beads, twelve attributes; some beads would have a mate.

As he concluded his work, he had an overpowering feeling he was wrong to separate the beads. They seemed to call to each other, the whole being more than the individuals. *Rubbish!* He shrugged it off and placed the envelopes in his satchel.

The next day, nineteen new Scoutmasters broke camp and assembled on the campsite for the closing ceremony. He thanked them for their willingness to devote time to the betterment of the country's boys. He told a few humorous stories of his work with young men in South Africa. Finally, with all in good moods and laughter dying down, B-P addressed them as the unique assemblage they were.

"Men, there will never be another group like this. You are the first of what I hope will be a long tradition of leaders to mold our youth, making the world a better place. As a symbol of this bond, I'd like to present each of you with something unique."

Clouds rolled in from the west and chilled the men. A light drizzle threatened but did not dampen their enthusiasm.

"As you know, thirty years ago I had the honor of defending the Crown's interests in South Africa. I encountered many strange and wonderful things and peoples during that time. The Zulus formidably fought all who dared trespass on their territory. Their leaders appeared to be ordinary warriors, yet commanded the unquestioned loyalty of members of the tribe. One such leader, Chief Dinizulu, courageously led his men against us in battle until he and all his followers lay slain. I found his body on the battlefield—under rather peculiar circumstances, I must say."

The image of the chief's face disrupted his thoughts, though he quickly dismissed this and refocused on the task at hand.

"Around his body circled a necklace of intricately carved beads, which I suspect originated from another place and time. I've kept this necklace packed away and found it only last night as I searched for something to pass on to you to commemorate this occasion—twenty-four special beads, different from the others.

"I would, therefore, at this time, like to present each of you with what I believe to be a very special token of leadership. I will keep five, binding me to this group. You will each receive one of these beads, which I hope you will wear during special Scouting activities and, when the time is right, pass it on to your successors. Treasure and protect them, for they are unique and irreplaceable, as is each boy under your care."

He lifted the small, dark satchel at his side. "I've taken the liberty of naming each bead to represent one aspect of the Scouting credo. Please do not read anything into the name chosen for your bead. I will pass them out randomly. The man receiving 'Clean' should not think himself any cleaner than his neighbor."

To that, there followed uproarious applause and laughter. The nineteen men queued at the podium. B-P received them in turn and, opening each envelope, placed the talisman around each man's neck, whispering the name of the bead in his ear. He did not admonish them from divulging which bead they received, but he suspected each new Scoutmaster would keep it to himself.

The skies darkened, and the winds picked up. The temperature dropped noticeably, and B-P whisked the men off to shelter just before the cold, biting rains began. He shuddered and cursed the ill effects this inclement weather had on his aging joints. Though the men's spirits were not dampened, B-P could not shake the feeling he'd done something dreadful. *Rubbish!*

CHAPTER ONE

LANGLEY, VIRGINIA, 2005

"He doesn't look that tough." Patrick Dartson wiped the sweat from his face and threw the towel toward his bag of gear just off the mat. His partner, Adnan Fazeph, shrugged. A cool spring breeze blew through the open hangar doors on the abandoned military airfield. Winter had not yet released its hold on the nation's capital. "What is he? Five eleven? Two hundred? I got him by a good two inches and at least twenty pounds."

Just off the mat on the far side stood a wiry, ordinary, middle-aged man peering at them through dull eyes, his expression one of boredom. His nose angled twice before flattening onto his upper lip. Gray-flecked stubble matted his cheeks and chin. His close-cropped hair receded to the top of his head. He inhaled deeply, then blew it out, pulling his sweatshirt over his head, revealing a muscled chest of matted hair patches. The flesh of his torso was a twisted array of old scars—slashes from knives, pocks of bullet wounds, burns where no hair grew. One long, midline surgical scar stretched from his sternum, around his navel, and disappeared into the top of his sweatpants.

"Holy … " Patrick stared at his opponent. "How is he still alive?"

Adnan glanced toward the man, then quickly turned away. "Some say he not. Pain is part of him. Make him very dangerous. He no care if live or die." Adnan's practiced Middle-Eastern accent did little to hide his concern. "I think maybe you call this off. Is bad idea."

Three brutally large Marines in sweats stood to the side, nightsticks in hand. Their job was not to ensure a clean fight, only to prevent serious injury … or worse. A fourth, the biggest of all, stood in the center of the mat, arms folded across his chest, head swiveling between the contestants, a whistle dangling from his lips. This ritual battle was not required or even encouraged, but it dated back many years. Most top field agents in the covert branches of government had at least tried.

"Watch my back and make sure those goons over there don't interfere." Patrick tilted his head from shoulder to shoulder, stretching his neck muscles, then slipped in his mouthpiece. "He can be beaten."

"Maybe, but no one has yet," Adnan said. "A guy named Rapp at CIA fought him to draw. Both carried to sick bay. Took weeks to recover. I think maybe you no look like movie star in few minutes."

The history of Patrick's opponent was one of great speculation among those who served near the nation's capital. A veteran of multiple covert missions in hot spots around the world, he'd been permanently restricted from all future work after escaping from a Taliban prison where he'd suffered months of inhuman treatment and torture. He had neither friends nor family and lived secretly—under guard, it was rumored—somewhere in the hills around D.C. and was brought out from time to time for training purposes such as this. He was known only by a moniker: "Granite."

Four GIs, who'd been playing basketball on the far side of the hangar, wandered over, more interested in the pending combat than in their pick-up game. One tucked the basketball under his arm. The absence of the noise of ball on hardwood and sneakers squeaking added to the mounting tension. One of them pointed at the man facing Patrick and whispered to his buddy. His eyes widened, and the pace of the group picked up. Soon they stood a respectful distance from the mat but with an unobstructed view.

The huge, muscular Marine in the center of the mat blew his whistle and stepped out of the way. No rules were discussed. None existed. His three comrades separated and assumed positions on the other three sides of the square.

Adnan stepped in front of Patrick. "Never let up. He can take a beating."

Patrick said nothing, but instead glared at his opponent and channeled his anxiety into focus. The scarred man walked partway onto the mat and stood flat-footed, arms at his side, his bored expression replaced with one of calm confidence.

Patrick bounced on the balls of his bare feet and wiped the sweat from his brow, working his mouth to adjust his protective guard. He danced toward Granite and extended a closed hand, expecting the traditional fist-bump. Granite stood motionless, as though Patrick did not exist.

Okay, Patrick thought, *if that's the way you want it.* With the next bounce off his feet, he sprang into the air, spinning with legs extended. The heel of his right foot caught Granite squarely on the jaw. Patrick landed in perfect position, ready to defend or lash out. Granite staggered only slightly and slowly turned his face back toward Patrick, blood streaming from the corner of his unprotected mouth. With some concern, Patrick noted that the man's arms had not left his side, either for balance or defense, his expression unchanged, as if nothing happened. His tongue slithered toward the blood stream, then darted back inside as he worked his jaw. The damaged corner of his mouth turned up in a sardonic grin, though his eyes remained lifeless.

Heeding Adnan's warning, Patrick spun the opposite direction, landing another blow to the opposite cheek. Granite reacted as before, slowly turning his head back to center.

This time, Patrick spun low to the ground. If he couldn't knock him down, he'd kick his feet out from under him. His sweeping leg caught nothing but air, and instinct told him to roll to the edge of the mat—fast. Milliseconds later, the thud of Granite's feet landing hard on the padding reverberated inches from his left ear. Patrick shot to his feet. Granite's demeanor was unchanged. *What is he doing?*

Patrick stepped closer, faked with his foot, and shot an extended arm toward Granite's exposed neck. Again, he caught nothing but air. He dropped and rolled away, just under the lashing blow of Granite's fist. A second attack should have landed, and Patrick braced for the impact, rolling one more time before bounding upright. None came.

The scarred man stood ten feet away, wiping the slowing trickle of blood from his mouth with the back of his hand. This time, as his head turned toward Patrick, Granite's eyes locked on his with a crazed ferocity.

The moment of truth had arrived. To this point, Granite had been gauging Patrick's reflexes and training, his lethal onboard computer mapping strengths and weaknesses. Apparently, he'd seen enough. With arms now raised in front of him, palms outward as though closing a church service, Granite approached, leading with his left foot, trailing his right.

Patrick was dimly aware of the cheers and taunts of the basketball players. Adnan shouted hurried commands. The Marine guards shifted uneasily.

"Hold it right there!"

The voice echoed off the bare walls.

One of the Marine guards fired a net-gun over Granite. The other three converged on him with lightning speed. Two were thrown backwards off the mat. The third wrestled Granite to the ground, his nightstick pulled hard across the scarred man's throat. The other Marines recovered quickly and piled on, each grabbing a limb. Only the taut netting prevented Granite from attacking with his one free arm. The Marine with the whistle worked one arm free, drew his pistol, and shot a dart into Granite's leg, right through his sweats. Slowly, the struggles ceased.

Patrick and Adnan exchanged puzzled glances, though the look of relief on Adnan's face was unmistakable.

Director of Homeland Security Michael Cisneros approached, flanked by two Navy MP's.

"Who authorized this?" Cisneros said, his voice strong and reverberating around the old hanger, the vein at his left temple standing out. The Marines on the mat ignored him and slowly released their hold on Granite, though all remained coiled and alert. Their concern was not with Cisneros.

Patrick let out a deep breath and shook his head.

Adnan sprang forward, his hands clasped before him as though in prayer, his skinny, six-foot frame bowing repeatedly. "Thanks be to you, boss, and a blessing on your family. May your days be filled with joy and your—"

"Can it, Agent Fazeph," Cisneros barked. "You two get your things and come with me—now!"

"I could've taken him," Patrick mumbled as he reached for his gym bag.

"Yes, of course you could have," Adnan said. "I think he was ready to give up. Next time."

Cisneros shot them an angry glance, halting any further talk. The two agents fell in behind him and followed to the waiting limo. Cisneros ignored them on the ride back to his office, studying a brief he'd removed from his case. Neither agent spoke. The hammer would fall soon enough.

———

From his top-floor office not far from the Capitol, the early spring view of Washington, D.C. was spectacular: trees blossomed, grass greened, and people milled about as though released from their wintry prisons. Director Cisneros plopped into his chair and waved the two agents toward the seats opposite his desk.

"What is it with you people and that man?" he asked rhetorically.

Patrick knew he expected no answer and hoped Adnan would keep his mouth shut. His partner drew a breath, but stifled it in response to a look of reproach from Patrick.

Cisneros leaned onto his desk, hands clasped. "It's not enough you're on admin leave for shooting a vet in Nashville?"

"That was a justified kill, sir. The man was waving a shotgun at civilians, one of them being my father. The inquiry board—"

Cisneros silenced him with an icy glare. "You shouldn't have been there in the first place." He paused and reached to the corner of his desk. "But sometimes, things happen for a reason. What do you make of this?" He passed a sheet of paper across his desk. Patrick took it and settled in his chair, leaning toward Adnan to allow his partner a chance to peruse it with him.

Along the left side of the sheet was a column of symbols—twenty-four by quick count. They made no sense, even to Patrick's trained eye familiar with Cyrillic, Arabic, and Oriental script. Beside each symbol was typed a word, the top twelve words repeating in identical order opposite the bottom twelve symbols. He recognized these as being the credo of the Boy Scouts: Trustworthy, Loyal, Helpful, Friendly, Courteous, Kind, Obedient, Cheerful, Thrifty, Brave, Clean, and Reverent. A third column listed twenty names, all sounding British. Many of these names were linked by what looked to be hand-drawn lines to additional names, and these to still others, and so on—like a family tree. Three of the names to the far right were circled.

Patrick started to pass the sheet back to Cisneros, but Adnan snatched it from him and focused on the left column. Patrick could almost see his partner's brain working. The symbols meant something to him. Shouldn't be a surprise. Adnan's encyclopedic knowledge had solved unsolvable riddles before.

"Mean anything to you?" Cisneros asked.

"Not really, sir," Patrick said. "Appears to be a list of Brits with admirable attributes and nonsensical symbols."

"Look at the names again," Cisneros said. "Particularly the last on the right."

Patrick held his hand out to Adnan, who made no move to relinquish the sheet. Patrick grabbed a corner and tugged, but Adnan held fast, lost in concentration. "Hey," Patrick barked at his buddy. Adnan looked up, startled, and slowly his eyes focused on Patrick. He loosened his hold on the paper, allowing Patrick to take it. He then slipped back into whatever trance he'd been in. Patrick knew he was visualizing the sheet now permanently etched in his brain. Best to leave him alone when he got like this.

Patrick glanced at the paper. "Freeman. So what?"

Cisneros held his gaze. "We think that's Dr. David E. Freeman the Fourth."

Patrick hesitated only a moment, then his eyes flew open wide. "David E. Freeman the Fourth—my roommate at Dartmouth?"

Cisneros nodded. "He's in Memphis, Tennessee—"

"Finishing his orthopedic residency," Patrick interrupted. "Yeah, I know. Dad's recruiting him for his practice in Nashville. Why's his name listed? And where'd you get this?" Patrick asked, suddenly more interested.

"Came in this morning over secure lines, we think from inside Great Britain, but that's all we know. Whoever sent this knew what he was doing and didn't want us backtracking. That by itself earned a red flag." Cisneros paused. "See the three circled names at the top right?"

"They're all dead," Adnan said, his focus now back with the group.

Patrick turned toward him and raised an eyebrow.

Adnan continued. "The three circled were recently killed— beheaded, as I recall. All of them old men living in or around London." He glanced toward Patrick. "Don't you keep up with the news, old boy?" he said in perfect Cockney—vocal mimicry being another of his skills.

Patrick did study the department's daily summary of current events, but Adnan took it a step further—speed-reading dozens of periodicals and somehow storing the information in his freaky brain.

"He's right," Cisneros said. "Scotland Yard considers these to be ritualistic killings done by a band of South Africans illegally in the country."

Patrick leaned forward. "Do the Yardies have this list?"

"We don't think so," Cisneros said. "Whoever sent this seems to have purposely left them out of the loop." Cisneros pointed at the paper Patrick held. "See the last name to the left of Freeman's—the one connected by that shaky line?"

"Alphonse Baroni?" Patrick said.

"Checked into the VA Hospital in Memphis last night. Guess who's his doctor?"

"Oh, no way," Patrick exclaimed. "Next you're going to tell me we've got some suspicious African nationals showing up in Memphis."

"Moses Donnelley is the other name connected to Baroni. We don't know much about either yet, except that they fought together in World War II—out of England," Cisneros said.

"You think my friend David is in danger? Might be a little tough picking out a group of illegal Africans from the general Memphis population."

Adnan snatched back the information sheet and focused on the left-hand column of symbols.

"What is it, Adnan?" Cisneros leaned further onto his desk. "What do you see?" He, like all the others in the department, gave the lanky Arab-American a great deal of respect. The agent's intellect and deductive powers had become legendary in the six years he and Patrick had teamed together.

"These hieroglyphs," Adnan said, continuing to stare at the paper and occasionally twisting it from side to side. He slipped into his stilted English; something he practiced often—helped when infiltrating sleeper cells. "They might tell story when put in proper order. Is now jumbled: A falling sun … a North African king … a serpent … a powerful box or container." He pointed to a particular symbol and held the paper for them to see. "This one peculiar—drawn to show devastating destruction and death … or blissful salvation—is interesting."

"What was the motive for the murders?" Patrick asked.

"Unclear," Cisneros said. "Nothing missing except…" He paused, as though unsure of what he was about to say. "…except a bead each man wore about his neck. The men were very old and infirm. It was the first thing their caretakers asked about and appeared distressed when informed the beads were missing."

Patrick grabbed the paper from Adnan. "These symbols are bracketed in rounded rectangles, I thought for emphasis or contrast. Wouldn't be the outline of the beads, would it?"

"Very good, Agent Dartson." Cisneros leaned back in his chair. "I can't believe this represents any real threat to Homeland Security, but at the moment, I don't have any other assignments for you. What's your gut tell you?"

Patrick and Adnan were the best of several two-man teams given wide latitude by the department. Their job was to follow sketchy, strange leads to prevent another 9/11, using any means necessary. Cisneros had come to trust their instincts.

"I'm uneasy about this, sir, but that might be due to my personal connection to Freeman." He glanced toward Adnan. "What do you think, buddy?"

Adnan shuddered visibly, and Patrick caught just a flash of something he rarely saw in his partner's eyes—uncertainty. Adnan turned his gaze to the floor. "It is irrational. I cannot explain. This is no good … no good at all. With every fiber of my being, I want to turn from this." Patrick felt his stomach knot. This was very unlike his partner, who feared nothing and could endure inhuman levels of pain without flinching. "Yet I feel we cannot ignore this. This was sent to us on purpose—to you and me. This will change things."

"What the hell are you talking about?" Patrick projected a bravado he didn't feel, and he knew Adnan would see right through it.

Adnan shook his head and gazed at the symbols. Beads of sweat collected at his hairline.

CHAPTER TWO

MEMPHIS, TENNESSEE

Dr. David E. Freeman IV, lab coat slung over his shoulder, yawned as he shuffled down the darkened halls of the Veterans Hospital. One of the long overhead bulbs flickered, threatening to die. The cries of the ever-present demented patient echoed from somewhere farther down the hall. Freeman ran his fingers through his thick, dark hair and felt the tender spot on his forehead where he'd slammed into the underside of the top bunk when responding to the nurse's phone call. His six-foot frame fit poorly in those government-issue bunks in the house-staff call rooms.

Today marked the beginning of his final three-month rotation as chief resident at Campbell's Clinic, a large, private orthopedic practice that served as the training program for the University of Tennessee and covered many of Memphis's urban hospitals. His mind wandered: fourth in a family line of surgeons. His father, grandfather, and great-grandfather had all experienced this moment; the beginning of the end of training.

He'd strolled these VAH halls before; once as a medical student, once as a general surgery intern, and again as a junior ortho resident. He'd volunteered to take the first night on call, not yet trusting the junior residents and students. Two hours ago, he'd sent them home and was hoping to catch some shuteye before the full day tomorrow.

A patient spotted him and rattled his bed side-rails. "Hey, Doc." A string of obscenities followed, leading to a fit of productive coughing and spitting. *DTs: delirium tremens from alcohol withdrawal.* As a medical student, he'd have raced into the room and fretted over the patient.

A night nurse strode his direction, syringe in hand, and waved him away. "Don't worry about that one, Dr. Freeman. He does this all the time."

Freeman nodded and continued toward the nurses' station.

"Oh, Dr. Freeman," a second nurse said. "Thank you so much for coming."

"That's okay." He didn't want to annoy the nurses on his first night. They could make his time here miserable. "What do you need?"

"Mr. Baroni in 512 insisted I call you. He doesn't look good to me."

"Baroni… Isn't he the new admit with intractable back pain? World War II vet?"

"Yes, sir."

"What's he need? A sleeper?"

"No, sir. It's nothing like that." The nurse paused for a moment. "He says he's dying… and I think he might be right."

"Are his vitals okay? Have you called his medical doc?"

"He asked for you by name, Dr. Freeman. He said you're the reason he checked himself in here today."

Freeman hadn't yet met this Mr. Baroni. The patient had been in x-ray during rounds, and the junior resident, Jim McCallum, had summarized his case: Elderly white male admitted to rule out metastatic cancer of the spine. McCallum ordered CT and MRI scans for tonight; bone scan tomorrow. Freeman had asked about family. McCallum stated none had come with the patient. An old, black man claiming to be Baroni's friend had driven him here from West Memphis, Arkansas.

Freeman rubbed his eyes and took the chart from the nurse's outstretched hand. The old man had spiked a temperature to 103.

"They had trouble with him in x-ray," the nurse said. "Very confused. Had a problem keeping him in bed."

"Probably just sun-downing. He's allowed at his age."

"Worse than that," she said. "He's sweating, and his blood pressure's down. I've seen a lot of older people get confused after dark, but this is more than that."

Freeman continued leafing through the chart. Admission lab work looked fine. He knocked and eased open the door. "Mr. Baroni?" He entered the room with the nurse. "I'm Dr. Freeman. How you feeling tonight?"

The patient turned toward them, his eyes sunk into dark, deep sockets. Ill-fitting dentures pushed his thin lips abnormally outward. He looked like Gollum from *The Lord of the Rings*, but in a more pathetic way. The room had the smell of death.

Freeman approached the bed and placed a hand on the old man's withered leg under the sheet. He leaned and planted his other arm on the bed beside the patient's head.

Baroni's hand shot from the covers and grabbed Freeman's wrist.

"Were you a … Scout?" the old man asked, his wispy voice barely audible, his loose dentures clicking an irregular rhythm to his speech.

"A Scout? You mean a Boy Scout?"

The old man's grip tightened on his wrist. He nodded slowly, his breathing labored.

"Sure," Freeman said. "For two or three years. Made it to First Class. Why?"

Baroni loosened his hold. With both hands, he removed from his neck a thong threaded through an intricately carved wooden bead. He took Freeman's hand in both his own, folding into it the small bead.

"I've searched for you." The patient struggled to get the words out. "There are … more."

"More what, Mr. Baroni?" Perspiration beaded on the old man's upper lip and his already pale complexion blanched.

"Chief … Scout. Helpful. He had more," the old man whispered, pressing the bead harder into Freeman's hand.

Freeman sucked in a breath. He'd been with patients as they died; some seemed to know beforehand. Baroni had that appearance.

The heart monitor alarm sounded.

Freeman felt for a pulse at the patient's wrist. Nothing. He glanced at the monitor. Flat line. The old man pulled Freeman closer and gasped, "I'm sorry. Find the others…"

Impossible! The old man with no heartbeat just spoke to him.

"That thing hooked up?" Freeman motioned his head toward the monitor.

The nurse checked the leads and controls, while Freeman checked for a pulse in Baroni's neck. Again nothing. He snatched the stethoscope from the nurse and listened to the patient's chest. Quiet.

He watched the old man's eyes cloud and his head loll over on the pillow. The nurse hurried to the phone. Freeman flipped to the front of the chart.

"Cancel that. He's signed an advanced directive for a 'no code.'"

She replaced the phone in its cradle, her forehead crinkled and lips pulled tight. Freeman stood at the bedside, rolling the unusually warm bead in his fingers. After a few respectful moments, he turned to the nurse.

"Mark his time of death as 11:23 p.m." He closed the patient's eyes. "God rest his soul. I'll call Dr. Canole and see if he wants me to notify the family. Canole *is* the attending physician of record, right?"

The nurse did not respond; she seemed shaken.

"What happened here?" Her questions came rapid-fire. "It was all backwards, as if he lived a few moments after his heart stopped. And what's with that thing he put in your hand? What do you think he meant by 'there are more'? And why ask for you by name? Do you know him?"

Freeman shook his head. "I think he was talking about this bead. Apparently, he thought there are more of these, and for some reason, it was important for me to know that." He wrapped the thong around his fingers and dropped the coiled necklace into his lab coat pocket. "I'll hang onto this until I hear from the family. May be of sentimental value to them."

"A little creepy, if you ask me," she replied. "I'd get rid of that thing."

"It's just a little wooden bead," Freeman said. He glanced past the nurse to the open door. In the shadows of the flickering hall light stood a slumped, old black man leaning on a cane.

"I'm sorry, sir, but visiting hours…" Before he could finish, the visitor vanished around the corner.

"I'll call security," the nurse said, having caught a glimpse of the man.

"Don't bother," Freeman said, fingering the bead in his pocket. "Probably Mr. Baroni's friend. I'm headed down anyway. If the front desk guards haven't spotted him, I'll mention it to them on my way to the call room."

"Thanks," she said as he made his way past her. "I'll try not to bother you any more tonight."

"No problem." He turned back one last time before leaving the room. The old man's head tilted slowly toward him. A shiver ran down Freeman's spine.

CHAPTER THREE

Pam Blanchard, like other nurses at the Veterans Hospital, both dreaded and looked forward to the beginning of each quarter when new interns and residents replaced the old familiar ones. Staff nurses had to reestablish routines and indoctrinate intelligent, headstrong men and women with government-style medicine. July was the worst month. New doctors fresh out of medical school, with little, if any, practical experience descended on teaching hospitals, eager to inflict their recently acquired knowledge on the unsuspecting injured and ill. The final quarter of the year wasn't so bad. At least the novices had nine months under their belts.

Though only thirty-three, Pam ran the fifth floor orthopedic ward. She'd developed her leadership skills while serving in Iraq in field hospitals. Dealing with the petty squabbles and bureaucratic inefficiencies of the VA, though frustrating, presented her little challenge. At first, the older nursing staff resented her rapid climb to nursing supervisor, but Pam gradually won them over with her no-nonsense approach. And her startling good looks quickly disarmed the male-dominated administration and medical/surgical staff—at least the heterosexual ones.

More difficult to manage was the ever-present sexual tension between single, male orthopedic residents and attractive female nurses, single or not. Pam's three-year relationship with an orthopedic resident, Dr. David Freeman, potentially undermined her authoritative position on such matters. Every three months, the administration conducted seminars on sexual harassment and what would and wouldn't be tolerated. Hormones, however, always trumped cognitive, gray-matter brain function. Hanky-panky was inevitable with resident physician personnel changes every three months, providing a constantly fresh, target-rich environment for nurses.

Inside the hospital, she and David kept their relationship purely professional, but the sparks that flew between them did not go unnoticed. It was no secret the young doctor wanted to slip a ring on her finger, and her friends were puzzled she didn't jump at the opportunity to land that good-looking, available surgeon, who just happened to be a nice guy. She adamantly avoided his obvious desire to take their relationship to the next level. Her reasons had nothing to do with David Freeman—she clearly recognized it'd be hard to find better. Her reasons were her own, and she didn't share them with her friends—or with the man who loved her. Her specialized field training and acquired skills of war obtained in Iraq hadn't prevented her heart from being crushed. One husband dying in her arms was enough.

David Freeman's second day as chief resident passed uneventfully. He assigned an orthopedic patient to each of the medical students, and after clinic that afternoon, he and Jim McCallum made teaching rounds with the students and Dr. Canole. As Freeman's thirty-six hour shift drew to a close, he turned the service over to Jim and prepared for the bike ride home.

Darkness settled on the Memphis landscape as Freemen pedaled his bicycle to his apartment. Tonight he'd sleep in his own bed. Three more months and he'd be out of training. No more nights tossing in uncomfortable beds, awakened for every little thing. Private practice had to be better than this. He'd sacrificed a lot. Most of his college buddies were married with kids in school and a real paying job. He'd put his life on hold for nine years to become what he'd chosen to be.

He pondered the pride and the burden of his legacy—the fourth in a line of Freeman surgeons. All had served in wars; his grandfather in two. When the time came, if war still raged in Iraq and Afghanistan, he knew he'd follow in their footsteps and sign up. Not something he looked forward to, but he didn't question it. Some things just had to be. As an only child, he worried at times he might be the one to break the chain of male heirs. Traditions dating back as far as the Boer War deserved preservation.

His thoughts shifted to Pam, his girlfriend of three years and a nurse at the VA. He hadn't seen her in two days. Her job kept her busy also, and their time together suffered as a result. At best, they had two or three nights a week to spend with each other and rarely, a weekend day. They'd kept their relationship light—at her insistence—maintaining separate apartments. His upcoming move to Nashville in three months added a sense of urgency to their arrangement. They'd talked of marriage, but she held firm against it, at least for the time being.

He pedaled harder, working up a sweat and pushing his body. He hadn't stayed in shape during his residency. The job demanded every bit of the eighty-hours-a-week limit imposed by the government, and left little personal time for exercise. His legs burned, and he thought of the training he'd done for his college rowing team. No way would he ever be in that kind of condition again, but he fought not to lose it all. Nearly a century ago, his great-grandfather rowed in the Olympics for England, and had stayed in remarkable shape until the time of his death. Mr. Baroni's appearance had stirred his childhood memories of the old man.

The days lengthened now, and twilight lingered. He turned into his apartment complex and coasted to the foot of the stairs. Breathing hard, he carried his bike and backpack full of clothes and medical paraphernalia to the second level. He liked that the doors opened to the outside of the building rather than into a dreary hallway.

Fumbling with the keys, he let himself into the apartment he'd called home since beginning his orthopedic residency. It came with cheap, sparse furnishings, and he'd made few improvements, though Pam badgered him to do so. He leaned his bike against an empty wall and collapsed onto the couch, flipping on the TV. He played "change the channel" for a few minutes until his breathing slowed and the burning in his legs quieted. Having been up most of the previous night at the Veterans Hospital, his longing for sleep supplanted interest in anything on the tube. He needed a shower and time between the sheets before starting over again at five o'clock in the morning.

Turning off the TV, he fished out the small wooden bead from his lab coat and peered closely at the carvings. The intricate geometric pattern appeared to be an ancient symbolic language. He thought of Baroni's last words before death—something about a Chief Scout and there being more of these. No rank of *Chief* existed in Scouting that he knew of. Strange last thoughts for a dying man? What was so important about this bead? Probably nothing. Just the ramblings of an aged mind getting too little oxygen. He draped the bead with its cord over the post at the head of his bed. Maybe the old man's family would want it after all.

He thought back to Baroni's death. It didn't make sense: The old man actually talked after his heart stopped. Occasionally, a corpse would do strange things immediately after death, but conversation was not one of them. Had Baroni's head really turned toward him as he left the room, or had that just been the workings of his own tired brain?

The phone rang as he stepped into the shower. Wrapping a towel about his waist, he checked the caller ID: Pam. He smiled.

"Hi there, cutie," he answered, stifling a yawn.

"Hey, Doc. You just get home?" she said.

"Yeah. Just getting into the shower. What's up?"

"So does this mean you're talking to me naked?" she asked.

"Close, but no cigar," he replied.

"Well, we could do that too," she laughed, borrowing a now famous line from a presidential conversation.

"Are you off?" he asked, turning on the water. "And more importantly, can you come over? I won't be much fun, but I do want to see you."

"You surgical residents don't take care of yourselves. Have you had dinner?"

"No. I'm too tired to eat." The last few words came in yawn-talk. "Up most of the night."

"I thought as much. Listen, I made a batch of spaghetti and I'm gonna need help eating it. I'll walk some over." When he didn't respond immediately, she added, "You have to eat, Doc."

"Yeah, that would be great. But I might be in the shower when you get here."

"Promise?" she said, hanging up the phone.

He pulled the towel from his waist, threw it over the rack, and stepped into the shower. Already, he felt better. Pam always did that to him.

Hot water washed away the drudgery of the last thirty-eight hours. He stretched his arms over his head and leaned into the wall, letting the water massage his back. He'd get to the task of cleaning in a moment, but for now, he enjoyed the peaceful solitude. His muscles ached from the ride home. Not long ago, that bike ride would've been easy. When he finished residency and started in practice, things would be different. He'd make time for working out and enjoying life—hopefully with Pam.

He rinsed off and stepped from the shower, reaching for the towel. Gone. He distinctly remembered throwing the towel over the rack before he stepped into the shower.

"Looking for this?" Pam said from around the corner. Her arm appeared in the bathroom doorway with his towel.

"Oh, come on, Pam. Throw me the towel, unless you're volunteering to dry me off."

Pam strolled around the corner, holding the towel out in front of her as a flimsy shield between their bodies. He willingly surrendered. She closed the distance between them and wrapped the towel around his chest, letting it hang over his nakedness, and pressed her body into his.

"Let me help you. I am a nurse, after all."

He stood quietly while she ran the towel through his hair and over his face. She dried each arm, and wrapped the towel around his torso, bringing the ends together behind him. His back must have been very wet, for she took a long time on it, using the front of her body to press the towel into his chest. He glanced down. Her v-neck sweater and tight jeans left little to the imagination.

Pam knelt before him and continued her work. She slowed as she reached his responding groin, but only long enough to dry him and glance up, smiling. Running the towel over his legs, her auburn hair rubbed against him, making the situation worse. He reached for her, but she brushed away his hands.

"Dinner first, Doctor," she scolded.

She stood five inches shorter than he, and kept herself in great shape; her body slim and muscular; her shoulders broad, like a swimmer's. The fragrance of her hair made his knees weak. Her smile and dark eyes hinting crow's feet at the corners could make any group of residents lose their place in rounds.

She dropped the towel and sashayed from the bathroom, leaving him standing in a state of readiness.

Freeman waited until his body relaxed, then crossed the hall into his bedroom and donned his bathrobe. Pam had set his small table for two and poured the Merlot.

"That was cruel," he said.

"Yeah, you looked like you were suffering," she replied. "Now sit down and eat your dinner before it gets cold. We've got something to talk about, but that can wait."

His belly flipped at the thought of a serious talk. That could mean only one thing. He kept the mood light. "Why'd you do that? I mean, I found it all pretty erotic. Took my mind off eating, you know?"

"David, you were up most of the night and worked all day today. If I'd bedded you a few moments ago, you'd be dead to the world right now, and I'd be here eating this spaghetti all by my lonesome," Pam said, taking his hand and leading him to his seat at the table. "Now, sit down and eat, and tell me about your day."

He did as told, feeling confused. His belly grumbled, but the spaghetti hit the spot. The addition of the wine capped the moment and took the last edge off the day. He hadn't realized how hungry he was until halfway through his first plate. Having not said a word, he looked up apologetically. She smiled and took another sip of wine.

"Sorry. Guess I didn't realize how famished I was," he said. "This spaghetti is super, as usual. One of my favorites you make."

"Flatterer. You say that about *everything* I make." She flashed that smile that still warmed him, even after three years. "There's more where that came from, if you need it."

They finished their plates over small talk, then Pam cleared the table. He sat with his back toward the kitchenette as she washed dishes.

"You need any help?" he called out.

"Forget it. You sit there and relax. I'll be done in a minute."

He watched her from his seat. This felt so normal. He had no problem seeing this as his life forever. He even dared to dream of children, perhaps the fifth generation of medical professionals.

He snuck up behind her and wrapped his arms about her waist. She leaned into him, but continued working. He nuzzled her neck, hopefully leaving no doubt in her mind what he had on his.

"I've been thinking about this summer," she said, still facing away and wiping off the last plate.

He didn't know if he wanted to hear the next line. "Can we talk about this in bed?"

She turned and pushed him away. "I'm serious, David." She leaned against the sink, but didn't cross her arms over her chest.

The dreaded arm-cross trumped any further advances until she'd had her way, and he took its absence as a good sign.

"Then you're just catching up with me." He stepped into her, pinning her against the counter top, hugging her close.

"This is hard for me, you know," she said.

He pulled back, but only a little. "You want to do it this way?" he asked. "I've told you before, there's nothing—no way, no how—that's going to change how I feel about you. If you want to keep that door closed, I'm okay with it."

She raised her pouting eyes to his and kissed him. "You're a wonderful man, David Freeman, and any girl would be lucky to have you. It's just that—"

He returned her kiss, cutting short her disclaimer. He felt her resistance melt away. He backed them out of the kitchen, the passion between them mounting. Their feet tangled as they reached his bed, and they fell laughing onto the mattress and into each other's arms again. They made love, not with the reckless abandon of youth, but with the maturity and knowledge of knowing what pleased the other.

Freeman closed his eyes, his breathing becoming deep and regular.

"You see. This is why I made you eat first." Pam laughed, bounding out of bed. She sauntered to the bathroom. He admired her figure silhouetted against the backdrop of the kitchen light. She disappeared into the bathroom and turned on the water. He must have dozed off because when he opened his eyes, Pam stood over him.

"Hey, Romeo," she said, holding her jeans and sweater. "At least wake up long enough to tell me good night."

"I'm sorry," he said, rolling onto his side. "You aren't leaving, are you? This has been a wonderful evening. I haven't felt this relaxed in ages."

"What time do you have to get up?" she asked. "Four o'clock?"

He nodded and yawned.

"Well, I don't, and I'm not going to. I'll be asleep in my own bed, dreaming of the next time. You owe me a dinner."

Slipping into her sweater, she clutched her blue jeans as she searched about the small room. He knew where her panties hung, but let her hunt for a while. The sight of her long, muscular legs topped off by one of the cutest bottoms he'd ever seen, never grew old.

"Looking for these?" he asked, pointing to the bedpost.

She gave him a look that usually comes over the top of a pair of glasses and retrieved her panties, the small necklace and bead catching in her hand.

"What's this?" she asked, examining the bead. "It's pretty."

"Oh, something a patient gave me today," he said through another yawn that earned him a reproachful look. "With his dying breath, the old man asked me about being a Boy Scout and kept saying there were more of these beads somewhere. He thought it important that I know. Then, he died."

"That's it?" Pam asked. "That's all he said?"

"Well, he did refer to the chief Boy Scout as having more. He also apologized when he gave me the bead."

"Why?" Pam asked. "Had he been rude to you?"

"No. It wasn't that," Freeman said. "He apologized for giving me the bead. Quite an old man. Flew bombers out of England in World War II. Reminded me of my great-grandfather, the one who gave me that sword hanging on the wall." He rolled to his back and clasped his hands behind his head, flitting his eyes toward the menacing weapon, the only wall décor in his apartment.

"That's where the Boy Scouts started," Pam said, zipping up her jeans and slipping into her high-heeled shoes. "England, I mean. My grandfather's an amateur historian, of sorts. He used to tell me tales of the early days of Scouting. He was big into that when he was younger."

"Those the shoes you walked over in?" he asked.

"You have some objection as to how I look?"

She did look sexy, hair mussed and that after-intercourse glow lighting her face. She struck a pose, arms akimbo, one leg slightly bent at the knee, tight jeans, low cut v-neck sweater with the sleeves bunched over the elbows, a few strands of her thick, auburn hair down in front of her face: enough to make him think twice about sleep. He made a move to get out of bed. She pushed him back.

"I didn't think so," she said, grabbing her purse and placing the bead on his nightstand. "Get some sleep, Tarzan. I'm going back to my place. We'll talk later."

She let herself out, and David nestled deeper into the pillow harboring the scent of her hair. The front door closed quietly. Sleep should have come easy. How could life be any better?

Yet something festered, depriving him of much-needed rest. He couldn't put his finger on it or dismiss it, and dozed fitfully.

Wind rustled outside his lone bedroom window, scraping bare limbs of the budding maple across the uncurtained pane. Moonbeams danced over his headboard, highlighting the old Zulu sword. David reached to his bedside alarm, tilting its face toward him, and groaned at what little time he had left. His hand flopped onto the nightstand and the bead. He clutched it in his palm and tucked his hand under his pillow. His last thoughts before drifting off were of Baroni's final words... *"Find the others... Find the others."*

CHAPTER FOUR

LANGLEY, VIRGINIA

Patrick packed for the trip to Memphis. The drive would take only slightly longer than air travel, and he wanted to swing through Nashville and see his mom and dad. As their only child, he felt a special obligation to stay close to them as they aged. His father still practiced as an orthopedic surgeon and his mother, being native Cuban, helped out with Spanish classes at one of the local high schools.

A career in medicine just hadn't been for him, even though his father and college roommate, David Freeman, were convinced he'd make a good diagnostician. Just wasn't enough action in it.

Instead, Patrick took after his mother who'd escaped Castro's Cuba in a small, barely seaworthy boat, leaving behind family whom she missed dearly. Through her, he developed his love of languages and an appreciation for life in the U.S. His study of history and languages at Dartmouth, as well as his athletic prowess on the football field, had attracted the attention of the State Department, ultimately leading to his job as an operative with the newly created Department of Homeland Security. Fate intervened when he was randomly paired with Adnan Fazeph, the Department's most prized Arab-American. Their personalities and skills meshed and soon, many considered them the country's most effective anti-terrorist team. The fact that they'd grown to be as brothers only added to their effectiveness.

Adnan burst through Patrick's apartment door without knocking. "How long you think we be in Memphis?"

"Okay, what'd I tell you about knocking? How'd you know I didn't have a date in here?"

Adnan plopped onto the bed beside Patrick's open suitcase. "You say this every time. Where is mystery date? I no see her now or ever."

"Why don't you take a day off?" Patrick asked. "I'm stopping in Nashville at least overnight to see my folks. You can join me in River City in a couple of days."

"I have not been to Memphis. Food is good there, yes? We go to Rendezvous for ribs."

Adnan's ability to pack away the food had become legendary, though somehow, he remained thin and lanky. All agents vigorously worked to stay in top shape, but in his case, that still left thousands of calories unaccounted for.

Patrick's phone chirped—Cisneros.

"Don't leave yet," Cisneros said. "Grab Adnan and meet me in Conference Room C in five. Someone here I think you should meet."

"Is this concerning Memphis?" Patrick asked.

"Only in that it may shorten your trip. Five minutes." The line clicked off.

"Good or bad?" Adnan asked.

Patrick shook his head. It was not in Cisneros's nature to waste their time or expose them to other people. The fewer people that could connect them to the department, the better. "Wants to introduce us to some guy—didn't say who."

Adnan's cheerful demeanor vanished. The last guy Cisneros *introduced* them to turned out to be a double agent and nearly got them both killed.

On the way over, Patrick shifted back to their earlier meeting with Cisneros. "Given any more thought to that bead thing?" He knew full well that at least a part of Adnan's brain had worked it from every angle since it was presented to them.

"Makes no sense," Adnan said. "Africans … murders … beads … covert British message … symbols. I plug variables into grid. Maybe computer find link."

"Still think it means something ominous?"

Adnan hesitated. "I have this feeling only once before in life, but I remember well—as child, right before parents killed." His voice drifted off and he turned his head away. Though they were nearly at their destination, he turned up the collar of his jacket against the cool breeze. Patrick thought he saw a shudder.

"You knew the car wreck was coming?"

"What? Oh yeah … the wreck." Adnan came back from wherever it was he'd been; probably reliving the violent death of his mom and dad in Beirut, where he'd lived the first eight years of his life until orphaned.

Patrick slid his badge in the scanner and pulled open the door. Adnan followed, hands shoved deep in his pockets and chin in his chest, stepping hastily by and down the hall toward the elevators.

"Hey," Patrick called after him, standing at the door and pointing at the scanner.

Adnan whirled about and fished his badge from inside his coat. He shrugged and ran it through.

"You okay?" Patrick asked. His concern was both genuine and professional. As a team, they needed to think and act as one. No secrets. No hidden agendas.

"Just bad memories," Adnan said. "Nothing you don't know about."

Patrick's instincts said differently, but he let it slide for the moment. "We'll talk later," he said, leading the way to the elevators and down two flights to the conference area.

Two Marine guards stood before Conference Room C. They parted for the agents and one pushed the door open. Whoever Cisneros had for them was no lightweight.

"Gentlemen," Cisneros said, rising up from his chair at the small circular table. "May I introduce Miss Shoshanna bin Amin of Israel."

Neither agent was quick enough to hide his apparent surprise. Cisneros chuckled under his breath, enjoying the rare moment.

Before them stood a shockingly beautiful woman, jet black hair cascading below her shoulders, dark eyes heavily made up, as was the custom in the Middle East. Her business jacket and skirt of expensive tailored cloth artistically hugged her strong, though very feminine body. A simple gold chain with the Star of David hung from her neck and against her olive skin, exposed by her silk blouse open at the neck. Her high heels brought her to about five-foot-seven. She extended her hand, the prominent veins of which belied a physical strength matching the mental toughness apparent in her demeanor.

Each agent accepted her greeting and mumbled something incoherent and marginally appropriate. Cisneros brought them back to business and seated them around the table.

"Miss Amin—"

"Shoshanna, please," she interrupted, the lilt of her accent adding to her allure.

"Yes, well, Shoshanna has come to us with a request for help," Cisneros said. "It seems her country—"

"My family is very wealthy and influential in our corner of the world." Shoshanna shifted in her chair and leaned into the table, her gaze fixed on the two agents. "We have information of a developing terrorist threat in northern Africa."

Patrick glanced toward his partner, who caught it and raised an eyebrow, as if to say, "So what else is new?"

Shoshanna also caught the non-verbal communication. "Please, gentlemen. I would not bother you with ordinary threats. Those are a way of life for my people. What you Americans are only now waking up to, we've been dealing with for over three thousand years."

"Please continue, ma'am," Patrick said by way of an apology.

"We view the world differently than your people," she said, glaring at Patrick, but casting a glance toward Adnan. Her intertwined fingers on the table top tightened. "You deal with events of today, as do we. But additionally, we have an eye on the past—on the prophecies of the ancients. We watch for signs of Biblical predictions, for the unfolding of events that will dwarf our present problems."

"Have you seen such signs?" Adnan asked, falling into his stilted English.

Shoshanna tilted her head, as though Adnan's accent threw her. "It is unclear," she said, now addressing Adnan. "Events are unfolding as we speak, but are too important to ignore. It is my plan to infiltrate the threat."

Patrick still didn't understand what this had to do with them. Israel was capable of securing its own intelligence and was certainly not short on manpower. "You intend to personally go among them, whoever these people are? Are you trained for that?"

Shoshanna bristled.

"Don't let her appearance fool you," Cisneros interjected. "Shoshanna is a sharpshooter in the Israeli army and a respected member of the Mossad with numerous covert missions under her belt. She's been useful to us in the past."

Patrick struggled to stay focused and professional: beautiful *and* dangerous. Adnan must have picked up on this and cleared his throat. "And how we can help you?" he asked.

"I don't need your help," she said. The corners of her mouth turned down. "I need your faith. If we should cross paths in the near future, and I think we will, I need you to appreciate the gravity of the circumstances. I need you to understand we may be dealing with events larger than mankind."

"Why us?" Patrick directed his question to Cisneros.

"Shoshanna asked for this meeting with a team—I don't recall exactly how she put it, but in essence, capable of thinking outside the box. She intimated that most Americans are skeptics and non-believers." Cisneros looked to her for confirmation. Shoshanna remained stoically trained on the agents. "In my judgment, you two fit that bill."

"You think we are religious?" Adnan asked.

Now it was Cisneros's turn to scowl. "I feel you have instincts above the norm that you're willing to trust. Am I wrong?"

"If I may be so bold, sir," Patrick said, "this is a bit of an odd request, and coming on the heels of our earlier discussion and trip we are preparing for at the moment, I'm a little puzzled myself."

Cisneros sat back in his chair and folded his hands across his small belly. "Patrick, from where I sit and from the office of the President, there are events and circumstances presented us that defy logical explanation. These things necessarily never see the light of day. We, Shoshanna and I, ask for your indulgence. I pray we'll never be called upon to use it, but if we are, I want you to remember this conversation and recognize this woman as someone to be taken seriously. Can you do that?"

The agents exchanged looks. Adnan raised an eyebrow giving Patrick the green light to speak for both of them.

"Yes sir. And we appreciate your confidence." Then to Shoshanna, "And if you should ever need us, please know we will respond with all urgency. Is that satisfactory?"

Shoshanna's countenance softened for the first time. The crease between her eyebrows dissolved and a hint of a smile broke at the corners of her mouth. "That is all I ask of you and the sole purpose of my long flight to the States. Now I can return to my country and my work. It has been my pleasure, gentlemen."

She pushed away from the table and again extended her hand. After salutations were exchanged, Cisneros shooed the agents away.

Walking back toward their quarters, Adnan again appeared lost in thought.

"Well that was certainly strange," Patrick said.

Adnan shook his head. "This day has been strange. I wish to wake up and start over."

"Think we should brush up on biblical history?"

"Twice in one day, we are presented with ties to the beginnings of recorded history: First with the inscriptions on beads and now this. Coincidence?"

"While you're working on that, I'm going to head out. I can still get to Nashville before midnight, if I push it. I'll drive down to Memphis tomorrow and call you. The van ready?"

"Needs restocking." Adnan stopped outside Patrick's door and laid a hand on his shoulder. "Be careful, brother. I have bad feeling about this one."

"You have a bad feeling about all of them."

"Not like this. You know how legendary teams have one case that defines them? And how they say it started out as a nothing?"

"You think this is it?"

"Just be careful. We go into this with little or no background. Bad guys unknown. Motives unknown. You know that inner voice you speak of? Is talking real loud right now."

Patrick laughed it off and ducked into his apartment. With Adnan gone, he took a few quiet moments to allow his mind to wander. Something disturbed him also. This didn't feel like their other assignments. His inner voice cried out for attention.

CHAPTER FIVE

MEMPHIS, TENNESSEE

Freeman gave up around four o'clock, before his alarm sounded. What little sleep he'd managed was fitful at best. Rest shouldn't have been a problem—physically and mentally exhausted, fed and bedded, he should have dropped off like a lead weight. Instead he'd thrashed about, his mind flitting from one strange scene to the next. Something pursued him in his dreams, something formless and powerful, and he couldn't make his feet work fast enough. Dense jungle tore at him. Oppressive, thick air filled his throat and choked him. Sweat poured from his body.

He kicked aside the damp sheets and lay staring up at his great-grandfather's sword, the little light from outside his window dancing off the polished blade. Thunder rumbled in the distance, and wind rustled the leaves outside his apartment, disrupting the beams from the streetlight across the way.

The cruel sound of the alarm formally halted his struggles. Only then did he notice the bead still clutched in his left hand. He draped it back over his headboard on the way to the bathroom. He stumbled into the kitchen. His automatic coffee maker had malfunctioned again. Grumbling, he reached into the refrigerator for a back-up source of caffeine.

He turned on the shower and stared into the mirror over the sink as the water heated. Some gray was creeping into his dark hair. The towel around his waist, still damp from the night before, pressed cold into his pelvis as he leaned on the sink, and despite his fatigue, he smiled at the memories of last night.

A long strand of Pam's hair hung over the faucet. He'd see her today on rounds at the Veterans Hospital, and they'd make plans to spend time together this Sunday. Maybe they could go for a drive if the weather cooperated. She wanted to see a movie, a chick-flick with Sandra Bullock, but he knew he'd fall asleep regardless of the show.

He hurriedly showered, donned his scrubs, and loaded his backpack with items necessary for life inside the hospital. Before leaving his bedroom, he paused in front of his headboard. Baroni's bead beckoned him. Surgical residents rarely wore jewelry, but it wouldn't hurt anything, and if the family asked, he'd have it with him.

He dropped the cord with the bead over his head and around his neck. For a split second, another desert scene of northern Africa flashed before his eyes—a nomadic tribe slogging its way through harsh land under a blazing desert sun. Dizziness forced him to brace himself on the wall. The episode passed as quickly as it came. He shook off the moment as one of low blood sugar and vowed to get something to eat at the hospital.

With his bike over his shoulder, he headed out the door and down the stairs. No traffic to worry about this hour of the morning. The ten-minute ride to the hospital would be his last time for personal reflection until tomorrow night.

He tried to clear his mind and enjoy the ride. The morning air threatening rain brushed cool and crisp against his cheeks; the bead warm against his chest. Invigorated, he took corners faster than usual. Banking hard, he turned right onto Madison Avenue.

Two black men sporting long dreadlocks and running full speed darted from between buildings. Freeman swerved right to avoid hitting them and crashed onto his side, the bike skidding from under him. Glancing up, he saw the two men sprinting all out, not slowing or looking back.

He scrambled upright and took inventory. A dark street in downtown Memphis was no place to loiter. The fall had torn the right leg of his scrubs, and he had a nice strawberry on that knee. He'd tend to that at the hospital. The palm of his right hand burned, but the skin appeared unbroken. His bike looked okay.

Shaking his head, he again glanced after the two running men. They disappeared down another dark alley.

As he climbed onto his bike, he stared down the alley-way from where the two had come. Back in the shadows thrown by street lights, something moved. Inner-city survival instincts told him to pedal away—fast. He paused, trying to make sense of the image.

An old black man stumbled from behind a dumpster and fell against the wall of the building. The poor light revealed an obvious street person; clothes tattered and unkempt, face unshaven. Blood trickled from a corner of his mouth. Shuffling forward, he again slumped onto the wall. The silhouette reminded Freeman of the man standing outside Baroni's room late last night at the VA. Could it be the same man?

Freeman saw him better now; the old man's tired, bloodshot eyes staring at him. Without asking for help, the man slowly slid down the wall, landing sideways on his left hip, his chin sagging into his chest.

He was here yesterday and he'll be here tomorrow, Freeman thought. He'd ridden past bums like this every morning for the past four years. He stood on the pedals, but couldn't ride away.

"You okay?" he called out to the old man.

When no response came, he dismounted, stepped into the alley, and leaned his bike against the wall. Cautiously, he approached the vagrant. He played his mental game of trying to imagine the man as an infant in his proud mother's arms. This usually helped when he found himself passing judgment too quickly.

"Hey, man. You hurt?" he asked. "Can I help?"

The bum turned his head and stared, but said nothing.

Freeman knelt by the man's side and started a cursory medical evaluation. Large bruises circled the man's eyes. Several small lacerations marred his chin and blood oozed from his mouth. Without warning, the old fellow vomited on the pavement and Freeman's shoes before he could jump clear.

"Geeez", Freeman moaned.

Shaking his head, he looked down at the poor old guy. His gaze shifted to his own ruined shoes, which now reeked of stale wine, bile, and blood. *No good deed goes unpunished.* His revulsion gave way to clinical evaluation of the situation. Freeman recognized the smell of digested alcohol and blood. The old man might be bleeding into his stomach. Scrambling back to his bike, he fumbled for his cell phone and called the VA Hospital, just minutes up the road.

"Hello, operator? This is Dr. Freemen. Emergency department, please."

After a few seconds, the ER night nurse picked up.

"Emergency Department," she yawned into the phone.

Freeman explained the situation. "Can you send an ambulance to pick him up? He's in pretty bad shape."

"Sounds like a case for the City Hospital," she replied.

"I don't care where they take him," he said. "He's just more than I can manage on my bicycle."

"Okay, I'll call Metro and send one out to you," the nurse said.

After giving directions, he returned to the alley and walked around the man's far side to avoid the pool of vomit. The backside wasn't much better. The old guy had lost control of his bowels. It reeked of blood mixed with stool—melena.

"I've called for an ambulance," he said, kneeling behind the man. "What's your name?"

The man looked up with sallow, sunken eyes. He stared for a moment and then reached out, putting his gnarled, old hand on Freeman's chest. His yellow eyes flew open, sparking to life.

"You're *Helpful*," he rasped.

"Well, not yet, I haven't been," Freeman said.

"No," he coughed, turning his head away to spit. Wiping his mouth, he reached back and this time, patted Freeman on the chest.

"You are *Helpful*," he repeated in a dry voice, barely audible.

An eerie sense of deja-vu gripped Freeman. The old man stared right through him. Again the vagrant reached and pressed his withered hand onto Freeman's chest. The pressure forced the bead uncomfortably into his sternum.

"Hang on, mister. An ambulance will be here in a minute," he said.

"No," the man rasped. "It's okay. Phony did good." A fit of coughing overcame him. More blood and mucous. He turned back to Freeman. "Find the others."

Freeman stiffened. "What others?" he asked. "Are more people in this alley? Do you have family?"

The old man grabbed Freeman's shirt and pulled him close. His rancid breath made Freeman's gorge rise.

"Find the others," the old man whispered, letting go of his shirt.

Freeman sprang backwards, nearly falling. He caught himself and gazed back at the old man, whose breathing became more labored and irregular. He felt the wrist for a pulse. Nothing. He felt the carotid artery in the man's neck. Again, nothing. *Oh, no! This can't be happening again!*

The old man grabbed his wrist. Freeman struggled to free himself.

"*Helpful*... find others," the injured man said one final time.

Freeman felt a cold shiver. The ambulance pulled into the alleyway. The paramedics grabbed their gear from the back of the truck and ran to where he knelt.

"What happened here, buddy?" one of them asked.

"What? Oh, yeah. Thanks. I'm Dr. Freemen. I was biking into work when I saw two guys run out of this alley. Found this old fellow stumbling around. He's in pretty bad shape. Losing blood from both ends."

"Know who he is?" the paramedic asked while his partner checked for vital signs. "Did he tell you his name or what happened?"

"No. He didn't tell me anything. Just rambled on about nothing."

"Well, no hurry now," the other paramedic said, wrapping his stethoscope around his hand and shoving it into his coat pocket. "This guy's been dead for a while."

"What!" Freeman exclaimed. "That's impossible. We just talked. He grabbed my shirt."

"Feel for yourself, Doc. His body's like ice."

Freeman touched the old man's forehead, the skin cold and stiff. The head moved under Freeman's hand, eyes open and staring.

Freeman leaped back. The paramedics didn't seem to notice. One of them moved to prepare the body for transport and the other returned to the ambulance. Something clicked in Freeman's mind. He shoved the paramedic aside, then squatted, and leaned over the body. With trembling hands, he ripped open the old man's jacket and tore away the ragged undershirt. The old cloth easily gave way. No bead like Baroni's. He sighed with relief and sat back on his heels.

"Hey, look. He's got dog tags," the paramedic said. "Must be a vet. We'll take him by the Veterans Hospital for the medical examiner to pick up later." He leaned past Freeman and wiped the dog tags with his thumb. "Can't make out the name in this light."

"If you don't need me anymore, I'm gonna head to work. I'm already late," Freeman said, casting a glance at his watch.

"Yeah. Go on," one of them said. "We've got it here. The medical examiner might want to talk to you, though. You say your name's Freeman, and you're a doctor?"

"Yeah. I'm an ortho resident at the VA Hospital. Thanks for your help," he said, pushing off on his bike. The body heat from the early part of his ride had dissipated, leaving him chilled. He checked his coat and pulled the zipper tighter. Pedaling hard the last half mile to the hospital warmed him.

He locked his bike to the rack inside the hospital, then reached under his shirt and touched the uncomfortable spot at his sternum. The bead felt oddly warm, and he wondered if this kind of wood stored and gave off heat. He remembered it being that way yesterday when Baroni died.

He shrugged off the thought. After stashing his backpack in his locker and changing into clean scrubs and different shoes, he slipped into his lab coat. Using supplies from the ER, he cleaned and dressed the abrasions on his knee and hand. The hand would hurt when he scrubbed for surgery later that morning. His junior residents were probably halfway through rounds. He'd have to hurry to catch up. As he scurried down the hospital corridors, he couldn't shake the sinking, unsettling feeling something wasn't right in his world.

CHAPTER SIX

"I don't understand what this fuss is about," the woman on the phone insisted. "I only want to talk with the young man. I understand he's a resident in training in your program and you're responsible for him. Why can't I speak with him?"

"Ma'am, I didn't say you couldn't speak with him," explained Kay Daugherty, staff secretary at Campbell's Clinic. "I need to know what this is about before I chase him down. He might be in surgery." The matriarch of the Clinic, having occupied this position for over thirty years, protected the residents as though they were her children.

"I've already spoken with the Veterans Hospital," the woman said. "They contacted *me*. They said Dr. Freeman might have been the last person to see my grandfather alive. I need to talk with him about something."

"Why don't you give me your name and number?" Kay said. "I'll have Dr. Freeman or someone on our staff call you later." In this lawyer-infested society, aggrieved family members might call the less experienced doctors-in-training to gather information for potential lawsuits. Kay had to make sure these calls were passed on to the attending physicians, keeping the residents sheltered, if possible.

"Okay, but please have him call me. Granddad always kept something with him, and according to the people at the hospital, it wasn't on him at the time of death. It's very important I speak with Dr. Freeman. He may know about this," the lady said.

Kay took the woman's name and number. First, she'd contact the staff physician at the VA Hospital, Dr. Canole. Like herself, he'd been with the Clinic for over thirty years and had seen many residents come and go. She reflected for a moment on her relationship with the older doctor. In his earlier days, Rocco

Canole had been the driving force behind the clinic. Nowadays, he prided himself with supervising training at the VA Hospital and left management of one of the world's largest orthopedic training programs to the younger staff. She text-messaged him and returned to work in the library, which served as her office.

In OR 2, Freeman helped a first year resident with a less than glamorous case: the amputation of a leg, so common in smoking veterans. Many novice surgeons began their careers with amputations of disvascular limbs of old soldiers. More experienced residents preferred joint-replacement surgery and other reconstructive procedures, something they anticipated doing once they finished training. But part of his job as chief resident at the VA involved training the younger guys.

"Bevel the edge a little more," Freeman said. "That's going to be the area of pressure on the prosthesis, and if the edge of the tibia is sharp, it'll lead to skin problems with the stump."

Freeman supported the leg at the knee while junior resident, Jim McCallum, cut through the bone with an oscillating power saw. A tourniquet around the patient's thigh prevented bleeding. As the young surgeon worked, an experienced, middle-aged, black scrub nurse, Gladys Vaughn, dripped water onto both bone and saw blade to prevent overheating. Despite this, some of the bone inevitably aerosolized, producing a burnt, chalky smell familiar in VA operating rooms.

Freeman shouted over the noise of the saw. "Take your time with the cut. Don't burn the bone any more than you have to."

Dr. Canole strolled into their operating room, tying his mask strings behind his head as he entered. He came up behind Freeman and leaned in to observe. McCallum paused and looked up at the older doctor.

"Good morning, Dr. Canole," he said.

Freeman glanced over his shoulder and echoed the greeting.

"Well, looks like you've got everything under control here, Freeman. Tell me, how would you do this if your battery-powered saw gave out on you?" Canole asked, addressing both of them, but really directing his comment to the junior resident.

Freeman, who had his back toward the old professor, rolled his eyes. *Oh please God, not the Gigli saw.* He kept his mouth shut, though, as he knew a lesson in "how we used to do it" loomed.

"I don't know, sir. I guess I'd use the rongeur, the bone-biting tool," McCallum answered.

"Really? You can make a smooth bone cut with a rongeur? You youngsters must be more talented nowadays. Nurse?" Canole asked. "Do you have a Gigli saw on the table?"

Freeman's shoulders slumped. This would add another fifteen minutes to an already boring operation, but he stayed quiet.

"Freeman? You think you can show him the proper use of this time-honored piece of equipment?" the professor asked.

"Yes, sir. I've had the course, but we really never use that anymore."

"Of course you don't. But one of these days, you'll be out in private practice and your equipment will break down and you'll be thankful old Dr. Canole made sure you knew more than one way to skin this cat. Nurse, hand Dr. McCallum the Gigli saw, please."

The bewildered young resident watched as the scrub nurse unwound a strand of what appeared to be very fine barbed wire with a wooden handle on each end. To hold the instrument, the surgeon had to pass the wire between two of his fingers. The wire detached from one of the handles to allow passage around the bone.

"Now, Dr. McCallum, pass that free end of the saw behind the tibia at the level of the planned cut," Dr. Canole instructed. "Use one of those long hemostats. Good. Now reattach the free end to the handle. That's right. Now hold your arms so the saw makes about a ninety-degree angle. Okay, complete the cut."

This made it harder for Freeman to assist. He imagined his great-grandfather doing the same thing over a century ago in South Africa with one steady swipe of his sword. Freeman now had to steady both sides of the leg being amputated. His junior resident pulled the wire back and forth, making little progress. Sweat beaded on his brow.

"Come on now. Put some muscle behind it," Canole goaded.

Fortunately, they'd completed the beveled part of the cut prior to the old professor's arrival. Ten minutes later, the winded junior resident completed the task and the leg came free.

"There," Dr. Canole said. "That wasn't so bad, was it?"

No, thought Freeman. *For Civil War medicine, that went pretty well*. The end of the bone needed to be reworked to accept prosthetic fitting, but hopefully Canole would lose interest and they could do this with power equipment and not with the large bone rasp Freeman knew lurked somewhere in the background.

"Now, nurse. Get these young surgeons that bone rasp of mine so we can rework that cut end. McCallum, I'll scrub in and help you finish. Freeman, you're wanted at headquarters."

Freeman looked up, surprised.

"I have no idea, son," Dr. Canole said in response to his unasked question. "Something to do with the family of a patient of yours. Sounded urgent. Better get going."

Freeman shrugged, silently apologizing to Jim McCallum, who looked uneasy, then pulled off his OR gown and headed to the locker room. This couldn't be good. Had some family complained about his care? Was he involved in a lawsuit? He didn't need this so close to the end of his training.

Freeman changed into street clothes he kept in his locker, hopped on his bike, and rode over to the University Clinic, the downtown office—a five minute ride away. What could they want with him?

Locking his bike to a rack, he headed upstairs to the staff office.

"Hi, Kay. Someone here need me for something?" he asked the all-knowing staff secretary.

"Well, actually, *I* called you. Oh, I tried Dr. Canole first, but you know how he is. He told me to find you."

"What's the deal?"

"Did one of your VA patients die yesterday?"

Freeman frowned. "Sure did. Mr. Baroni died shortly after admission. Why?"

"Baroni. That's right. His granddaughter's been calling here. Said it's important she talk with you."

"Is she mad about something?" Freeman asked. "Did she say what it concerned?"

"She wouldn't say, but did mention you were the last person to see her grandfather alive. I tried to pass it off to Canole, but he wouldn't take it."

"Did she sound litigious?"

"I don't think so, Dr. Freeman. I've been doing this a long time and I can usually smell a lawsuit coming, but I don't think that's the case. Here's her number." She handed him a small Post-It note with the phone number. "Dr. Canole said for you to call her."

Freeman fingered the wooden trinket around his neck. He walked to the back of the library and found a phone. Before calling, he went over the details he could remember about Mr. Baroni's admission. Nothing out of the ordinary, except for the manner in which he died. Strange, but not criminal. He dialed the number.

"Hello," said a soft, feminine voice.

"Hi. I'm Dr. David Freeman, an orthopedic resident at Campbell's Clinic in Memphis. You called earlier wanting to speak with me?"

"Oh, thank you for returning my call. My name's Lisa Baroni. I was afraid I'd never hear back from you. Did you know my grandfather, Alphonse Baroni?"

He chose his words carefully, not sure where this might lead. "Barely. He was admitted to our service yesterday, and passed away shortly afterwards," he replied, not volunteering more information.

She must have sensed his wariness. "Please, don't feel defensive. That's not why I'm calling. Grandpa was very old, and I'm sure you did all you could. I wish I could've been there with him when he died."

Her voice broke and she paused. Freeman began to feel better about the conversation, and like Kay, sensed this was not a malignant situation. Still, he would let Ms. Baroni lead the discussion.

"He seemed like a nice old gentleman," he added. "I'm sorry for your loss."

"Thank you. Listen, Dr. Freeman, would it be all right if we got together for a few minutes, maybe for lunch? I'm just across the river in West Memphis, Arkansas, and would be happy to meet you someplace near your work. It won't take very long. I promise."

"I don't know, Ms. Baroni. My work keeps me pretty busy. One of the professors had to spell me in the operating room just so I could call you this morning." He'd have to deal with bereaved family once out in private practice, but as a resident, he wasn't yet comfortable with it.

"Please. It's really important to me, and I think it will be to you also," she said. "I won't take much of your time. I could come over right now, if that would work for you."

Freeman glanced at the clock on the library wall. Almost noon. The amputation they'd just finished completed the operative schedule for the day, barring any emergencies. Clinic didn't start until two o'clock. His resolve softened.

"Okay. I can't promise I'll be available, but I'll try. You might make the trip for nothing if I get tied up," he said, half hoping to discourage her.

"I understand. I know you're busy and I'm imposing on you. Tell me where to meet you."

Freeman gave directions how to find the VA hospital cafeteria. She said she'd be there in an hour or less. He walked past Kay on his way out of the library.

"What was that all about?" she asked.

"The granddaughter of my patient who died yesterday wants to meet with me. I really don't think it's anything medical-legal," he said in response to the askew look she threw him.

"You agreed?"

"Yeah. What the heck. It'll be good practice for when I'm a *real* doctor."

"Well, tell Dr. Canole," she said. "He's ultimately responsible, you know, not you. Legally speaking, Mr. Baroni wasn't really your patient."

"Yeah, sure. I know the routine." He hurried out the library door. "See you later."

Three more months, he thought on his way back to the VA. Three more months of this servitude, then they *would* be his patients.

Normally, he spent the workday in surgical scrubs, but now dressed in street clothes, he thought it'd be nice to do clinic in a shirt and tie. That might confuse some of the old vets, he laughed to himself. Besides, he had this meeting with Ms. Baroni.

Before he locked his bike at the VA, his beeper sounded. Recovery room. The amputation patient was bleeding from his stump, and his blood pressure had fallen. Freeman wondered if Dr. Canole had let the tourniquet down before closing the wound. Some of the older docs didn't worry about post-op bleeding. They were famous for saying, "All bleeding stops … eventually."

Freeman dashed straight to Recovery, where he found Jim McCallum holding pressure on the stump and looking worried.

"He wouldn't let me deflate the tourniquet before closing," McCallum said. "It's been like this since we got here." Bright red blood streamed through the dressing and around his gloved fingers.

"That's arterial. You're not going to stop that with pressure. Call the OR, tell them we've got a take-back for bleeding. Shouldn't take very long. Probably one lone pumper needing a stitch." Turning to the nurse at his side, he asked, "Is he typed and crossed?"

"Two units of packed cells," she replied.

"Go ahead and hang one. We'll probably need both," Freeman said, heading for the locker room. So much for street clothes.

Though the VA Hospital was notoriously slow with most things, arterial bleeding onto the bed served as a great motivator. Within ten minutes, they had the patient in the OR, ready for exploration. As expected, the blood emanated from a calcified branch of the popliteal artery and, once ligated, the wound dried rapidly. The two residents watched the open wound for a few minutes to make sure nothing else would break lose, then began the closure. He'd have to report this at the monthly Morbidity and Mortality conference as an "unexpected take-back" to the OR; part of their quality-assurance program. Being the chief resident, the blame would fall to him. Dr. Canole, if he even attended the conference, would not be expected to come to his rescue. One more reason he wouldn't miss being a resident.

"Dr. Freeman. There's a guest waiting for you in the hospital cafeteria," the circulating nurse said as she entered the operating room.

"Has it been an hour already?" he asked, glancing at the clock. "Tell her I'll be there in a few minutes. I have to stay until this patient is safely in Recovery."

"How did you know it was a 'her'?" the nurse asked, eyes smiling over top of her mask.

Freeman's mind wandered elsewhere. It wouldn't do to leave this patient again and have more trouble develop. That would be a *real* problem at M&M.

Completion of the closure, dressing the wound, and taking the patient to Recovery took another twenty minutes. He left the paperwork and the conversation with the family to Dr. McCallum. His lab coat over his scrubs, he hurried to the cafeteria.

Lisa Baroni sat in a booth at the far end of the dining area. Freeman wasn't sure what he'd expected, but not this. Ms. Baroni looked every bit the Wall Street professional. Her smart business suit was tailored to the slim contours of her body. Her briefcase on the worn, vinyl cushion of the booth, sat tucked under her left arm. She tapped her fingers nervously on the tabletop and surveyed the cafeteria through wire-rimmed glasses, her otherwise stern appearance softened by her blonde hair pulled back in a ponytail. She watched for him to come in the main entrance. Entering through the staff dining area gave him a few seconds to study her, the only unaccompanied woman in the room.

As he approached her table, she started to stand and extend her hand.

"Please, don't get up. I'm Dr. Freeman. You must be Ms. Baroni," he said, taking her hand. The strong grip of her skeletally thin hand felt cool to touch. *Strange*, he thought. Her nails appeared chewed to the quick.

"Thank you so much for meeting with me. I got here as quickly as I could. I hope I'm not interrupting anything," she said in a strong, determined voice; no southern lilt to her speech.

"That's quite all right. I hope I didn't keep you waiting long. We had a problem with a patient I had to personally take care of," Freeman replied, sounding a little too self-important to his own ears.

"I understand. I wouldn't be here except that I felt this important. You are the doctor that took care of Grandpa, Alphonse Baroni, before he died, aren't you?"

"Yes, ma'am," he replied, thinking he caught a hint of a British accent. "But I really never got to know him before he passed away."

"Did he say or do anything unusual before he died?"

"I'm not sure what you mean by *unusual*," he said, going over the events of the previous night in his mind yet again.

"Oh, I don't know what I mean either. Such a special person—always into something. Kept to himself, mostly, in his later years after Grandma died. He'd begun a search of some sort, months ago, and it seemed to consume him. He spent hours in our public library in West Memphis. Didn't like the internet. Sometimes, he even traveled to Little Rock or Nashville in search of information. Seemed so important to him."

She paused for a moment, searching in her briefcase.

Freeman let her look through her things uninterrupted. So, the old guy had a hobby or an interest in something. What's so important she had to drive all the way here to speak to him in person?

"Last week, I received phone calls from a group in England very interested in coming here to meet with Grandpa. They wouldn't tell me much, but said they'd make it worth my while to help them. Sort of scared me. I mean, Grandpa wasn't rich or anything, but he wasn't poor either. Sounded like a scam to me. Then, yesterday, one of them shows up at my house. I didn't tell him where Grandpa was. But it wouldn't be hard to find him here at the VA. Has anyone else contacted you about him?"

"No, ma'am. You're the first." He fingered the wooden bead through his scrubs.

They talked for several minutes about the last day of Mr. Baroni's life. She asked about Baroni's personal articles. Freeman didn't mention the bead. The conversation again came around to those interested in finding Baroni.

"Well, I thought you should know. They were persistent, to come all the way here from England, I mean. I had to pick up Grandpa's personal effects anyway. He hadn't brought much with him; just his clothes and such." She gathered her things to leave. "You sure there was nothing else of his not with his belongings?"

Freeman reached across the table and put his hand on her arm.

"There is one thing that wasn't with what the hospital gave you." He removed the cord with the wooden bead from around his neck and passed it to her. "As he died, Mr. Baroni pressed this into my hand. He thanked me for being helpful and said there were more. Then he apologized for something—I don't know what. He seemed to attach a lot of importance to this necklace."

Lisa took the artifact and her shoulders slumped. Holding it in her hands, she stared at him. For a brief second, her serious continence changed to one of pity, but quickly reverted back.

"I hoped this had gotten lost. This is what those men asked about, Dr. Freeman. Tell me exactly what Grandpa said as he gave this to you."

"Well, he asked me if I'd been a Boy Scout. And, as I said, he thought there were more of these somewhere. He said something about the Chief Boy Scout. I didn't even know there was such a position. Then, he said I'd been helpful, apologized and said nothing more." Freeman leaned forward onto the table. "Ms. Baroni, what's this all about?"

"Did he say: 'You've been helpful' or 'You are Helpful'?"

"I don't recall exactly. He may have just said the word 'helpful.' He was pretty weak at the time. Why is that important?" Freeman's concern grew. His life had taken a strange turn since Baroni gave him the bead.

Lisa drew a deep breath. She passed the bead back to him and wrapped it in his hand.

"For some reason, Grandpa wanted you to have this. He wore it since returning from World War II. A dying soldier he'd flown with during the war gave it to him. When I was a little girl, Grandpa used to tell me this made him part of a special group of men— others around the world wore similar beads. He called his bead 'Helpful.' I think all the research he did before he died centered on this thing." She swallowed and looked away. "I can't take this from you, Dr. Freeman. He always told me it was his duty to pass this on to the next 'carrier,' as he called them. That would be you. I'm sorry," she whispered.

"Why does this bead always come with an apology? Are you sure you want me to have this? I knew him for such a short time."

"Foni never did anything haphazardly," she said. "If he gave it to you, it served his purposes and you must take it. Besides, I don't want those other men to get it. They have no reason to think you have it, so it should be safe."

Something clicked in his memory. "What did you call him?" Freeman asked.

"Grandpa? Oh, his nickname: Foni. His friends gave him that during the war. I think they liked to say 'Foni Baroni,'" she said, smiling.

His mind raced. The old drunk in the alley had said something about 'phony.' Or had he been referring to 'Foni'?

His beeper sounded. Reaching down, he silenced it.

"Listen, I know you have to get back to work and I have to leave now. It would be best if we didn't see each other again or communicate on the phone. Take good care of the bead, Dr. Freeman, and thank you for all you did for Grandpa," she said, clutching her briefcase and heading toward the door.

"Wait. What am I supposed to do with this? Who are those men looking for it?"

Lisa turned and waved as she hurried away.

What was Baroni's connection to the old drunk in the alley? Was it the old black man who'd brought him to the hospital? His beeper sounded again.

"Damned thing," he said aloud as he studied the message. The world of medicine pulled him back in. Before responding, he checked to see if he still had Lisa Baroni's phone number. Yes—in his wallet. He started to slip the bead in the pocket of his lab coat, hesitated, and put the necklace around his neck, then plunged back into the bowels of the hospital.

Something rubbed him wrong about Lisa Baroni. Was the old vagrant in the alley connected to "Foni" Baroni? What was the importance of this bead? What did some guys from England want with it? Why had Lisa not taken it from him? All these questions going through his head would have to wait.

CHAPTER SEVEN

Nights sometimes dragged long and boring at the Veterans Hospital. The emergency department really served as a night clinic and true emergencies funneled to one of the downtown ERs or to the Elvis Presley Memorial Trauma Center. Freeman used this time to catch up on his studying. He had boards to take two years after finishing training. Apparently, the inpatients were sleeping quietly, and the floor nurses resisted bothering him with inane requests for laxatives or heating blankets. He struggled to stay awake and finish the latest issue of The Journal of Bone and Joint Surgery. The recliner in the surgeon's lounge provided little comfort, but it didn't have to. He'd spent many nights grabbing an hour or two of sleep in this very chair.

His head bobbed, waking him from his drowsiness until finally, he gave up. Grabbing his lab coat, he headed for the on-call room and the government-issue mattress that would serve him tonight. He'd postpone his shower until morning—it'd help him wake up.

Not bothering to change out of his scrubs, Freeman flopped onto a bed in the dark room. A second bunk occupied the far wall; the nightstand between holding a lamp and phone. Another resident slept noisily in one of the other beds. Without turning on the light, Freeman lifted the phone and dialed the hospital operator for a wake-up call at five in the morning, four short hours from now. He placed his beeper on the night stand and turned toward the wall. The previous night with Pam seemed long ago and far away.

He'd barely fallen asleep when the phone rang.

"Good morning, Dr. Freeman. Five o'clock," the operator said.

"No. That's not possible. I just got into bed," he mumbled.

"Sorry," she said and hung up.

Freeman sat on the side of his bed, his head in his hands. He'd slept hard and uninterrupted, which was unusual, but he could use a couple more hours. He stood, grabbed his coat and headed to the locker room for a quick shower and change of scrubs. Afterwards, he found Jim McCallum, and together they started morning rounds. By seven o'clock, they'd changed all their patient's dressings, entered notes into their charts, and still had time before they had to be in the OR.

"You up for some breakfast?" Freeman asked his junior resident.

"Never pass up an opportunity to eat or void," McCallum said. "One of the resident survival rules I faithfully follow."

As they turned the corner to leave the third floor, Pam Blanchard nearly ran them over.

"Oh, excuse me," he said before realizing who he'd nearly bumped into.

"Hi, Doc. Surprised to see you here so early," Pam said sarcastically.

"Yeah, right. You know me better than that. I've been here all night," he replied with a smile as he signaled to McCallum he'd catch up with him.

"Then what was all that going on in your apartment last night?" she asked.

"Nothing I know anything about. What makes you think something happened in my apartment?" he asked, trying not to be obvious as he checked her out. Not even the drab nursing outfit of the VA could completely hide the sensual woman underneath.

She paused and smiled. "Are you through? Do I pass inspection?" she teased, cocking her head to one side.

"Huh? Oh, sorry. What do you mean about my apartment?" he repeated, now back in the present.

"Well, I had the three-to-eleven shift yesterday so I drove home around 11:30 last night, and of course, I passed right by your place. A dim light was on and I saw you—or someone— moving around behind the blinds in the front room. I almost stopped, but it was late and I was pretty tired." She grinned. "Besides, I figured you needed the recuperative rest."

"You sure it was my place and not the clown next door? He's always throwing parties. I was here all night."

"Oh, it was your place all right. Keeping someone locked up in there?"

His beeper sounded. He glanced at it, noting the number for the operating room.

"Listen, I've got to go. We'll talk later," he said, touching her arm before hurrying into the stairwell. They'd decided long ago to keep the public displays of affection to a minimum while at work.

Their first case was a total hip replacement. Jim McCallum wanted desperately to do this one. The junior resident had not yet been lead surgeon on one of these. Today, Freeman would function as McCallum's first assistant, which sometimes proved harder than actually doing the case. McCallum had helped on a few hips earlier in the year. Still, it was different actually doing one, especially your first. With luck, Dr. Canole wouldn't make an appearance, or at least be late enough for them to have most of the case done before he intruded to show how they used to do it back in his day.

Freeman decided to skip breakfast and headed straight to the OR. The nurse in the pre-op area paged him with concerns about the patient's lab work. Freeman checked the chart and determined the operation could proceed as planned. He ran into McCallum at the scrub sink, who nervously fiddled with his protective helmet and the fan battery clipped to his scrub pants.

"Sorry I skipped out on breakfast. Did you get something to eat?" Freeman asked, trying to calm the younger surgeon's nerves.

"Nah, too nervous to eat," McCallum said.

Freeman nodded. A good sign. False bravado leads to errors. Being nervous meant he would be able to help McCallum instead of fight him through the case.

Freeman's mind wandered back to his apartment. Who could have been there? If it'd been a thief, the only thing he had of value was a cheap television.

The last two days had been bizarre. He touched the small bead against his chest. He'd had it less than forty-eight hours. Surely the thief wasn't after this. Nevertheless, during that time, he'd witnessed two strange deaths and had an unusual visit from one Lisa Baroni.

The two residents finished scrubbing and the staff helped them into their sterile gowns. The patient was positioned on his right side, his left leg painted a dingy orange from the antiseptic soap. The two young surgeons draped off the sterile field. Dr. McCallum assumed the position of the lead surgeon, standing to the patient's backside. Freeman stood opposite him, in front of the hip.

"Ready to start?" Freeman asked the anesthetist.

"Go ahead," came the response from behind the drapes at the head of the table.

He nodded to McCallum, who reached for the scalpel on the Mayo stand. Gladys, who'd worked at the VA for generations and seen hundreds of young surgeons come and go, slapped his hand away.

"I'll keep my hands out of your wound, and you keep your hands off my table," she scolded. "Just tell me what you want."

"Uh … knife?" McCallum said.

Gladys slapped the scalpel into his palm and placed two clean, absorbent sponges on either side of the proposed wound site. She was a rarity in the VA system: an experienced, talented scrub nurse who took a personal interest in the training of young surgeons, her forte being etiquette between doctors and nurses. For an operation to go well, the team had to work together; everyone doing his job. She managed the tools of the trade prepared for the surgeon's use on the back table. After years of doing this, she knew where everything lay and could put her hands on the next tool without so much as a glance back at them. That is, unless some rude surgeon took it upon himself to reach out of his domain and into hers.

He and Jim smiled at each other from inside their space helmets. All the residents knew Gladys and her rules and respected them. She'd grown up in the projects and feared no man. McCallum had had a momentary lapse of concentration in his nervousness about the case. Gladys' scolding broke the ice and calmed the young surgeon's jittery nerves.

McCallum visibly relaxed and set about doing the operation he'd assisted on many times. Freeman held back the soft tissues, exposing the anatomy and making the steps of the operation easy. They talked little during the case. The hoods they wore for sterility, and the small fans that circulated the air within them made conversation difficult. Requests of the scrub nurse had to be shouted over this din.

Hip replacements at the VA took about two hours, barring complications. Freeman and McCallum quickly exposed the hip joint, then came to the part requiring real judgment: placement of the components. If the cup or the stem of the hip replacement were placed even slightly out of line, the hip might dislocate post-operatively—a complication every surgeon dreaded. McCallum needed Freeman's experience at this stage of the operation.

"Looks like we got company," Gladys said.

Dr. Canole, scrubbing his hands outside the OR, peered in at them. He wore the protective helmet required during total joint replacements.

The two residents looked up at each other. McCallum's eyes seemed to plead, "Please don't leave me." Freeman motioned back to the patient as if to say, "Let's get as much of this done as we can before things grind to a halt in the name of education."

Dr. Canole burst through the door, hands held high.

"How you boys doing?" he shouted loud enough to be heard through the hoods.

"Good morning, Dr. Canole," Freeman replied. "We're actually almost done here. You really don't have to scrub in, if you don't want to."

"Yeah, we're almost done," McCallum echoed.

"Well, let me just take a look. I've done more than a few of these in my time. Besides, Dr. Freeman, you have someone here who needs to see you. Says he knows you from college. Says it's important. Came in from D.C. this morning." Canole stepped to the table to take Freeman's place.

Freeman looked away from the operation and at Dr. Canole. This marked the second time in two days Canole had had to relieve him from an operation to take care of personal business.

"He's in the surgeon's lounge," Canole said, taking the retractor from his hands.

Freeman was too startled to feel empathy for Jim, who looked as though he would reach across the table and grab his arms. Freeman felt as if caught in a web not of his making. A sinking feeling washed over him.

He left the OR and grabbed his lab coat as he exited through the locker room. Who did he know from college, now in D.C.? One of the nurses stopped him before he entered the surgeon's lounge.

"If that tall, dark hunk is available, I want him," she said.

He entered the lounge. "Patrick Dartson!" He embraced his roommate from his last two years at Dartmouth. "Good to see you, man. What brings you down here?"

"Good to see you too, *Doctor*," Patrick replied, stepping back and holding out David's lab coat to show the printing over the left breast pocket.

"Yeah, how 'bout that? Who'd a thunk it back then, huh?" David said. "What brings you way down south? Whatcha doing in D.C.? You're not President yet, are you?"

"Not hardly. Wouldn't want that job. I'm with the Department of Homeland Security. Been there since we left Hanover. Listen,

I need a few minutes of your time. Is there somewhere we can go and speak privately?"

"Yeah, sure. We can use one of the on-call rooms. Won't be anyone there this time of day. Might be a little rank, though, if housekeeping hasn't gotten to it."

"Be just like old times, huh?" Patrick said. "Lead the way. I'll grab my briefcase and be right behind you."

Walking through the hospital, the two talked about others in their college class and what had become of them. When they reached the on-call quarters, David threw open the door and sank onto one of the bunks, offering the room's only chair to Patrick. After closing the door, Patrick pulled the chair around to face his friend.

"Part of my job, David, is to keep track of foreign nationals with questionable purposes. Most turn out to be innocent travelers. Some are here on shady business, but if there's no threat to national security, we don't get involved. Two days ago, something was brought to my attention with your name on it."

"Okay, I know I'm a little outspoken about politics," David said, "and may have written a letter or two to the editor of *The Commercial Appeal*, but I didn't think it'd attract national attention."

"No, it's nothing like that. The British have had trouble with a group of Africans who're apparently stalking British citizens. A few older Brits have turned up dead. So far, they have no motive. No demands have been made and nothing has turned up missing. Nothing important, anyway. The killers are a strange group though, and as of this moment, thought to be dangerous." He shifted in the chair. "Two days ago, some people from South Africa fitting this profile landed in the U.S. and made their way here to Memphis. They had a list of names with them. Don't ask how I know that." He paused. "Your name was on that list."

Patrick held his gaze, a serious expression on his face. "What do you mean: 'my name was on the list'?" David asked. "A list for what?"

Patrick ignored his question. "Do you know a Moses Donnelly?"

"Never heard of him," David said, getting a little anxious.

"Yesterday morning, Moses died in your emergency room," Patrick said. "Seems he'd been beaten to death by some street thugs."

"Wait a minute. Old guy? Black?"

"Yep. And your name was on the report turned in by the paramedics," Patrick added.

"I didn't know the guy's name. And for the record, he didn't die in the ER. He was already dead when they brought him in."

"That's the one. Had you seen him in the hospital before that morning?"

"Come on, Patrick. What's this all about? My name on some list, you coming down from D.C., and now a dead bum in the ER? Is this going somewhere?"

"Another name on the list was Alphonse Baroni. I understand you were one of his doctors."

David clutched the bead at his chest. Patrick's expression changed.

"Is that the wooden bead?" Patrick nodded toward David's hand at his chest.

"What? How'd you know that? This is all too strange. Ever since Mr. Baroni gave me this thing, weird stuff has been happening. Is that what this is about? The bead? Here, you take it. I don't want it," he said, taking it from around his neck and thrusting it toward his friend.

"It's not that easy, I'm afraid," Patrick said, refusing to accept the bead.

"His granddaughter wouldn't take it either," David said, rolling the bead around in his hands, examining it.

"What granddaughter?" Patrick bolted upright in his chair.

"Lisa Baroni, from Little Rock or West Memphis, I think. She came to the hospital yesterday to talk to me about her grandfather's death. Seems they were pretty close."

"Could you describe her well enough for an artist to sketch a picture?"

"Better than that, I have her phone number. Why don't you call her?" David said, handing him the scrap of paper from his wallet.

"Have you tried the number yet?" Patrick asked.

"Just the one time when I first returned her call."

Patrick reached for his cell phone. He paced around the room as he dialed the number and waited. Seconds later, he dialed the number again, this time handing the phone to David.

David stared at the phone in Patrick's hand and hesitated. Finally, he took it and put it to his ear.

"The number you have dialed is no longer in service. If you think you have reached this number in error, please—" David cut it off. Looking confused, he handed the phone back to his friend.

"Alphonse Baroni had no children," Patrick said. "Therefore, I doubt he had a granddaughter."

"I don't understand any of this." David jumped up from the bunk. His beeper sounded. "Damn this thing. How does it always know the worst time to go off?" He pulled the beeper off his hip and glanced at the number.

"Is that important?" Patrick asked, nodding toward the beeper.

"Just one of the floors. Let me take care of this. Don't run off." David reached for the phone on the nightstand.

"You and I need to have a talk—right now." Patrick left no doubt about the seriousness of the issue.

David stared at his friend and talked with the floor nurse. He then called the hospital operator and instructed her to put all his pages through to Dr. McCallum.

He hung up the phone. "Start talking."

CHAPTER EIGHT

David told Patrick the whole story, starting with the strange death of Alphonse Baroni and the gift of the bead, through the death of Moses Donnelly, and concluding with the visit from a woman claiming to be Baroni's granddaughter. He started to tell his friend about Pam, the special woman in his life, when he remembered his last conversation with her.

"Damn," David said. "Running into you almost made me forget."

"Forget what?" Patrick asked.

"A few hours ago I bumped into Pam, who said she saw someone in my apartment last evening. I was here at the hospital all night taking calls," David said, glancing at his watch. "I haven't had a chance to follow up on that."

"I assume Pam is your girlfriend."

"How'd you know that?"

"Let's head over to your place. Get your stuff and we'll leave now."

"It's not that easy, Patrick. I can't just run out of the hospital."

"Well, do whatever it is you have to do, and let's get going," Patrick said, pushing him out the door of the call room. "My car's in front of the hospital. Shouldn't take us long."

David made a few phone calls and then walked with Patrick to his car.

"Okay, I've spilled my guts. How's about a little *quid pro quo*?" David said as they climbed into the car.

"Fair enough. I'll tell you what I know." He backed out of the space and threw it in drive. "As part of my job with the Department of Homeland Security, I have access to lists of, let's say, less than desirable people entering the country. We look for trends in their travel pattern. Our computers tell us if there's any unusual influx of people from a particular region. The British do the same. Several weeks back, the Brits had a string of murders with no obvious motive, the victims all elderly men. Some eye-witnesses described tall, thin, black men in the area who seemed out of place. The Brits think they're from South Africa—members of a Zulu tribe."

"What would Zulus be doing in Great Britain, and why would they murder old men?" David asked, his mind jumping back to his encounter with Moses Donnelly in the alley.

Patrick turned left on Madison.

"You know where I live?"—more an exclamation of surprise than a real question.

"That information's not hard to come by," Patrick said. They pulled into the parking lot of David's apartment and Patrick took charge. "Don't go in. Stay with the car while I check out the building."

David threw him a look demanding an explanation.

Patrick paused before exiting the car. "I've been in this situation many times. It's my job. I'm not looking for clues on this trip around the perimeter of the complex. I'll take them if I find them, but my real objective is to look for escape routes and defensive positions before entering your place. My partner, Adnan Fazeph, and I have been ambushed more than once entering strange buildings. Knowing the lay of the land ahead of time saved our lives on those occasions. I feel particularly vulnerable doing this alone." He stepped from the car. "Be right back."

David got out and patiently leaned on the car. Minutes later, Patrick slinked up behind, startling him.

"Okay, 007. Can we go in now?" David asked.

"Let me enter first. You follow when I tell you it's safe." Patrick headed up the stairs.

They slowed, approaching his apartment. There'd been a forced entry. The frame opposite the latch appeared broken and although the door was pulled shut, the latch didn't catch. The complex had not installed burglar alarms, and David made a note to talk to management.

"Looks like your friend was right. You did have visitors while you were out."

With his foot, Patrick nudged the door. A large semi-automatic pistol appeared in his right hand.

David stood dumbfounded at the appearance of his door and at the sight of Patrick's gun.

"Shouldn't we call the police or something?" he asked.

Ignoring him, Patrick cautiously proceeded into the apartment. Looking over Patrick's shoulder, David saw his personal things scattered about. His television, the only thing of value, sat on its stand, untouched. After a few minutes, Patrick signaled him to come in and stood aside as David took inventory.

"Anything missing?" Patrick asked, breaking the silence.

"Nothing except my peace of mind," David said. "Am I supposed to stay here tonight?"

In the corner of the bedroom, something must've caught Patrick's eye. He brushed aside some scattered clothing and carefully reached down, lifting a palm-sized wooden object; ball-like and finished with a dark stain, except for the flat bottom, which looked smooth and light; the color of unstained wood.

"What's this?" Patrick asked, holding the object for David's inspection.

"I'd say it used to be part of my bed frame." David pointed to the left side of his headboard. On top of the right bed post sat its mate; the left bed post missing its round top. A small splinter of wood peeled away from the post where the ball once sat.

David took a closer look. The cut surface of wood felt remarkably smooth except for the last bit where it had come loose.

"There aren't many weapons in the world that will cleave wood like that," Patrick said, still examining the bedpost. "This wasn't done with a blunt object or even an axe. Whatever took this off had a very sharp edge—and some heft to it."

David glanced over the headboard and noticed for the first time his great-grandfather's sword was missing, the bare nails from which it hung protruding rudely from the drywall. He clenched his jaw and ran his fingers through his hair. "That meant a lot to me."

Patrick cocked his head, waiting for an explanation.

David explained about the missing heirloom.

"It was a Zulu weapon? Sounds more Islamic to me," Patrick said.

David glanced at his watch. "I've got to get back to the hospital. It's time for afternoon rounds and my junior resident will wonder where I am. Can you give me a lift back?"

"What are you going to do about your place here? The door won't close, you know."

"Oh, yeah. Guess I forgot about that." David surveyed the mess in his apartment and frowned.

"Listen," Patrick said. "My P.C.'s in the car, and I've got some paper work to do. Call your building super about the break-in. I'm sure he'll want the police to look it over before fixing the door. I'll stay here after I've dropped you off at the hospital."

"Thanks. That would be a help. I shouldn't be at work much longer, then I'm gonna need some shut-eye. You think I should stay here tonight?"

Patrick hesitated before answering. "Only if I can stay with you." He smiled. "The couch doesn't look too bad. If you've got an extra blanket and towel, it'll be like old times back in Hanover."

"You're serious about this, aren't you? Do you really think I'm in some kind of danger because of this bead?" David pulled the cord from his shirt.

"Put that away!" Patrick said. "Damn right, I'm serious. And I wouldn't be waving that around in public unless you want to be separated from your head like the bedpost here." He sucked in a deep breath. "I haven't told you the manner of death of the older Brits who got caught up in this, have I? If the Zulus indeed killed

Moses Donnelly, he's the first to go to his grave with his head still attached." Patrick tossed the wooden ball to David. "The Brits have kept that information under wraps for fear of alarming the public. My partner calls them the *denogginators*."

David stared at his friend in disbelief. He saw in Patrick's expression the seriousness of the situation.

"Yeah, okay. If you don't mind, I don't. Take me back to the hospital after I call the superintendent. Better yet, let's go over there. His office is in the next building. That way, I can introduce you, and he'll know you're with me."

They did just that, then headed to the hospital. Patrick dropped him off and left to return to the apartment. At the hospital, David caught up with Jim McCallum and they finished rounds. Leaving the hospital with his pack over his shoulder, he ran into Pam, also finished for the day.

"Need a ride home, Doctor?" she asked.

"No. My bike's chained in the locker room. I'm on my way there now," he replied, his mind elsewhere.

"Got plans for the evening?" she asked.

"What? … uh, no, not really. Some personal stuff to take care of, that's all. I'll call and tell you about it later." He turned down the corridor toward the locker rooms.

"Maybe sooner than that," he heard her say, more to herself than him.

David used the ride home to sort things out. He felt bad about blowing off Pam. So much had happened. Who'd ransacked his apartment, and why had they taken his sword? Who was that mysterious woman pretending to be Baroni's granddaughter? What did this have to do with him? And why now—with only three months of training left?

He was glad to have Patrick along on this strange ride. Sorting this out on his own would have been a daunting task. Patrick had never been above using his all-Ivy line-backing skills to solve problems off the field.

What day of the week was it, anyway? Probably Wednesday or Thursday, but he truly didn't know. Working thirty-six hour shifts, the days tended to blur together. Before he'd answered any of these questions, he found himself home and carried his bike up to his apartment.

The door frame had been hastily repaired and would at least shut, but not securely. It needed some finish work and paint, but at the moment, that didn't bother him. Inside, he found a note from Patrick.

> Having second thoughts about spending the night. Call me when you get in ... Patrick.

What now? Fatigue dulled his mind. Even though he'd dozed a few hours at the hospital last night, it hadn't been good sleep. He'd learned his first year to sleep lightly in order to rapidly respond to emergent situations. Right now, he needed a shower and some sack time. Surely, the crooks wouldn't hit his place two nights in a row. They didn't find much the first time. Why would they come back? His hand wandered to the bead hanging around his neck.

Dropping his pack, he picked up the phone and dialed Patrick. He heard a series of clicks and beeps, then finally, his friend's voice.

"Hey, David. Make it home okay?"

"You tell me. What's that noise on the phone?" David collapsed on the sofa. "You got my place bugged or wired or something?"

"Maybe. Just a few precautions. Listen. I've done more research on the perps, and according to the Brits, they're tenacious about getting what they're after. They stalk their victim until catching him alone, usually at home. Pack a bag, and I'll pick you up in a few minutes. I'll put you up here in my hotel room for a few nights and let's see what happens. No need to take risks," Patrick hung up, giving David no chance to argue.

He gripped the receiver and stared at the mess around him. Oh well, the hotel would have nicer accommodations. He spent the next few minutes putting his stuff away and cleaning. Gave him a small feeling of being in control of something.

———

Pam ran a few errands before heading home. First, she stopped by the grocery and picked up a couple of pork chops. She had this great recipe for chops with an apple glaze that David said was "to die for." Wild rice and asparagus would round out their meal. Now, what to wear? Her other outfit of jeans, sweater, and high heels had worked wonders. Maybe she should stick with that, but wear a different sweater. She'd have to hurry to make it home, fix dinner, shower and do her hair. David said he had errands to run. He'd get home late, and that meant close to being asleep. In any case, she'd wake him up, and he wouldn't regret it. He seemed distracted at the hospital today, but the old spark had surfaced.

Pangs of guilt stabbed her. It had been four years—time to move on. Still, she paused long enough to glance at the photo she kept tucked in a zippered compartment of her purse. They'd been so happy, despite being in Bagdad and at war. Robert's smile warmed her, even over the years and from the grave. The tattered edges of the photo had yellowed. She knew David wanted more than just a girlfriend, but until recently, she had no more to give. Maybe it was time.

She finished checking out at the grocery and sped home. The pork chops needed time to cook; time enough for her to clean up. She stepped into the shower and thought back to a couple of nights before.

Blow drying her hair took the most time, and she nearly burnt dinner in the process. She'd prepare the rice and asparagus at his place. On second thought, he had none of the necessary cooking utensils, so she hurriedly made the dishes before leaving. He did have a microwave.

The proper wardrobe gave her pause. Should she even bother with undergarments? A sexy bra under a sheer blouse. That'd work. She selected her most seductive bra; one all but transparent itself. The thong always pushed his buttons, so that was a no-brainer. Over this, she squeezed into a short skirt and slipped on a thin, white blouse that looked more like a man's shirt. With the top two buttons open and her hair down over the collar, he'd be helpless. Maybe loafers rather than heels. That'd give him something to say about her wardrobe and get the conversation centered on her appearance. From there, she could take him in any direction. Men were so predictable. She knew she didn't have to go to all this trouble, that he'd be happy with her dressed in burlap. But she enjoyed his response to her efforts.

Pam loaded the food into a wicker picnic basket, checked herself one more time in the mirror, and headed out the door. The short walk to his apartment chilled her. The lights in the parking areas lit the way. Winter dragged on endlessly. When would spring come with the switch back to Daylight Savings Time and longer days? It'd been a long, cold season.

No security lights shined on his apartment door. She knocked and waited, key in hand if needed. When no answer came, she tried the knob. The locked handle held fast, but the door came open as she jiggled it. *Well, that's not good.* He'd have to get that fixed. This wasn't a high crime area, but he should at least have a secure door. *Had it been like that two nights ago?*

She leaned her head into the apartment. The only light filtered from the kitchenette.

"Anyone home?" she called out. "Hello? Dr. Freeman? David?"

He must not be home yet from his errands. Calling the whole thing off briefly passed through her mind. He'd be back soon. This gave her time to fix up his place.

She stepped into the apartment and closed the door. The latch caught, but with just a little tug, opened again. She pushed the door closed, shaking her head.

The table cloth and candles added a nice touch. She put the oven on low and slid the covered food dish inside. Surely, he wouldn't be much longer. Straightening up his apartment proved irresistible. The sloppily made bed took no time to fix. With the covers partially turned down and the pillows arranged, it actually looked presentable. She noticed the missing piece from the bedpost. Now that was new. That dreadful sword was gone also.

Next stop, the bathroom. Some last minute primping. Her watch showed it to be nearly seven. One last check of the apartment and she settled onto the couch and flipped on the TV. The coffee table made a good footrest. She leaned back into the corner of the couch, careful not to mess her hair. For cheap apartment furniture, the sofa felt pretty comfortable. Better than the one in her place.

It had been a long day. An episode of *Survivor* played on one of the channels. She'd have to pour herself a glass of wine and start without him. Reluctantly, she rose from the couch and checked to see if the remnant of their first bottle still sat in the fridge. Luck was on her side, and she did as planned, pulling the small blanket from the back of the couch over herself. She'd hear him coming in time to straighten up before he got through the door. Wouldn't he be surprised and pleased to see her here with dinner ready?

The wine hit fast; the couch so warm and comfortable. She'd just close her eyes for a moment. He'd be home soon.

A noise outside the apartment startled her into wakefulness. How long had she been asleep? She glanced at her watch. Ten thirty! She scurried toward the bathroom. How had it gotten to be so late? Would he even want to eat now? Was the food in the oven still good? She turned it off and pulled the dish out on her way by. Many questions raced through her mind as she stood in front of the bathroom mirror.

The front door opened as she continued fussing with her hair. Let him get into the apartment and then turn the corner and surprise him.

She sensed him coming up behind her and glanced sideways into the mirror. What she saw was not David. A dark, thick-featured face stared at her; the ebony skin streaked with paint and partially covered by a frightening feather headdress. Bare-chested and hairless, around his neck hung a string of three beads. The black man lurched at her. In his right hand, he wielded a large knife—David's sword.

Pam screamed as his arms locked around her torso. She struggled against his overpowering strength, the grip about her chest stifling any further cries. Flinging up her right arm, she cut it against the razor edge of the weapon. The sight of her own blood sickened her, but she kicked and fought as he effortlessly carried her from the bathroom. Twisting in the giant's stifling grip, Pam saw two other men. One lashed out at her, striking her in the eye as she stood helpless, her arms pinned. Her knees gave way. The room grew dark.

CHAPTER NINE

SOUTH AFRICA, JANUARY 1967

Banta Manjabe finally turned age twelve—old enough to join his local troop. Scouting had many participants in South Africa. Some saw it as a paramilitary organization. Banta had often watched his older brothers in their Scouting uniforms head to meetings or outings and begged to come along. Now he could go on his own. The hand-me-down status of his ragtag uniform from his older brothers didn't matter. It was now his. He wished for a full-length mirror in which to admire himself. Surely, he looked as regal as his brothers. No matter. He was a Scout.

Through the open window of their shanty home, Banta spotted his three brothers, Jarmangi, Tungata, and Pantal, heading off to the meeting. He raced after them.

"Well, look who is finally a Scout come to join us," Jarmangi, the oldest, said.

Banta knew he was their pet and they loved him, but he wanted their respect also.

"Lead the way, Scout," Jarmangi said. "Take the spoor. Show us to our meeting."

Banta had secretly followed them many times as they had made their way down the dirt road through the hills of South Africa to the grass thatched hut that served as their meeting place. He knew the way well.

He and his brothers thought nothing of the hot, dusty path. Barefoot like the rest, he sprang into the lead and ran down the road toward the first hill. He turned and laughed, taunting his brothers to try and catch him. The game was on. He ran fast, but Jarmangi had earned the reputation as the fastest boy in the village. Banta grabbed the cloth cap from his own head so he wouldn't lose it, and sprinted away. Through his laughter, he could hear his brothers gaining on him. Never had he run so fast. He was a Scout.

He crested the hill and turned left down the dirt trail. Now he would really pick up speed. He breathed rapidly, no longer laughing. He felt it important to become one of them, not just the little brother. Beating them in this footrace would go far toward acceptance. He heard their footsteps closing in behind. One more hill. Get over the next hill, and the hut would be in sight. If he could outrace them to that point, it'd be a victory.

At the bottom of the hill, the path jutted right around overgrown, shoulder-high shrubbery. As he reached the bend in the trail, he glanced over his right shoulder, but saw only Tungata and Pantal. Suddenly, he crashed into something or someone. Jarmangi had leapt out of the brush and blocked his way. Banta never saw him. The two tumbled onto the dusty road. The others joined in this rolling heap of laughing, wrestling Zulu brothers.

"How did you do that? How did you get ahead of me?" Banta asked, brushing himself off and arranging his cap and neckerchief.

"Ah, Banta. You have much to learn. The cleared path is not always the best way," Jarmangi said. "Come, let us march as brothers to the meeting."

The eldest lined them up and inspected their uniforms, straightening here, tucking there. He then assumed the lead position, and off they marched, proud and in step, to join their friends.

The meeting was already in progress as they entered the hut. The Scouts sat together on the dirt floor listening to the Scoutmaster. Banta and his brothers joined them at the back of the group.

"One of our troop has been selected to go to the Jamboree in America later this year," boomed the old Zulu Scoutmaster. "It is to be held in the state of Idaho in Farragut Park. Our Scout will join others from troops elsewhere in Africa. We will present a gift to the Jamboree officials. The nature of this gift has not yet been determined, but it must be something from Africa to Scouting worldwide." He paused. Banta knew going to America was a once-in-a-lifetime chance for the lucky boy chosen. The room buzzed with the excited chatter of the youngsters.

"Jarmangi Manjabe! Come forward please," the Scoutmaster shouted above the ruckus.

Jarmangi looked to his brothers and then back to the front of the room. His brothers pushed him to his feet and forward. The oldest and tallest of the Scouts, nearly fully developed and already six feet tall, he'd earned the respect of his younger comrades. The boys parted for his brother as he made his way to the wooden platform that served as their stage. Banta could barely contain his excitement, his chest bursting with pride.

"Jarmangi," said the old Scoutmaster, "your work with the Scouts and your efforts to help others has been rewarded. The leaders of this troop have selected you to represent us at the American Jamboree."

Thunderous applause and dancing erupted in the hut. Banta and the other young Zulus spontaneously launched into the celebratory dance of their ancestors and formed a large circle of bodies, chanting for Jarmangi to enter. The circle opened as he approached and closed behind him. They chanted and danced in their native tradition. To Banta, their Scouting uniforms seemed to transmogrify into the native garb of loin cloths and feathers, the aura respectfully joyous. Finally, their leader called them back to order and they settled into a ring around Jarmangi and the Scoutmaster.

"Jarmangi, show the younger Scouts your Wood Badge and explain to them the significance," the Scoutmaster said.

Banta's oldest brother seemed to grow taller. He reached inside his shirt and pulled out the small bead Banta had seen many times, but had attached no significance to.

"Many years ago in the Matabele war with the British and the Dutch, a string of beads very much like this one was found on one of our ancestors, Chief Dinizulu, after he died in battle," Jarmangi explained. "A man named Baden-Powell took these beads to England. Years later, Baden-Powell formed the Boy Scouts. He gave these beads to the first Scoutmasters he trained in Gilwell Park, England. Since then, the order of the Wood Badge has come to represent great achievement in Scouting." Banta and the others sat spellbound. "Each Scout to reach this pinnacle is awarded a replica of those original beads. That is what I wear around my neck today. The Wood Badge ties us to our roots in Scouting and to our roots in Africa."

"Where are the original beads, the ones taken from Chief Dinizulu?" Banta blurted out. Those around him and his other brothers quickly hushed him into silence. He had spoken out of turn in his first meeting.

"Forgive my young brother. He does not yet know the ways of a Scout, but he will learn," Jarmangi said to the group, casting a stern look his way. "His question is a good one, though.

"The original beads are scattered round the world. Some were lost in the World Wars. Others have been handed down from their original owners to relatives or other Scouts. They are very valuable to those of us who know their history," Jarmangi said.

"But they belong to Chief Dinizulu's people," Banta blurted out. His other brothers jostled with him in an effort to quiet him. He jerked free and remained standing.

"What my impudent young brother says is true," Jarmangi said. "The original beads do belong to us, the Matabele people, and the descendants of Chief Dinizulu. They are a part of our history. However, it is unlikely they will be returned." He paused here and paced within the circle, obviously in deep thought.

"My younger brother's questions have stirred something within me." Again he paused and looked to the Scout leaders, who stood apart from the circle of boys.

"In celebration of my trip to the Jamboree in America and to honor the history of Africa and Scouting, I propose we make a replica of Chief Dinizulu's necklace. I propose we take this as a gift to the Scouting leaders in America. In fact, we should make several necklaces." Jarmangi seemed inspired and his enthusiasm contagious. "We will keep one with us in Africa. We will take another three to America and present one to the Jamboree, one to the American Scouts and one to the British Scouts. Our efforts will be famous throughout the world." He concluded, his hands raised over his head, his chin thrust proudly forward, defiant.

Again, the boys erupted into spontaneous chanting and dancing as the troop took up the cause. Jarmangi had whipped them into a fever pitch.

The old Scoutmaster allowed them their celebration, then stepped into their midst. "Scout Jarmangi is wise beyond his years," he said. "This task he proposes is good. There is much to be done, however, and we will need help from other troops if we are to make so many beads. Let us conclude our meeting today. The leaders of your troop will make plans for the upcoming months prior to the Jamboree."

The circle disintegrated and the Scouts lined up in their patrols and repeated the Scouting pledge before heading home in their separate ways.

Banta and his brothers hurried down the mile-long trek to their home.

"I don't get it," Banta said. "If the beads belong to Africa, why must we make more to give to those who took them from us?" His chest swelled with pride to see his oldest brother consider his question.

"Banta, the beads were taken from us many years ago. If we had known then what would become of them, would we not have given them freely? If they in some way led to the movement of Scouting, have they not served a good purpose? Should we not then, symbolically, give them to those who took them from us, as a gesture of forgiveness?" Jarmangi paused, his eyes slanted in wisdom toward his little brother.

This logic confused him. Jarmangi might be right. Banta kicked up dust from the path. Still, he felt troubled. He vowed one day to set things right. At the moment, though, he decided the best tactic was to change the subject. With a burst of speed, he raced passed Jarmangi and leaped high, snatching the cap from his brother's head.

"Now I've stolen your cap, you must give me another," he said, laughing and running as hard as he could down the road. The ensuing footrace ended in a mass of tumbling arms and legs and shrieks of laughter. It had been a good day for the brothers.

CHAPTER TEN

IDAHO, AUGUST 1967

Twelve thousand eleven Scouts from one hundred five countries assembled in Farragut State Park, Idaho, for the start of the 1967 Scouting Jamboree—the theme for this event: For Friendship. The long trip for Jarmangi and three other Scouts from the Zulu nation took them through London, New York City, Seattle, and finally, into a van for the long trek to the northern Idaho campsite: a journey of over twenty-two hours. They would have been dead on their feet were it not for the excitement and wonder of being in this new land. The Scoutmasters, as well as their young charges, stared wide-eyed and speechless at the sights and sounds of America and its people. They'd seen places like this on television but felt unprepared for what they now experienced.

The day of arrival at the campsite, the leaders arranged a stay in a local motel. Officially, the Jamboree didn't begin until the next day, August 1st. As the van pulled into the small resort motel buried deep in the Idaho woods, the Scouts could barely contain their eagerness. Jarmangi, the oldest and tallest of the group, tried to assume the air of an experienced leader, but even he bubbled with anticipation.

Before the van doors opened, their expedition leader, Scoutmaster Banaganga, pivoted in his seat and demanded their attention.

"Before you step from the van and begin this incredible adventure, I want you to listen to me. There will be much time for fun and exploration later. While our local host and driver, Scoutmaster Jackson, checks us in, I want you to assemble with me to the edge of the woods beyond the picnic table to the right of the building. Does everyone see that?"

He waited as four heads nodded acknowledgement.

"Good. Now go use the restrooms inside and meet me there in five minutes. Do not be late."

The three adults remained seated as the four young Scouts burst from the van. Stan Jackson, Danbi Banaganga, and the other African leader watched their young charges explode with barely containable joy out the sliding door of the vehicle and through the entrance of the motel.

"Will they be all right here—in America, I mean?" Stan asked the African Scout leaders.

"I think we have chosen these boys well," Danbi answered. "The tall one, Jarmangi, is a natural leader, and the others will look to him for guidance. They will be fine."

"Still, at the moment, America is a troubled land," Stan said. "As you no doubt know, there are many riots in major cities protesting the Vietnam War. Many of these have taken racial overtones. Even here in this remote part of Idaho, there are people who will look upon your boys with hatred because of their skin color. You must keep them close to the campsite where they'll be safe."

The Zulu Scoutmasters did not reply, but turned to watch after the boys making their way toward the picnic table. They'd been chosen not only because they were good Scouts, but because of their maturity and knowledge of English. Still, a look of concern spread over the faces of both African men.

Danbi Banaganga slid from the van and accompanied their host to the registration desk. After picking up the keys to the boys' rooms, he walked outside and turned toward the waiting group of young Zulus. True to their native upbringing, they sat not at the picnic table, but on the ground beside it. Jarmangi commanded their attention and coached them in something. The three younger boys fidgeted, but quietly listened. As their Scoutmaster approached, Jarmangi either concluded his remarks or cut them off.

"So, what do you think of America so far?" the Scoutmaster asked.

The boys let out a chorus of whoops and cheers.

"This land is very different from ours in some ways and very like it in others," Banaganga continued. "As you have already noticed, the trees and grasses are diverse and beautiful in their own way. The animals in these forests are not the same as those at home. The people also are unique. Mostly, they are good people." He paused and studied each boy. "You know of the problems with apartheid in our country. America is no different, and at this time, is perhaps more troubled with racial problems than South Africa. Just two years ago, in a city called Watts, a large race riot burned many buildings and hurt many people. This state of Idaho is far removed, but even here, there are those who will look upon you with evil in their eyes because of your skin color."

The boys exchanged nervous glances. Banaganga continued.

"I wish for you a wonderful time during this adventure. But I also want you to be wise and careful in your actions. Do not wander alone. Explore with a friend. Watch out for each other. Be Prepared, right Scouts?" Four heads nodded in unison.

"Here are your keys. We are on the border of a large National Park. The trails leading into the woods have signs explaining the wonders of the forest." He checked his watch. "We have two hours before dinner. Go to your room and settle in. Then you will be free to explore. Explore as a group, at least for now." He pointed to the one he knew he could depend on the most. "Jarmangi?"

"Yes, sir," the tall Zulu boy responded.

"You are the leader of this patrol," Banaganga said. Addressing the others, "When there is no adult, you will listen to Jarmangi and follow his council. Is that clear?"

"Yes, sir," they responded.

"Good. Now go," he said, handing out room keys.

Paired in two rooms, Jarmangi and his roommate, Gonza, entered theirs and felt immediately chilled by the blast of conditioned air.

"This is like the airplanes," Gonza said. "Why do they keep the air so cold?"

"I think Americans must like it like that," Jarmangi replied. "They are unaccustomed to the heat, as we are. I think that is the machine that keeps the air so cold," Jarmangi said, pointing to the air conditioner in the window. "Maybe we can turn it off." He approached the unit and played with the buttons until finally the stream of cold air stopped.

Gonza turned on the television and nearly stumbled backwards, finger pointing, mouth agape.

"Jarmangi! It is color! The picture—it is color!"

The two stared in wonder at the images on the television. Gonza changed the channel. Of the three stations, two broadcasted in color.

A loud, excited knock on the door pulled their attention from the TV. Gonza opened it and the other two Scouts rushed in.

"Have you seen the television?" the Scout called Bon exclaimed. "Yes! Look! The pictures are colored!"

All four Scouts sat on the beds in one room watching the television when their Scoutmasters walked by their open door. The boys acknowledged the two men and turned quickly back to the TV. Jarmangi saw the adults shaking their heads and laughing as they continued down the hall.

The next morning, August 1st, marked the beginning of the Jamboree. Scouts from all over the world set up campsites and prepared for the next week of competitions and events. The campsite occupied a large, cleared area of land surrounded by pristine forests of the Great Northwest. In summer, Idaho could be hot and even humid, but this night, the air felt cool and crisp.

A few thin clouds streaked the horizon, seeming to catch fire as the sun reflected off their undersides. That evening, at sunset, all 12,011 Scouts and their adult leaders gathered in front of a large campfire. A speaker's podium stood to the side of the fire.

R. T. Lund, Acting Director of the Jamboree, called them to order. He led them in reciting the Scouting pledge, as though at an ordinary weekly meeting of some small troop. He then covered the ground rules of making such a large camp work. When the formalities concluded, he turned the stage over to their special guest for the event, Vice President Hubert H. Humphrey.

"Is that really the vice president of America?" Jarmangi asked Scoutmaster Banaganga. The older man nodded, his eyes never leaving the speaker on the podium thirty feet in front of them.

"Maybe you should do the presentation," Jarmangi said. "I cannot stand with such men."

"Nonsense," the Scoutmaster replied. "He is only a man, and you have traveled longer and harder than he to be here. The beads were your idea and you should have the honor. You will do well, Scout Jarmangi."

The vice president concluded his remarks to thunderous applause and turned the stage over to R. T. Lund, who introduced the next speaker, Lady Olave Baden-Powell, the widow of the founder of the Scouting movement. Though slow and frail with age, she stood on her own after being helped to the podium, and with a strong clear voice, addressed the young men.

"My husband would have been so proud of you," she began. "Sixty years ago, this movement started when Stephe, my husband, invited twenty-two young men to a campsite off the coast of England on Brownsea Island." She waxed for a few minutes about her husband, Lord Baden-Powell, and the early days of Scouting.

Jarmangi could hardly contain his excitement and nervousness. "Her husband took Chief Dinizulu's beads to England?" he asked.

Banaganga again nodded. "He is dead now, God rest his soul."

This seemed surreal to Jarmangi. These names had been part of his life for the last six months as the Scouts of Africa carved the acacia beads he'd present later this same evening. But they had only been names. The importance of the moment overwhelmed him. He thought of his youngest brother in Africa and wondered what questions directed at Lady Baden-Powell Banta might blurt out. This made him laugh and calmed him. Banta would probably accuse the Lady of thievery and have to be physically restrained.

Jarmangi's mind wandered far away in Africa when he heard his name called over the loud-speaker. His Scoutmaster, already standing by his side, reached to help him to his feet. The young Zulu nervously glanced about. All eyes trained on him.

"... the Wooden Badge. And here to make the presentation is Scout Jarmangi Mangabe, representing the Scouts of South Africa."

During Jarmangi's daydreaming, R. T. Lund had replaced Lady Baden-Powell on stage, and now gestured for him to come forward. Scoutmaster Banaganga accompanied him to the podium, but did not ascend it with him. Jarmangi had rehearsed this moment many times, but that seemed so long ago. He stood and stared out at the sea of Scouts.

"Scout Jarmangi? Do you have something you'd like to present to us?" R. T. Lund asked. Jarmangi stared back at him and for a moment, stood silent. He looked to his three friends who gave him the Zulu hand salute for courage. This bolstered his confidence and he stepped to the microphone. At first, the boom of his own voice startled him, but he rapidly regained composure.

"The Scouts of Africa would like to present to this Jamboree three replicas of the necklace found in our land many years ago by the Chief Scout of the World, Lord Baden-Powell. The beads of the necklaces are symbolic of those given by Lord Baden-Powell to the first Scoutmasters he trained in Gilwell Park, England.

We have made four of these necklaces. One will stay with us in Africa. The other three will be presented tonight to Mr. Lund, Mr. Joe Brunton, the Chief Scout of the United States, and to Mr. John Thurman, the first Camp Chief of Gilwell in England."

With that, Jarmangi produced a leather pouch that had been at his side the whole evening, and from it removed the three beaded necklaces. Each of the men walked to him on stage, and he had no trouble placing the beads about their necks, for he stood easily as tall as or taller than they. What happened afterwards passed as a blur. A few more speeches and instructions; then before he knew it, they all headed back to their campsites.

"You did well tonight, Jarmangi." Banaganga put his hand on the young Zulu's shoulder. "Your beads were well received."

"I was so nervous," Jarmangi said.

"Let us now go back to our tents and give thanks to our ancestors for the gift of the beads and for bringing us here to America," Banaganga said, addressing the four Zulu boys. "The bugle will sound in the morning to raise us from our beds, then after breakfast, the competitions begin. Sleep well, but do not wander from your tents."

The days of the week passed quickly for the young Scouts. The activities left little time for idleness. Part of their fun included aquatic activities on Lake Pend Oreille; canoeing, sailing, fishing, even swimming for those who braved the chill of the water. The hike to the lake was a short one.

Lake Pend Oreille, the largest natural lake in the state of Idaho, stretched some thirty miles with depths of over eleven hundred feet. It had served as a naval training center in World War II, preparing over a quarter million sailors for war. The small town of Bayview sat at the southern edge of the lake. Farragut State Park, where the Scouts camped, stood just outside Bayview. This southern end of the lake held a boat moorage in Buttonhook Bay, so named because a peninsula of land curved outward, sheltering the bay from the main body of water. Heavily wooded public lands and steep cliffs with snow-white mountain goats surrounded the rest of the lake. Whitetail deer, black bears, bobcats, and coyotes inhabited these woods. Varieties of pine, fir, poplar, and western larch comprised the forest.

"I haven't seen anything larger than a squirrel all week," complained Gonza, as he and Jarmangi prepared for sleep on their last night in America. "I'll bet if we went to the other side of the lake, we'd see many native animals."

Jarmangi watched as Gonza stood upright outside the tent flap, gazing into the darkness toward Lake Pend Oreille. Tomorrow, they would begin the long journey back to Africa.

"Let's explore, Jarmangi. Let's go to the water now. Night is when animals come from the hills to drink. We will see many. We could take one of the canoes across the bay. Come, Jarmangi. Let us not sleep through our last night."

Though tempted, Jarmangi felt the responsibility of leadership. "We can't go off and leave the others, Gonza. You heard Banaganga. Stay together at all times."

"Fine. I'll get Bon and Kintu. They will want to go. I know it," Gonza said, ducking back into the tent, returning with his flashlight.

Jarmangi knew he would have to physically restrain Gonza to prevent this from happening. He'd seen his new friend get ideas like this before, and once he made up his mind, there was no changing it.

"Okay, Gonza," Jarmangi said. "We will go for just a few hours, but to avoid detection, we must wait until all are in bed. Go tell the others we will come for them in thirty minutes."

That half hour seemed to stretch forever as the four boys waited to leave camp. Moving quietly through the forest at night came second nature to them, and they had no trouble crossing the camp boundaries undetected. They stalked through the woods and toward the lake, the night air cool and still. They listened for the sounds of nature and animals. Though they had flashlights, the clear sky and moonlight provided enough light for their purposes. Minutes later, they boarded the canoes and quietly headed for the other side of the bay.

Some believe native Zulus can see into the future. Jarmangi had come to accept this ability more as a unity with the earth, a oneness with nature, like feeling the approach of a thunderstorm. Tonight, he harbored such a feeling... and it was not good.

CHAPTER ELEVEN

Gerald Johnson had lived outside Bayview, Idaho all his life, working ten hours a day at a garage to stay off welfare. Ten years earlier, after the eighth grade, he lost interest in school and dropped out. He lived to hunt and fish. He and a friend, Darrel Gaspar, spent every spare moment either in the woods or preparing to go.

Darrel wasn't any smarter than Gerald. He worked for the Parks Department, in sanitation. Neither had fathers they knew, and both had learned the ways of the world hanging around bars and dives. Each topped six feet and proudly carried a beer belly the size of a basketball. Gerald had bushy red hair and a beard to match. Darrel tried to grow a beard once, but didn't like it and kept his dark hair cut military short. Each sported a tattoo of a naked woman on his left shoulder, the result of a drunken night years ago in Seattle.

Late one afternoon, Darrel stopped by the garage to see Gerald, who, at the moment, lay beneath an old Chevy in one of the bays. Darrel leaned against the wall and stuffed a pinch of Beechnut chewing tobacco between his cheek and gum.

"I know huntin' season don't open for a month, but I'm tellin' you, I saw signs of the biggest buck on the west side of the bay. Hoof prints were huge. Must've come down from the mountains. If we don't get him now, he's likely to be gone by the time he goes into rut."

Gerald said something, his words lost in the blare of the radio and outside traffic. Darrel kicked the foot sticking out from under the chassis. "Can't hear you, big fella," he said through his chaw of tobacco.

Gerald, looking perturbed, slid from under the car on his creeper. "I said, so what do you want to do about it?" He wiped his greasy hands on a rag.

"Don't know. Thought I'd talk to you and see what you wanted to do."

"We got stands out there?" Gerald asked.

"We don't, but some other guys do, and they won't be using 'em for another month," Darrel said, looking out at the traffic.

"Any rangers in that area?"

"Sometimes. But I know their schedules, and tonight they're goin' to the other side of the lake, some thirty miles away."

The mechanic sat up and considered this. Darrel knew Gerald wasn't against breaking the law. He couldn't afford to get caught, though. One more time before Judge Parker and his friend would be doing time in lockup.

"You sure there's no one out there?" Gerald asked. "You've screwed up before and nearly got us nabbed."

"Look. I told you there won't be no one there. Just be you and me and that big buck." He accepted Gerald as the leader of this two-man band.

"Yeah, I guess it'll be all right. You got enough whiskey to keep us warm all night in those tree stands?"

Darrel reached with both hands to the back pockets of his official Parks coveralls and pulled out two pints of Jack Daniels, like a pair of six guns; his toothy grin marred by bits of tobacco.

"Okay. Let's head out around ten," Gerald said. "We'll leave the truck off the road so as not to attract attention. Is it a long hike to the spot?"

"Not too far. Stand's a big'un and we can easily fit in it. One of us could sleep while the other keeps watch."

"Yeah, what the hell. We'll probably get drafted and killed in Vietnam anyway. Now get out of here and let me finish up," Gerald said, sliding back under the car.

Bon and Kintu beached their canoe ahead of Jarmangi and Gonza. Jarmangi had them pull the boats from the water and into the woods, far enough for concealment. Then the four gathered, squatting in a circle to make plans for the next move, excited about exploring the forest, but also about doing something forbidden.

"Should be easy to pick up the spoor by the water and track it into the trees," Jarmangi whispered. "We must watch the time. Everyone check his watch. It's now eleven forty-five. We should be back to the canoes no later than two. If we get separated, come back by then, understood?"

They nodded agreement.

Within minutes, the young Zulus discovered a large set of cloven hoof prints heading to and away from the water. At the point where the trail led into the woods, Gonza spotted a pile of droppings. He stuck his finger into the middle of it.

"This is fresh," he whispered. "Soft and warm. Can't be more than thirty minutes ahead."

The boys worked as a team, cutting the spoor as they had done with their friends and fathers so often back home. The others followed Jarmangi, and when he lost the spoor, they separated and crisscrossed the area until someone picked it up again. All of this with the stealth of the natural hunters they were born to be. Jarmangi estimated they'd gone about a mile when he got his first glimpse of the large buck.

He heard it before he saw it, froze, and signaled to the others. They'd tracked up a densely wooded hill. Approaching the crest, the trees ahead silhouetted against the moonlit sky. Jarmangi pointed up and to the right. At first, no one appeared to see it, then the giant buck shifted and stepped from behind a large fir. Its massive head sported a rack of at least sixteen points; his outline, black against the star-studded horizon. No one breathed. This is why they'd come that night.

Gonza leaned into Jarmangi. "Let's get closer," he whispered.

"Wait until it moves and quits looking about. Then we'll get as close as we can without spooking it," Jarmangi replied, barely audibly. Gonza passed the message to the others.

The buck ambled away. A soft breeze cooled their faces. Instinctively, they stayed downwind as they crept closer.

Gerald and Darrel climbed into the deer stand, fifteen feet off the ground and well hidden in the branches of a Ponderosa pine. The two hunters settled into their familiar seating arrangement, back to back, to watch from all directions. The air breezed colder up here, but not uncomfortable. A nip of whiskey would fix that.

"It's four to five hours 'til sunrise. How we supposed to see that buck even if it comes right up to us?" Gerald said.

"The moon's bright enough. Your eyes'll get used to it. Besides, we can't be here when day breaks. Now be quiet and keep a sharp eye. You got your pint, right?"

Gerald grunted. He was the leader, but when they entered the familiar parks, his friend tried to act the big shot. Gerald shifted his position. He'd tolerate Darrel's attitude unless it got out of control, then he'd have to slap him down and reestablish authority.

The hard part with this kind of hunting was staying awake, and after about thirty minutes, Gerald could tell that his buddy had nodded off. No harm, unless he started to snore.

The solitude soothed him, away from the rest of the world constantly telling him what to do. He thought of Vietnam; his chances of being drafted were pretty good. Might not be so bad over there. Probably like now. Just be shooting gooks instead of deer.

A dry branch snapped. Shifting only his eyes, Gerald focused in the direction of the sound. Something moved. Gerald looked away from the sound, using his peripheral vision. The large beast stopped, testing the air. He and Darrel were upwind. Would it smell them and run?

Gerald elbowed Darrel whom he hoped would awaken gently. "Quiet," he whispered in Darrel's ear.

Darrel jolted up and craned his neck in every direction. Gerald pointed into the darkness. Darrel stared and shook his head and then nodded as something moved. They readied their rifles, positioning themselves with slow, deliberate motions, never taking their eyes from their quarry. The long shot would not be accurate in this light. The big buck ambled towards them. Gerald would call the shot, as usual. Both hunters trained their high-powered weapons in the direction of the beast. Scopes proved useless. Too dark.

"Wait," Gerald whispered. He knew Darrel lacked the nerve for this part. Patience was low on his short list of attributes. Darrel clicked off his safety.

The Zulu Scouts crept closer. They took turns rising up to admire the huge stag. Their palpable excitement didn't interfere with their woodsmanship and playing the game of seeing how close they could get.

A small, metallic click alerted both the buck and the band of boys. It had come from off in the distance, and though faint, was definitely not a sound of the forest. The buck raised its head and sniffed the air, appearing jumpy.

"He'll run," Gonza whispered to Jarmangi.

Jarmangi slowly rose from the brush for one last look at the magnificent animal. The buck bolted at the same instant the report of the rifle reached the boys. Something warm and wet splashed over Gonza. Jarmangi fell back into the brush.

Gonza wiped his face and stood upright, stealth no longer important. He recognized the feel and smell of the liquid, but refused to come to grips with what that meant. The buck vanished. The three boys looked to where Jarmangi lay. A sense of dread paralyzed the young Zulus and no one moved or spoke. Then Gonza knelt by his friend.

"Jarmangi? Are you okay?"

The rhythmic splash on the forest floor at Gonza's feet became fainter and more rapid. He touched his friend's shoulder and shook him. Jarmangi's head rolled and came to rest on his left shoulder in an unnatural position. The last of Jarmangi's blood pumped onto the forest floor. Kintu cried out and they all jumped back, away from the corpse, staring at each other in shock and disbelief. Gonza sank to his knees, singing out in his native Zulu tongue.

———————

"Did you get it?" Gerald asked. "I didn't tell you to shoot. It was too far off."

"Naw, I missed," Darrel said. "It took off just as I shot, like he heard me pulling the trigger. It's gone now. We'd better get out of here."

"What's all that noise out there?" Gerald asked. "You sure you didn't hit it?"

"I saw it run off. It didn't look wounded to me." Darrel looked in the direction of the racket. As the ringing in their ears from the rifle faded, the night air suddenly filled with a piercing wail.

"What the hell was that?" Gerald asked. This wasn't good. He had a bad feeling in the pit of his stomach. They were supposed to be alone out here.

"I don't know. I think it's coming from past where the buck was," Darrel said. "Think we ought to check it out?"

"Name me one good thing that can come from us going over there," Gerald said. "You're the one who shot. You want to go out there, go ahead. I'm haulin' my ass out of these woods."

"Yeah, you're right. I'm right behind you."

With that, the two men scrambled the quarter-mile back to their truck and sped away into the night.

CHAPTER TWELVE

Gonza stayed with the body while the others went for help. The camp staff called the authorities, then canoed with Bon and Kintu across the bay to where Jarmangi's body lay. The police rescue squad examined the scene, then carried the body out of the woods to the hospital. A coroner flew in from Spokane. After the autopsy, he prepared the body for travel back to Africa, doing his best to sew Jarmangi's head onto the torso. Except for a small flap of skin and muscle, it had been completely torn off by the high-powered rifle bullet. The coroner explained to the police investigator, to cause that much destruction, the bullet must have struck a small branch in flight and yawed end-over-end like a small buzz-saw into Jarmangi's neck.

The long, somber journey to South Africa weighed heavily on the Scouts and those who awaited them. News of the tragedy preceded the Scouts, and throngs of grieving Zulus met them at the small airport. Banta would not believe it. Certain it was all a big joke, he knew his older brother would bound off the plane, laughing and pointing at them. The scene of the casket being carried off the twin-engine aircraft burned into his mind, there to remain for the rest of his life. He refused to come to grips with Jarmangi's death until the funeral.

As the family filed past the open casket, Banta stopped and stared at the body of the brother he'd idolized, a line of sutures around the neck clearly visible above the tribal burial garment. Banta screamed and climbed into the casket. He grabbed Jarmangi's body by the shoulders and shook him repeatedly, disrupting the sutures holding the head, causing it to tilt gruesomely. The family embraced Banta and physically restrained him, but his wails would not stop until a local doctor sedated the boy.

During the last few weeks of summer, Banta drew farther into himself. Though his brothers, Pantal and Tungata, tried to engage him in activities; he would have none of it. Only hunting held his interest. He fashioned his own spears and arrows, and tirelessly stalked the small game of the African countryside. Sometimes his friends tried to join him in the hunt. Though he didn't discourage their efforts, he would lose them and soon be off on his own. His school attendance suffered. If Pantal and Tungata hadn't dragged him to school, he would have dropped out altogether.

Banta's mother died the following year.

The boy's conduct drew the attention of the elders in the village. They decided he'd grow out of this behavior and left him to his family. But Banta did not mature into a stable young adult, as they'd hoped. If anything, his anger increased. His hunting became ruthless; he killed for the fun of it, not even bringing home the game needed for food. Several pet dogs in the village turned up missing and were later found beheaded. Some suspected Banta, but he'd become adept at covering his actions.

In the late '60s, South Africa, much like the United States, struggled with racial issues, and apartheid divided the people. In this climate, Banta found a natural vent for his anger. His interest in Scouting died, and he no longer joined his brothers at meetings. He took up the cause of the downtrodden native and joined a local group of malcontents. Through them, he learned to fight, not as his brothers had taught him and not for defensive purposes. Splinter groups of the more radical broke off and he followed them, anxious to be in front of the action. In the early 1970s, he spent time in jail and juvenile detention.

Banta worked odd jobs, but with a purpose. He hung around garages and picked up work from the owners, gradually becoming skilled at auto mechanics. His interest in firearms drew him toward the local military encampment and eventually led to his enlistment. Here, he found what he looked for and moved rapidly up the ranks. His superiors noticed his lack of fear of injury or even death. This, combined with his athletic abilities and size, made him a natural leader among new recruits. Banta had grown to be larger than even his idolized older brother. Like so many in South Africa, his ancestry stemmed from a combination of Zulu, Xhosa, Hottentots and probably a few others. This gene pool occasionally produced massive men. He stood a head taller than the average Zulu and worked at his physical strength, sculpting his body to impressive proportions.

The more violent among them drew to him, like jackals thirsting for blood. He did not cultivate their friendship, but he did win their loyalty and respect. Soon, they turned to him for protection and guidance.

Border skirmishes developed and Banta always volunteered his men for action. He learned to be a hunter of men. His security force became the most sought after in the country. There would be no trouble at large government rallies if Banta and his men stood visible. Some people complained his tactics too brutal. One of his more vocal detractors turned up missing.

Banta spent the years leading up to 1987 becoming more and more dangerous and hard to control. Even his military superiors came to regard him with suspicion and fear. They routinely assigned him the most hazardous missions, half in hopes he wouldn't return. But he always did, more experienced and menacing. Thus, it surprised him when they assigned him crowd control at a large Scout rally; an easy gig, not worthy of his talents.

Hundreds of young Boy Scouts assembled with their leaders in the coolness of mid-July. Twenty years had passed since Jarmangi's body had returned to Africa, but to Banta, the scene with all these Scouts made it seem like yesterday. Chief Minister Mangosuthu Buthelezi served as the guest of honor that day and probably the reason Banta had been given this job. After preliminary talks by other dignitaries, the Chief Minister addressed the Scouts.

"Today," he began, "we are assembled to complete the circle. Nearly one hundred years ago, items very precious to the Zulu people were taken from this land. Many lives were lost protecting these symbols. Twenty years ago, another young man lost his life as replicas of these symbols spread around the world."

Banta, who'd paid little attention to that point, felt his blood chill. Suddenly, he knew the purpose of this rally. Emotions buried for twenty years surfaced and hot tears of anger and resentment filled his eyes. His throat constricted and his legs threatened to give way.

"Jarmangi Mangabe was a Scout, just as you," the Chief Minister continued. "He traveled to America carrying replicas of these beads as gifts. He returned in a casket. After nearly one hundred years, four of the original Zulu beads have been found and today will be returned to their rightful owners—you, the Zulu people."

Chief Buthelezi then walked to an older woman sitting on stage. The chair in which she sat stood on yet another platform, making her perch higher than the others. Full ceremonial tribal garb hung loosely on her withered frame. A crown of feathers sat atop her shortly cropped head of graying hair. Her skin, sagging beneath her sharp eyes, bore the ravages of over eighty years in the hot African sun. She did not stir as the Chief Minister approached.

"Princess Mahoho, daughter of Chief Dinizulu and beloved mother of my own wife," Chief Buthelezi continued, "I bring back to you four of the original beads taken from your father nearly a century ago."

With that, Chief Scout of South Africa, Garnet de la Hunt, arose from his seat on stage and proudly walked to the Chief Minister. From a darkly stained wooden box, he removed a thong on which hung four of the original Dinizulu beads. He passed it to Chief Buthelezi, in the symbolic act of returning the beads to their rightful owner. The Chief then placed the thong over the head of Princess Mahoho.

Banta's head spun. Images long buried in his subconscious flooded back. He saw his older brother in the casket. He saw Jarmangi's head come loose from the row of stitches. He remembered the beads they had worked so hard on that fateful summer. Through the mist of his tears, he saw Jarmangi standing in the Scout meeting announcing his plans to make the beads. He recalled his rage when learning the original beads had been taken from his people. Why did his fellow Zulus not share his anger? Did they not know the story? Now, only four beads returned. Who would bring back his brother? Where were the remaining beads? Who had them?

Suddenly, Banta knew why he lived. He knew his purpose. It made sense now. If the other beads existed somewhere on this earth, he would find them and bring them back. Those who held them would suffer the same fate inflicted upon his brother. Unknowingly, all his adult life, he'd prepared for this mission. No matter how long it took or how far he had to travel, he would make things right. Nothing would stand in his way.

CHAPTER THIRTEEN

MEMPHIS, TENNESSEE, 2005

The wake-up call came at four o'clock. David picked up the phone and started to say something, then heard the recording click off. Patrick had insisted on sleeping in the rollaway bed. David stepped around it as he headed into the hotel bathroom.

"What time is it, anyway?" Patrick mumbled, pulling the pillow over his face.

"Four a.m. Go back to sleep."

Instead, Patrick sat up and yawned, running his fingers through his hair. "You going straight to the hospital?"

"Yeah. Why?"

"For the next few days, I need to know your whereabouts at all times," Patrick said. "Help should arrive from D.C. later this morning. My partner, Adnan, will be joining this little party, and one of us will be sticking close to you for a while."

"You really think that's necessary? You coming in the operating room with me, too? How about rounds? I could use some help with the scut work the medical students can't handle," David said, sticking the toothbrush in his mouth.

"Hey, man. This is *not* a joke," Patrick said, scooting to the end of the bed. "There's some crazy person or persons out there killing people, and I think they're the ones who broke into your place yesterday."

David finished brushing his teeth and rinsed his mouth.

"And you think all they want is this bead? Let's just give it to them and be done with it. I don't care. I'm only three months from leaving here and joining your father's practice in Nashville. I don't need the hassle."

"Not that easy," Patrick said, swinging his legs off the side. "Maybe I should tell you more about these guys. You need to keep this to yourself, though. This is the kind of thing the media loves to scare the public with."

"Okay, but make it fast." David turned on the water in the shower. "I've gotta get to work."

Patrick stumbled out of bed and into the bathroom. "We give these guys credit for three murders in England; all old men, all beheaded for no apparent reason. We've traced the victim's family lines. The fathers of two were best friends during WWI. Turns out, these fathers had been to the same Scoutmaster training camp in 1919 in Gilwell Park, England, during the early days of the Boy Scouts. The man who ran that camp, Lord Baden-Powell, a retired officer in the British army, fought in South Africa before the turn of the century."

"My great-grandfather did, too. I think he might have been with Baden-Powell." David said, stepping into the shower.

"The third victim was over one hundred years old and in a nursing home. He actually attended that first Scoutmaster thing," Patrick said, examining his face in the mirror. "Your patient, Alphonse Baroni, had an uncle who also attended that camp. We've fed this information into our computers and the common link seems to be that 1919 Scoutmaster camp in England."

David stuck his head out of the shower and peered at his friend. "As long as we're making 'jumping to conclusions' an Olympic sport, you might check out that old black guy I found beat up in an alley yesterday on my way into work. He seemed to know Baroni, and he kept touching my chest where this bead hung. The guy died before the paramedics could get him to the hospital. Remember, they took him to the VA? He was on your list of names."

"Yeah. We talked about him. Moses Donnelly," Patrick said. "Turns out, he served with Baroni." Patrick rummaged through his case. "After I see you safely to the hospital, I'm going over to your place and look around again. I may try to find some of the people who live and work in the area. Maybe one of them saw something on the night of your break-in."

David finished his shower without further interruption. Opening the bathroom door to let out steam, he noticed Patrick hanging up the phone.

"Still thinking of joining my father's group?" Patrick asked.

"It's way past the stage of thinking." David worked the towel through his hair. "I've told them I'm coming and have signed a contract."

"You know about the trouble Dad had earlier this year with an insurance company? Some rogue lawyer trying to ruin him?"

"Yeah, I heard about that. It's all resolved, isn't it?"

"Yeah, but it left Dad with a bad taste in his mouth. I don't know if he's going to stay with the group, or even practice much longer," Patrick said.

"I hope he stays. I'd like to get to know your dad better. May shed some light on why you turned out to be such a prick."

Patrick laughed. "You got time for breakfast before taking off? I could call for room service."

"Nope. I'll get something at the hospital. Call me if you find anything of interest at my apartment." He finished drying off, shaved, put on his scrubs, and headed for the door. Patrick paused in the middle of his set of sit-ups.

"Hey, you need a ride?" Patrick asked.

"I can walk to the hospital from here. My bike's still there, so I'll get back tonight on my own." He shouldered his pack. "Have a good one. I'm out of here."

The chill of the morning air helped clear his head. The walk to the VA Hospital, only three blocks from their hotel, provided him much needed quiet time to think. What was this all about? Was he really being stalked for this little bead he still had about his neck? It seemed too much.

After completing the uneventful walk to the hospital, David and the other members of his team made rounds and arrived at the operating room on time. The light case load included a bunion procedure and three knee arthroscopies. David assisted Jim McCallum doing these operations. It turned into one of those rare, low-stress days ... or so it seemed.

As they finished their first case, David's pager beeped. The text read, "Call me on my cell ... now! Patrick" —followed by a string of numbers. David went into the surgeon's locker room, slumped onto one of the recliners, and reached for the phone. Patrick picked up immediately.

"How'd you get my beeper number?" David asked. "I didn't give it to you, and that's not something you can call up and get."

"Never mind that," Patrick said. "I need you to come to your apartment—right now!"

"Hell, no! I've got work to do here. I can't just take off. What is it this time?"

"I'm calling from your place," Patrick said. "Something happened here last night—something bad."

"What do you mean, 'something bad'?" David asked, afraid of what the answer might be.

"When I got here, the door was flung wide open and—"

"Oh, that's because management didn't fix it very well," David said. "Probably swung open by itself sometime during the night."

"Don't think so, buddy. There's been a fight here. Blood's all over your bathroom."

David paused to let the news sink in. His heart pounded against his chest wall.

"Whose blood? How much blood?" he said, still dazed and apprehensive. "Anything else?"

"Won't know for a while. I've called our local forensics people and they're on the way. Can you think of anyone who might have been here last night?"

David had a sinking feeling in his stomach. It would be just like Pam to come over in his absence. She knew he was off last night. Hadn't they spoken in the hospital as he was leaving?

"Pam has a key. Let me check out here and call you back. I'll get there as soon as I can."

"I'd like you to look around before the forensics guys get here," Patrick said.

"Okay. Give me fifteen minutes." David hung up phone and bolted out of his chair. He nearly ran over Jim McCallum.

"What's the hurry?" Jim asked. "Problems?"

"Maybe. Can you handle the other scopes by yourself? I've got to go." David hustled down the hallway.

"Sure." Jim smiled. "Take your time."

David ran up two flights to the third floor and found the charge nurse. "Where's Pam Blanchard?" he asked, out of breath. "Did she come into work today? Is she scheduled to work?"

"No. She never showed up," replied the charge nurse. "I called her home and no one answered. We're really shorthanded today, too."

He tried her cell with no luck. Minutes later, he pedaled hard to his place. Patrick was on the phone as he arrived. David started through the door, but Patrick held up a hand and stopped him.

"Yeah, it's not far from the University. You'll see it. Bye." Patrick hung up. "Let me show you where not to step." He pointed to small drops of what appeared to be blood leading from the bathroom.

"Apparently, whatever happened in here was later taken outside." He motioned for David to follow him. They stood outside the bathroom, the scene grisly: shower door broken off, one towel rack pulled loose, blood spattered over the mirror and wall, some smeared on the floor. David recognized this wasn't a life ending amount of blood, gruesome as it was.

"Any ideas?" he asked.

"It looks to me as though the victim was cut, and then in the ensuing struggle, sprayed the bathroom with her blood."

"What makes you think it was a 'her'?" David asked, holding his breath.

Patrick pointed to the sink. "Unless you've got some guys around here with shoulder length, dark hair, I'd say that used to belong to a woman."

"Oh, no," David said. "Pam didn't show up for work this morning. Her apartment is in the building next door. She comes over sometimes with dinner." He glanced at the uneaten prepared food on the kitchen counter top. "She was here, Patrick."

Patrick's phone rang and he stepped out to take it, indicating to David not to touch anything.

David fell onto the couch. Suddenly, his training didn't seem so important. He tried to imagine life without her, and couldn't. He'd been stupid not to think of her safety when deciding to spend the night with Patrick at the hotel. Should have at least called her. *Let her be all right*, he prayed silently, *and I won't make that mistake again.*

Patrick interrupted his reverie and entered the apartment accompanied by a tall, thin, olive-skinned man, about their age, in a wrinkled suit. His black hair stood slightly mussed, and a day-old beard covered his chin and cheeks. His sharp, dark eyes took in David's apartment with one quick scan of the room.

"David Freeman, meet Adnan Fazeph, my partner."

The two men shook hands, and Patrick explained to Adnan what they knew about the events of the last two days. The three of them left David's and walked to Pam's. The locked door showed no signs of forced entry. Adnan pulled something from his pocket, worked the lock for three seconds, and the door popped opened. Inside, they found no signs of foul play.

Though panicked about what they might find, he felt uneasy being in her apartment like this and hurried them out, but not before Adnan had pocketed a small address book sitting near the phone.

"I guess you'll want me in protective custody until this resolves," David said, becoming more distressed by the moment at the thought of what might be happening to Pam. He hoped she was still alive.

"What! Not on your life—so to speak." Patrick said. "You're the bait." He turned and resumed his conversation with Adnan.

Bait? I'm bait? For what or whom? He wasn't sure he liked the sound of that.

CHAPTER FOURTEEN

Pam awoke, cold and shivering. Her head throbbed and her right arm hurt. Where was she? What had happened? She rolled over on the hard wooden floor and touched her face. Her numb lower lip felt swollen, and something tender and crusty perched over her right eye. The dark room disoriented her. She remembered being in David's apartment and hearing him come in and then— it wasn't him! She bolted upright. Her head felt as if it would burst. A wave of nausea forced her to lie down, closing her eyes as the room spun.

The nausea passed. She opened her eyes. A dark form squatted in front of her. She screamed and tried to scoot away. The pounding in her head stopped her struggling. The man stood, his dark silhouette outlined against the backdrop of light from the hallway. He towered over her, tall and menacing. She remembered seeing that face in the mirror earlier in the evening. Terror gripped her. She froze, unable even to scream. Two more figures entered the room. Her fear mounted, heart racing, mouth parched.

As her eyes adjusted to the poor light, she noticed other things about her captors. The black skinned, lean, muscular men wore only what appeared to be loincloths. Each sported a headdress of leather and beads, their facial features thick and menacing, their bodies musty. Heavy bracelets encircled their wrists. The tallest wore a beaded necklace. Had she been raped? Taking quick inventory of her body and clothing, she determined that wasn't the case.

"Who are you? Where am I?" she said, trying not to sound frightened.

The tallest answered, his English broken and heavily accented.

"Do not try escape. If you try, I kill you—or worse," he said calmly. The three men then turned and left her alone in the small room.

"What do you want with me?" Pam called after them. No response. With some difficulty, she struggled to her feet. Her head still thundered, but the nausea abated. She leaned against a wall to steady herself, then worked her way toward the door. Light shone from a room to the left. She stood in the doorway and looked herself over. Her left knee was swollen with a small abrasion over the knee cap. Her right ankle throbbed, but appeared uninjured. A bloody bandage wrapped around her right wrist. Her fingers worked, but moving her wrist side to side brought pain. Her little finger tingled, but had feeling.

She unwrapped the bandage. On the little finger side of her forearm, a large gash ran parallel to the wrist. The wound had clean edges and appeared made by a sharp instrument, probably that sword of David's. Blood oozed from the laceration. Her left shoe was gone. The torn neckline of her blouse exposed her bra on the left side; her short skirt twisted, but intact.

Pam rewrapped the bloody bandage around her arm. Leaning carefully into the hallway, she looked left and right. The men assembled in the lighted room to her left. They spoke a language she'd never heard and paid no attention to her. She limped to the bathroom across the hall and searched for a switch. Working it up and down produced no light. She leaned back into the hallway, peering toward the room occupied by her captors. The light from that room flickered, possibly from a lantern.

Great. No electricity. She drew a deep breath. *Wonder if the plumbing works.*

She tried the knob on the sink. The faucet sputtered and spat water. She leaned out the door to see if the noise attracted attention. One of the men stood in the hall, leering at her. He made no attempt to help or hinder though. He nodded at her, turned and joined the others. Laughter erupted from their room.

Pam's fright now turned to anger. Who were these men and what did they want with her? She turned back to the sink. A broken mirror hung on the wall. In the scant light, she could see her face and the reflection made her head swim. To avoid falling, she sat on the toilet. Holding her head in her hands, she took deep breaths and tried to think. When her head stopped spinning, she tried the handle on the toilet. Surprisingly, it worked. No door to the bathroom, but she needed to urinate, so without rising, she shifted her clothing to accomplish this, flushing again when done. She arranged her clothing back into position, and reexamined herself in the mirror. Her puffy right eye had developed a nice shiner; the small cut above it scabbed over. Dried blood covered the right side of her face. Her bottom lip was swollen and split in the middle. Teeth appeared okay. She unwrapped her arm and used part of the cloth as a wash rag to clean her facial wounds. She let the water run over the gash in her arm. The pain cleared her head. Cleaning her wounds as well as she could, Pam rewrapped her arm with the damp bandage. That would have to do.

She explored the small house and found another room opposite her captors—without furniture, its window boarded, drywall crumbled; floors of cold, bare boards; obviously one of the many abandoned shanties littering the Memphis landscape, intermittently inhabited by the homeless. How long had she been out? Was she still in Memphis?

When she found no obvious escape route other than the front door, she decided to confront her situation head on. She drew up to full height and marched to the room where the three men talked. Standing in the doorway, she saw her purse against the far wall, its contents spilled onto the floor. One of the men spotted her, then turned back to his comrades and resumed studying what appeared to be a map.

"Hey!" Pam shouted. "What the hell is going on here?"

The tallest of the three said something to the others, rose to his feet and slowly walked toward her. She held her ground, though her heart climbed to her throat. Without so much as breaking stride, he lashed out and hit her full in the face with a closed fist. Pam stumbled backwards, crashing into the opposite wall, striking her head. The terrible pain returned. She fought to remain conscious. As her vision cleared, she saw her attacker standing over her. He studied her for a few seconds, then walked back into the room and picked up what appeared to be a worn blanket. Returning, the dark-skinned man grabbed one of her ankles and dragged her back into her original room. She submitted, too stunned to resist. Her skirt rolled up around her waist. He deposited her in the middle of the room and threw the blanket at her. Before leaving, he turned and stared, apparently unaffected by her state of undress.

"My name is Banta," he said. "If you want something, you call me. You stay here. No more trouble."

Pam tried to clear her head. Her whole body shook from fear or cold or both. Wrapping the blanket around her, she curled in the middle of the floor and reached up, touching her face. Her left cheek ached from the blow. Fatigue and pain weakened her resolve, and though she fought them, tears rolled from her eyes. Finally, she broke down and wept. Shivering and sobbing, her head and face hurting, she succumbed. She'd need help to get out of this.

Sunshine streamed through the boarded window and startled Pam awake. Her limbs ached; her neck so stiff, she could barely turn her head. Yawning sent bolts of pain through her jaw. Dust particles danced about the cold room through the streaking beams of light. Her first attempt to stand failed, but she struggled to her feet, left shoe still missing. Wrapping the blanket around her, she limped into the hall, timidly looking about. No sign of her captors. Thoughts of escape flashed through her mind, but more immediate needs took precedence. She made her way into the bathroom and relieved herself. Still no sign of the men in response to the noise she made. Her face looked worse this morning, or was it just that she could see better now?

Again using the cloth around her wounded arm, she cleaned herself. Her blanket served as a towel. The wound on her arm appeared red. Infection? A gritty film coated her teeth, and she brushed with her finger. Water from the sink made a poor substitute for her usual morning cup of coffee. Wiping her mouth, she rose from the sink, and saw the dark reflection of Banta's face staring at her in the mirror. Flashbacks to the night before in David's apartment came crashing down upon her, and leaning hard against the wall, she nearly fainted. Banta made no attempt to help. Instead, he grabbed her bandaged wrist, and pulled her back across the hall into her room. The pain in her wrist cleared her head.

"Sit," he commanded.

When Pam hesitated, he forcefully pushed her down.

Banta wore the rags of a street person. Tattered, dirty clothes layered his body, but failed to hide the muscular athlete beneath. The disguise came complete with the stale smell of cheap wine. From his jacket, he produced a length of rope and proceeded to bind Pam's hands behind her back. The pain in her wrist caused her to cry out.

"Quiet," he barked.

Pushing her to her left side, he then bound her ankles and hog-tied her hands and feet together behind her. After inspecting his work and testing the knots, he rose and started to leave the room.

"I'm cold," Pam said softly, her voice trembling.

Banta stopped in the doorway. The blanket lay on the floor in the bathroom. Walking back into the room, he kicked part of the blanket over her and left.

"Hey! Where are you going? You can't leave me here like this!" Pam cried out. She knew she wasted her breath, but couldn't help herself.

The door to the shack opened and closed. She was alone. Struggling against her restraints only brought more pain. Finally she turned her efforts to arranging the blanket to cover more of her body. She cursed herself for choosing such a skimpy outfit to wear the night before. Was it only last night?

She thought about screaming for help, but dismissed the notion for fear of reprisals. Instead, she squirmed into a less painful position and said a short prayer. She hadn't prayed in years. The hypocrisy of this was not lost on her, but what else could she do? Despair threatened to paralyze her. She willed herself to think. There must be something.

The events of last night played over and over through her head which, though still painful, was not throbbing as badly. She tried to remember every detail: their faces, the rooms of the shack, the bathroom, the contents of her purse scattered on the floor—

Wait! Had her cell phone been there among the items on the floor? Surely, they took it. Maybe not, though. Cell phones could be traced now, couldn't they? Would these foreign men know that? Either way, she felt a spark of hope.

Traveling across a hard floor, hog-tied, proved difficult. With an excruciating combination of small pushes and squirms, she progressed toward the door, into the hall, and to the entrance of the room used by the men last evening. Her purse, with its spilled contents, lay against the back wall. She couldn't rise up enough to see if her phone was still there. Struggling across the room, she stopped every few minutes to rest and listen for the return of her captors. Finally, she got within reach and nearly laughed out loud when she saw her phone. Turning around, she grasped it with her tied hands. Then she realized she wouldn't be able to see the phone and punch the numbers at the same time. She had no other choice but to position the phone on its side and turn back around to memorize its keypad. Repeating the move, she soon had the phone in her hands, and dialed 911. Hearing the phone ring, she quickly turned back around to face it. Maneuvering came easier, though no less painful. The operator answered before she fully turned.

"911. How can I be of assistance?" answered the woman on the other end of the line.

"Oh, thank God. My name is Pam Blanchard and I'm being held somewhere, I don't know where, and my hands and feet are tied and—"

"911. Is anyone there?" the voice asked.

"Yes, I'm right here. I can't reach the phone. My hands are tied and—"

"If you can't speak, touch one of the buttons on the key pad."

Pam stared at the display on the phone. To her horror, she saw "mute" lit up. She must have hit the mute button by mistake! Trying desperately, she reached the phone with her nose but couldn't work the buttons. She cried out in frustration.

At that moment, a car pulled up next to the house. She nosed the phone's disconnect button, pushed it toward the other items from her purse and began scrambling out of the room. She succeeded in reaching the hallway and partway to her room when the front door opened and people entered. Her back to the door, she couldn't see them, but from the strange language, she knew it to be Banta and his men. Their conversing stopped.

The men mumbled quietly as they walked toward her. Suddenly, someone dragged her by her bound arms into her room. She screamed. Her shoulders felt as if they would dislocate. The pain stopped when they reached the center of the room and the pulling ceased. She lay on her left side, her blouse ripped away from that arm, leaving her uncovered, her skirt rolled up around her waist. With her legs and arms tied behind her, she felt naked and exposed.

One of the other men knelt facing her. He grinned and said something to his friends. He tugged at her clothing, further exposing her. This seemed to excite his friends, who egged him on. Pam struggled against her restraints and tried to roll away, fearing this was a prologue to something much worse.

The chiming of her phone saved her. All three sprang up and rushed from the room. Banta returned with her phone and approached, holding it out to her.

"You make call while we gone?" he said. "Maybe you now want talk someone." He pressed the talk button and held the phone to her.

"Hello. Pam, are you there?" said the voice on the phone.

Shock almost prevented her from responding, having gone from the beginning of a rape to now talking on the phone.

"Hello? Pam?" the voice said again. David's voice!

"David! I'm tied up and being held by—"

Banta switched the phone off. "Good. Maybe he come to us now," Banta said. He studied her lying on the floor. She could feel her wrist bleeding again. Stepping behind her, he loosed her bonds. As fast as she could, she pushed away from him into the corner. There, she huddled, covering herself with what little remained of her clothing and the blanket.

"Clean yourself. My men not bother you," he said, leaving her alone in the room.

Pam wanted to run from the room and out the front door, but she couldn't move from the corner. She shivered and snuggled the blanket around her neck. Now was not the time for weakness, but she couldn't help it. Her emotions spilled over. Not even her war experience and training in Iraq had prepared her for this. Turning her face toward the wall, she wept.

CHAPTER FIFTEEN

David sat in his apartment with Patrick and Adnan, awaiting the arrival of the police. Patrick had phoned headquarters that he and Adnan would be here for a few days. Adnan flipped through Pam's address book. David couldn't sit still any longer and paced nervously about the apartment.

"I don't care about work." He glanced from Patrick to Adnan. "Tell me what I need to do to help you find Pam. The VA can get along without me for a while." He knew this would be reason enough to lose his position in the training program, putting his entire career at risk, but with clarity of purpose he didn't know he had, he didn't care. Must be the warrior in his bloodline.

Ignoring him, Patrick turned to Adnan. "Find anything?" he asked.

"Yes. I find her personal information. That very strange to be in her address book, but very lucky for us and her," Adnan answered in his heavy, Middle Eastern accent.

"Cell phone number?" Patrick asked.

"I could have told you that," David said.

"Yes. See. It right here," Adnan said, pointing to any entry under "Blanchard."

"Will you cut it out? You sound like a cartoon," Patrick said.

"That's only because you know it's an act," Adnan answered back in perfect, unaccented English.

"We use him to infiltrate Middle Eastern groups here in the U.S.," Patrick explained to David. "His English is so good, he has to practice sounding like he's from his home in Beirut."

"Why?" David asked.

"The terrorist cells that have been in the U.S. for years have shed their accents," Patrick said. "We've found if we're to plant someone amongst them, the agent needs to sound like he's been in this country for just a short while. Therefore, the accent."

Adnan shrugged and smiled. "We should call her number," he said, converting back to his broken English. "Maybe she answer. I find her then."

Patrick nodded, and Adnan dashed out to his car, returning moments later with a large laptop computer and a small antenna. Setting this on David's table, he entered Pam's phone number and glancing up at Patrick, hit the send button. The noise of the phone ringing spilled from his computer.

"If she answer, you talk," Adnan said, pointing to David.

After several rings, it sounded as if someone answered, though nothing was said. Adnan motioned for David to speak.

"Hello, Pam? Are you there?" he said, leaning down toward the computer. When he got no response, he repeated, "Hello, Pam?"

Her voice boomed out of the machine. "David! I'm tied up and being held by—"

David looked startled and searched his friend's face for answers.

"That enough?" Patrick asked Adnan.

Adnan didn't respond, but instead punched a few commands into the computer. A picture of planet Earth appeared on the screen and in rapid sequence zoomed onto an aerial view of Memphis. Seconds later, they focused on an image of a slum just northeast of Memphis, off Highway 51. With a few more key-strokes, one shack singled out. A car sat next to the house and the address printed across the screen along with instructions of how best to get there from their present location.

Adnan smiled and leaned away from the keyboard. "Google, with a few modifications," he said.

Amazed, David said "Is that where she is? How'd you do that?"

"Well, that's where she was two seconds ago," Patrick said. "I suggest we get out there now, before the scene changes. You get a make on the car?"

"Dark, four-door sedan. American made," Adnan answered, shaking his head. "Probably ten years old or more."

"Do they, the bad guys, know you can do that?" David asked.

"*I* didn't know he could do that," Patrick said. "But nothing he does surprises me anymore. Come on, let's go."

"Me, too? If I can help, I want to go," David said.

"Of course, you too," Patrick said. "We don't know what Pam looks like."

With that, Adnan turned the screen toward them. On it was Pam's picture from her driver's license. Adnan smiled.

"He's scary," David said.

"We need you with us," Patrick said. "Pam doesn't know us, and we'll need you along to get her confidence. I imagine she's pretty traumatized," Patrick headed toward the door to greet the police officers who'd just arrived. He showed them his federal credentials and explained the situation, giving them his card.

"We'll need to speak with the tenant of this apartment," said the officer.

"I'll personally bring him to you later today," Patrick said. "Right now, we need him." Grabbing David by the arm, he stepped past the officers and headed to his car. Adnan followed, holding his computer case as he ran.

Patrick and Adnan took the front, David in back. Adnan plugged his computer into the car and barked directions to Patrick. Impressive teamwork. They'd obviously done this before.

Turning to David, Adnan said, "Hand me case beside you, please."

David passed the stiff, heavy leather case over the front seat. Adnan opened it and rapidly assembled the short barreled shotgun, while continuing to copilot the car. Patrick talked to someone on his cell phone, explaining their situation.

"Guys, this is a little out of my area of expertise," David said. "I hope I don't get in the way."

Patrick ignored him. Adnan loaded shells into the shotgun.

"How many does that thing hold?" David asked.

"Eight," Adnan said.

"Isn't that illegal?"

Patrick swerved hard onto Danny Thomas Freeway, throwing David against the door, and headed north toward Highway 51. Adnan secured the shotgun into a holder attached to the dashboard and pulled out a large semi-automatic pistol from the holster under his jacket. Racking the slide, he chambered a round.

David decided he could either sit back and shut up, or jump from the speeding car. He chose the former. They sped by a police car parked off the side of the road. David felt sure the cops would pull them over. The patrol car ignored them.

"Why didn't we get pulled over?" he asked.

"When we get there, stay in the car and don't let anyone in," Patrick said, ignoring his question. "We'll come back for you."

"There," Adnan said, pointing to a crossroad.

David shrank into the back seat as Patrick slowed the car and followed his partner's directions into a collection of shanties. The shiny government car attracted the attention of the local inhabitants. Dark faces turned to watch as the vehicle rounded another corner and descended farther into a world he knew only through occasional contact with its injured inhabitants.

"There. Third house on right," Adnan said. "The one with loose screen."

Patrick pulled around another corner and killed the engine. Both men put something in their ears and strapped a thin belt around their throats, apparently for communication. Patrick mumbled something and Adnan acknowledged.

"Stay with the car," he said to David in the backseat. 'We'll only be a minute. I suspect they're already gone."

The two agents exited the vehicle. Adnan reached back into the car and extracted the short-barreled riot gun, known in this part of town as a street sweeper. A few people gathered but scattered and disappeared into the surroundings at the appearance of the shotgun. The two agents dashed out of sight, and David found himself alone in a late model car in the middle of the day in one of the worst areas of Memphis.

It wasn't long before the car got stuffy. He noticed people watching him from the safety of their homes. A few ventured outside for a closer look. He checked to make sure the doors were locked. Nothing to do but wait for Patrick and Adnan to return. What if they didn't return? What if they got into trouble or got hurt?

He glanced over the front seat, relieved to see the keys in the ignition. Making himself as small as possible, he settled against the door on the driver's side, gripped the arm rest and stared in the direction the two had gone. He didn't feel much like the soldier of his lineage, though he took some small comfort knowing his male ancestors had survived worse.

Minutes crept by. David's mouth felt dry, his hands sweaty. His heart beat rapidly. A heaviness developed in his chest, or was it *on* his chest? He reached up and fingered the wooden bead through his scrub top. Was it his imagination or was this bead getting hotter and weightier? Damn this thing!

A small metallic noise on the door at his back startled him. He jerked away and turned, brushing his head against the roof of the car. The thick, dark face staring back at him through the window scared him. Panic threatened to paralyze him. The bead on his chest felt crushing.

The black face showed no emotion. The man wore a fur-pelted headdress. He stood and his head vanished above the car. He wore no shirt, and his hairless, muscular body filled the window. Without warning, a large club slammed into the glass. Surprisingly, the glass held. The club crashed into the window twice more, the fury of the blows mounting. David looked about, his hands shaking. He wondered if he should get out and run or climb over into the front seat and try to drive away. Instead, he scooted as far from the attacker as the back seat would allow.

A loud blast caused him to jump, hitting his head harder on the roof. Stars danced in front of his eyes. A sharp pain shot through his neck. He turned to see Adnan running towards him, brandishing his shotgun in the shouldered position. David glanced back toward his attacker who had vanished. Looking quickly about, he saw no signs of the bare-chested man. How could he disappear so quickly? Could he be down beside the car, out of sight?

Adnan rounded the vehicle, soon followed by Patrick, who squatted to inspect the underside of the car. David reached forward and unlocked the front doors. The two men climbed in, and Patrick started the motor, pulling away from the curb.

"Where'd he go?" Patrick asked. "How'd he disappear like that?" He turned to David. "Are you all right?"

"Yeah, I'm okay. What'd you find? Any sign of Pam?"

"No, they'd left already," Patrick said. "They'd been there, though. We found Pam's purse and some of her stuff in one of the rooms—and blood in the bathroom sink."

"I have sample. We find out if belong to Pam," Adnan added.

"Do you think that guy beating on the car was with them?" David asked.

"Hard to tell," Patrick said, pulling out of the slum and onto Highway 51. "I doubt it was just a curious neighbor come to offer help."

"How come the window didn't break?" David asked. "He sure hit it hard enough."

"Government issue," Patrick said. He turned to Adnan. "Where do we go from here?"

"Well, it's a cinch—they still be after David, and come to us," Adnan said. "I must learn more about them. We go now either to hotel or David's place. I need some time with computer. David, tell me again how this start."

On the return trip, David summarized the events related to the bead, convinced now this was the lynch pin in the story. He was also sure if he purposefully lost the bead, those who wanted it would still come after him. "What's next? What do we do now?" His anxiety for Pam grew. What was she going through?

"The cops might want to question you about Pam's disappearance," Patrick said.

"That's it? We're quitting? She's got to be close by. How far could they have gone on foot?"

The two agents exchanged knowing glances. "We'll get her, David," Patrick said. "But not by making any more of a spectacle of ourselves here in shanty town. They'll come to us. It's not Pam they want."

David clutched the bead at his chest. Mr. Baroni was right to apologize when he surrendered this thing. If only he'd refused to accept it. Too late for that now. Who were these people stalking him? What was so precious about this bead? How does that woman posing as Baroni's granddaughter fit in? And why has this attracted so much attention from Patrick and the government?

David could not know the path down which he headed. He only knew it was dangerous and he sensed his life had changed … forever.

CHAPTER SIXTEEN

The trunk of the car felt cold and uncomfortable. Pam's hands and feet were tied, but not tightly. Or maybe she was getting used to the bindings. What she wasn't getting used to was the idea of being a captive. She listened to the voices coming from the car. The men had picked up another person—a woman. That might be a good thing. Maybe she'd be treated better.

The darkness of the trunk and the gag in her mouth made her claustrophobic. She fought the panic rising in her chest. *Breathe deeply and relax. Just breathe.* They'd have to eventually stop and let her out.

Going in circles; lots of turns. Finally, the car slowed to a stop. Doors opened and people got out. From the sound of their voices, they walked away! Pam struggled against her bonds and screamed into her gag. They couldn't just leave her! News stories of bodies found in trunks of cars flashed through her mind.

The trunk lid popped open. Two of her captors reached in and untied her. She wanted to bolt from her small prison, but her joints hurt too much for rapid action. As soon as they freed her arms, she reached up and removed the gag.

"What do you people want with me?" she yelled.

Ignoring her question, the two men led her into a rundown building; this time, an abandoned warehouse. Pam looked about, but recognized nothing. She'd lost her other shoe. As she walked, the gravel sent sharp pains through the soles of her feet. The men on either arm ushered her through a garage door big enough for tractor trailers, the interior poorly lit. They threw her into a small, barely ten-foot square room—no furniture, high ceiling, bare walls, and no window to the outside.

As soon as they closed the door behind them, she started to beat on it. "Hey! How about a bathroom? Let me out of here!"

After a few minutes, Banta opened the door and stepped into her cell accompanied by a white woman, presumably the one they'd picked up. The woman led her to a restroom down the hall and followed her in. Banta remained outside.

Momentarily ignoring bodily needs, Pam turned to the woman. "Who are you? Who are these men? What do they want with me?"

"Use the bathroom, if you must," the woman said. "Drink water from the sink. I'll bring you food later."

Pam detected a faint British accent. She stood facing the woman and decided to make use of the facilities. She continued talking, determined to get as much information as possible from this new person.

"You've got to tell me what this is about. Are they going to kill me?" Pam asked.

"No. I doubt they'll harm you unless you try to escape," the woman said. "These men are here on a mission, and they're using you to help accomplish their goal. Just be a good girl. Play along, and you might live through this."

Pam exited the stall and crossed to the sink. She examined her face in the mirror. Enough light came through the skylight for her to see. Her face was a mess: one eye swollen, lower lip split and crusted, left cheek purple, and her hair looked like she'd just crawled out of bed. As she washed, she studied the reflection of the other woman in the mirror. Tall, thin, professionally dressed, blond hair pulled back in a ponytail; she hardly looked the part of a thug.

Pam took her time. The woman paced about the room. The door to the bathroom swung open. Banta barged in.

"Enough time," he said, motioning for them to leave.

"I'm not going anywhere until I get some answers," Pam said.

Banta stalked toward her; eyes scowling, fists clenched. Pam cowered against the far wall, remembering the last time he'd approached her like this. He grabbed her bandaged right wrist and dragged her from the room. Pain shot up her arm. The wound felt like it had broken open again. Crying out, but not resisting, she stumbled behind him into the first room. Once inside, he removed a length of rope from one of his oversized pockets and started to bind her arms.

"Please don't tie me. I won't try anything. Please," she pleaded, near tears.

Banta hesitated, staring hard into her eyes. She held his gaze, her lower lip quivering.

"You try escape, I kill you," he said. Turning to the other woman, he motioned toward Pam. "You stay here. Watch. Call out if trouble." He left and locked the door.

The air in the room hung heavy and hot. Light filtered in through a small separation between the roof and wall, where the aluminum had warped. Dust coated the tile floor. Faded paper peeled halfway down one wall. An old fluorescent light fixture hung useless from the ceiling, the wall switch torn away.

Pam tried the door—locked. Pacing about the room and looking up at the separation of roof and wall, she caught her toe on a damaged tile and stumbled forward, catching herself before hitting the floor. Her wrist was bleeding again. Now her toe hurt. She sat immodestly on the floor, rubbing her foot, trying to control her emotions. The other woman leaned against the far wall, arms folded across her chest, as if bored with the whole situation.

"If we're to be held prisoner together, at least tell me your name," Pam said.

"I am not a prisoner," she said. "Banta trusts me."

"If you say so." Pam picked up on the uncertainty in the woman's voice. "My name's Pam."

"Call me Lisa. He'll come back for me soon—you'll see."

"How'd you get involved with these guys?" Pam asked. "I doubt you attended the same finishing school."

"You know nothing about him," Lisa said. "He's a good man, a strong man. He wants only what is his—and he will get it."

"What is it he wants? What has this to do with me?" Pam said, hoping to keep the woman talking.

"I'm not just here for his amusement," Lisa continued. "He needs me. I can get things he can't get on his own. It's not like back in South Africa. There, he could do anything. I was just his plaything. Now, he needs me. I'm important to him."

Pam decided to keep her talking, regardless of the topic. "What were you doing in South Africa? You don't look African," Pam said, glancing at her injured foot so as to seem uninterested.

"Oh, but I am. I was born and raised in South Africa. My work as a missionary took me north to underdeveloped areas. Not everyone there is cruel. Banta saved me from a band of rebels. They had hurt me—hurt me many times. Banta took me in. He never hurt me like they did. He's gentle when he comes to me," she said, hanging her head and turning away from Pam.

"What about the other men?"

"Most of the time he keeps them away from me. Sometimes, he gives me to them, but only for a short while, and then he takes me back. He needs me now."

Momentarily, Pam forgot her own plight. She felt sorry for Lisa, or whatever her name was, obviously an emotional cripple, pathologically tied to Banta, and perhaps even to his men. She began to think in terms of escape for both of them. But first, she'd have to throw a lifeline to Lisa and hope she'd grab it.

"Do you have family here in the States?" Pam asked.

Lisa looked away, offering no response. Pam decided that line of questioning was no good.

"You mentioned Banta wants something," Pam said. "What is it he wants? Maybe I can help."

"No, he doesn't need *your* help! He has me. I'll get him whatever he needs."

This wasn't working. She tried turning the questions away from the two of them. "What did he want in Dr. Freeman's apartment? Or did he want Dr. Freeman for some reason?"

"Banta is not a thief. Years ago, things were taken from his people. He wants them back. That's not stealing, is it?"

What could David have that Banta would want? Like most residents, he was broke and had no possessions to speak of. Something clicked in Pam's mind.

"Does this have anything to do with that old bead a patient gave him a few days ago?" Had it only been a few days? Seemed like months.

"It's not an old bead! It is a sacred relic belonging to the Zulu people. You can't begin to understand the importance of it," Lisa said, pacing around the room. "When is he coming back? I shouldn't be in here with you. I'm not a prisoner."

"If he wants the bead, I'm sure David will give it to him. Why doesn't he just ask for it? Why all this sneaking around? Is he in the country illegally or something?"

"He is not illegal. Banta is an important man. I arranged all the paper work. He has every right to be here." Lisa grew more agitated, her breathing rapid and shallow.

"Okay, okay. Settle down. Why don't you sit with me so we can talk? I'm sure they'll be back soon," Pam said, patting the floor beside her.

Lisa's emotional turmoil boiled over. She dropped to her knees in the far corner of the room and vomited. Pam struggled to her feet and went to her aid. Lisa did not fight her, but accepted her help. Pam held Lisa's hair back out of the way until she'd emptied her stomach. Lisa coughed and dragged the back of her wrist across her mouth, then collapsed into Pam's arms.

"They say the owner of the bead steals some of its magic. The full power only returns to the bead once the owner dies. That's why..."

Her voice trailed off as noise outside the door signaled the return of the men. The two women separated, assuming their roles as prisoner and guard. Wouldn't do for Banta to know any different.

It wasn't Banta, though. One of the other men walked into the room carrying a paper sack. Dressed only in a loin cloth and sandals, he posed a frightening figure in the small room. He held the sack out to Pam, leering at her. She made no move to take it. He then offered it to Lisa, who walked hesitatingly toward him and reached for the sack. As she neared, he dropped it and grabbed her wrist, yanking her to him. He twisted her arm behind her back and with his other hand, began to open her blouse. Lisa whimpered, but did not put up a fight. Pam rushed to them and grabbed Lisa away.

"Leave her alone!" she shouted.

The warrior's countenance darkened and his expression turned murderous. Shouts from the hallway saved the two women. He scowled and turned, leaving the room.

"I think that's the same one that tried to molest me," said Pam.

"His name is Shinto. He has a large appetite," Lisa said.

Pam now felt a bond between them. Lisa did not pull away from her as Shinto left the room. She pressed the advantage. "If you'll help me, we can probably both get away," Pam said. "You don't have to live like this."

"No!" Lisa shouted. "Banta needs me. I can't leave him. He takes care of me." She resumed her pacing.

Pam decided to give it a rest for the moment. She opened the sack, which contained pieces of fried chicken and rolls. She hadn't realized her hunger until she smelled the chicken. Reaching greedily into the bag, she extracted a breast and tore into it. Offering the food to Lisa, Pam sat down on the tile floor to consume the meal. Lisa shook her head and looked away. Too hungry to argue, Pam wolfed down two large pieces and ate half the rolls. A glass of iced tea would have been wonderful. Satisfied, she leaned back against the wall and studied her wrist, which still hurt. The wound looked infected. She needed to wash it.

Rising from the floor, she hobbled to the door. Her first instinct was to bang on it, yelling for attention. She couldn't recall if Shinto had locked the door on his way out. Hesitatingly, she tried the knob. It turned and the door cracked open. She threw a glance toward Lisa. Friend or foe? Lisa huddled in a corner, paying no attention. Was she asleep? Pam decided to chance it.

Slowly, she cracked open the door and scooted into the dimly lit hall, stopping to listen every few steps. Conversation came from another part of the building. Quietly closing the door, she hobbled away from the voices, toward the open end of the hall into the large garage. The bright sunlight momentarily blinded her. The asphalt burned her feet. Having no idea where she was and wanting to be anywhere but here, she took off running toward another cluster of abandoned buildings. She could hear the roar of the interstate ahead. Scaling a small wire fence, she made her way toward the road. The heavy air traffic overhead convinced her she was near the airport on the south side of town. Not someplace she wanted to be in a torn blouse and short skirt, but that couldn't be helped.

Scrambling up the embankment, she hurdled the guardrail and stepped onto the shoulder of the busy interstate. As luck would have it, the third car to pass her was a police cruiser. He flipped on his lights and pulled over about a hundred yards down the road. Pam laughed out loud with relief, never so glad to be pulled over. She'd see these flashing lights differently from now on.

From beside one of the buildings, Banta watched as the woman ran up the hillside to the highway. Nodding, he returned to his comrades.

CHAPTER SEVENTEEN

The familiar surroundings of the VA provided him some comfort. Usually, David couldn't wait to get out of the hospital, but now he wrapped himself in its sounds and smells and felt as though his life might get back to normal. The sound of his pager showing Patrick's cell phone number shattered that illusion. He toyed with the idea of not answering it, but anxiety over Pam won out.

"What is it now?" he asked, as Patrick picked up on his end.

"Pam's been found," Patrick said.

"What do you mean, 'been found'? Is she all right?"

"A little beat up, but okay. Cops picked her up off the interstate near the airport. She says she needs to see you."

"That's great news," David said. "Can you pick me up right now?"

"Not so fast. The cops need to question her first after they get her back from the hospital—"

"Hospital? Is she all right?"

"I don't know. Call me when you get through."

"That may be seven or eight tonight."

"If they get done with her before then, I'll let you know."

The rest of the workday dragged. David found it difficult to concentrate; his thoughts turning to Pam. Jim had to frequently bring him back into focus.

"What's going on with you, anyway?" Jim asked.

"It's complicated," David said. "Involves the police, robberies, abductions. If I turn up missing one day, don't think I've skipped out on you."

"If I can help, let me know," Jim offered.

"Thanks. I guess I worry about you feeling dumped on and complaining to Canole. Last thing I need is to get kicked out of the program."

"If it's that important, don't worry about it. I'll cover for you. Canole will never know you're gone."

"Tonight might be one of those nights, Jim. I need to get out of here as soon as possible. Would you mind doing rounds with the medical students?"

"Got you covered. I'm on call tonight anyway," Jim said.

David helped finish clinic and rounded on the total-joint patient from earlier in the week. He called Patrick, who said he'd be there in a few minutes, though he had no news on Pam yet. David's thoughts again turned to Pam and what she must have gone through in the hands of people who meant him harm. Visions of women brought to the ER flashed through his mind, and he dismissed those thoughts as soon as they popped up. He grew more anxious to see her.

Changing into street clothes, he walked out to the curb at the prearranged pick-up spot, his senses alert to the surroundings. Wouldn't do to be alone at dusk and daydreaming in downtown Memphis. Traffic thinned, but remained active in front of the hospital. A vagrant shuffled down the walk on the other side of the street, pushing a grocery cart full of who knows what. Probably his entire worldly possessions. Moses Donnelly had looked like that.

David fingered the bead at his neck. Why was it all the sudden so hot?

The vagrant stopped opposite the hospital. He reached into his grocery cart and fumbled between some bags. David watched out of the corner of his eye, not wanting the man to think he was being observed. Suddenly, the stooped-over street person moved quickly and athletically, pulling something from his cart. David caught the movement and alarms sounded in his head. He dove to the ground just as the blast from the shotgun took out a section of the wall behind him. Scrambling behind a car parked at the hospital entrance saved him from injury as a second blast took a bite out of the structure.

Patrick's car roared into the entryway, tires squealing. The door on the passenger side flew open and Patrick rolled out onto the ground, putting the car between them and the gunman. Pistol drawn, he peaked over the trunk toward the road. The cart lay on its side, wheels spinning; assailant gone.

"Geez! Am I glad to see you," David said from behind the car.

"Stay down! I don't know where the SOB is. Are you hurt?" Patrick asked, keeping his eyes on the road.

"No, I don't think so."

"When I tell you, jump in the car and slide over to the driver's side. It's in park and the brake's off. Keep your head low. Tell me when you're ready, and I'll get in. Then, burn rubber and get the hell out of here. Don't worry about traffic."

"Patrick, I—"

"Now! Go, go, go!"

David dove into the car. Patrick remained at his station behind the trunk, scanning the area over the sights of his gun.

"I'm in," David yelled.

"Once I join you, mash the accelerator to the floor. Be ready. It's gonna jump."

David heard the back door on the passenger side open. In the mirror, he saw Patrick dive in.

"Hit it! Take off! Now!"

With both doors open on the passenger side, David stomped on the gas. The car shot forward, slamming the doors shut. Tires screeched and smoked as they leapt out into the traffic of Madison Avenue. A blast of buckshot hit the car, cracking the back window, but the safety glass remained intact. The car fishtailed across the road, barely avoiding an oncoming vehicle, whose driver leaned on the horn. Patrick rolled over into the front seat.

"Where to now?" David asked, staring straight ahead at the road, his hands gripping the wheel.

"It's okay. You can slow down," Patrick said, holstering his gun. "I doubt we're being pursued. After all, they know where they can find you, right?"

David let up on the gas, his heart pounding.

"What?" The reality of that statement began to sink in. "What are you saying? That I can't go back to work?"

"No, of course not. We also know where we can find *them*," Patrick said.

"So, I'm still the bait, is that what you're saying?"

"Not alone. Think I can pass for a medical student?"

"You're kidding."

"No. It's perfect, really. I can tag along with you everywhere you go, wearing a bulky white coat over a small arsenal. What do you say?"

"I say you're nuts. But I don't have any better ideas. At the moment, I'm still clinging to the thought of becoming a real doctor one day."

"Take us back to the hotel. Adnan's there piecing this puzzle together. The cops will call us to come for Pam when they're through, which should be any time now."

"So how is Pam? Hear anything more?" David asked.

"She's had a thorough medical going over by the doctors at Methodist. Apparently, she's fine, but they wouldn't tell me much over the phone."

Patrick's cell phone rang. He answered and almost immediately, hung up. "That worked out well. She's ready now. You know where police headquarters is?"

Pam sat opposite the front desk, barefoot, with a blanket around her shoulders. As soon as she saw them, she raced into David's arms, the blanket falling away. David stood shocked at her appearance. Though she'd obviously had time to clean up and brush her hair, there was little she'd been able to do to hide the bruises and cuts about her face. With the blanket gone, her short skirt didn't begin to cover the bruises on her thighs and the rope burns about her ankles. He wrapped her in his arms as relief washed over him, and silently vowed to never let her go.

Patrick signed them out, and the three walked to the car. They'd spoken little to that point, Pam crying softly on David's shoulder. Patrick got behind the wheel and motioned for the two of them to get in back.

"I'm so sorry about all this. Are you really okay?" David finally asked.

"Do I look okay?" Pam answered with a mixture of anger and fatigue.

David could think of nothing to say that didn't sound trite. "You look fine, all things considered."

"You really know how to show a girl a good time, David. If you don't want me coming to your apartment unannounced, just say so next time," she said, hitting him on the shoulder.

David smiled. Some of the old spunk was creeping back. She'd be fine. "Do you feel like talking about it now?" he asked.

Patrick cut them off. "Why don't we hold off until we reach the hotel? I want Adnan to hear this, and you shouldn't have to relive it anymore than necessary."

"Hotel? I need to go to my apartment," Pam said. "In case you haven't noticed, my clothes aren't in such good shape, I need a shower, my make-up—"

"Later. Let's get you checked in first," Patrick said. "Hope you don't mind, but I've had Adnan get you two a room next to ours. Pam, you shouldn't be alone at your apartment tonight."

"Fine, but can one of you take me by my place later to pick up my car and some other things?"

David and Patrick agreed to work that out. They drove in silence to the hotel, David cradling Pam in his arms. She willingly submitted, the bravado melting away.

Adnan hunched over his laptop as the three of them entered the room. David introduced Pam and tried to explain the connection between him and the two agents.

"So, a patient of yours dies, a street person gets whacked and all of the sudden, I get abducted, and you've got the Department of Homeland Security putting us up in a hotel," Pam summarized.

"Well, it's a little more complicated than that, but—yes," David replied.

"Pam, before you go, please tell us everything you remember about what happened to you," Adnan said, again with a heavy Middle Eastern accent. "It very important for catching men."

"Do we have to do this now?" Pam asked. "I need to go by my place and pick up some things, and I *really* need a shower. Then, I'll be happy to stay up as long as I can and tell you everything."

"I could use a change of clothes myself, as long as we're headed that way," David said.

"Okay, but I'll have to go with you," Patrick said. "They know where both of you live, and my guess is they're none too happy about you getting away, Pam."

"How would they know where I live?" Pam asked. "I was at David's when they found me."

"Anything in your purse have your address on it?" Patrick asked, not looking up from the forms he sorted through.

"Well, sure, but I don't—oh, yeah. I guess they have that, don't they?"

"What's the bandage on your arm?" David asked.

"That's a cut I got in your apartment," Pam replied. "The docs at Methodist said they couldn't stitch it because it was too old and would get infected. Said I'd have to let it heal in."

"Did they attack you with a knife or something?" he asked.

"I think it was an 'or something.' In fact, I'm pretty sure it was that sword that used to hang over your bed," she said, nodding at David. "I cut myself on it when I was struggling."

David looked to Patrick. He could see his friend was thinking the same thing. Lucky she didn't lose her arm.

"Well, if we're going, let's do it," Patrick said. "I think we all need some down time to rest and relax. Adnan, we'll be back in less than an hour."

Adnan looked up from his computer. "Pam, before you go, did you learn name of any of men?"

"Well, I don't know if it's his real name, but the one in charge told me to call him 'Banta.' Also, the woman with them called herself Lisa."

"Woman!" David shrieked. "That's the first I've heard that. What'd she look like?"

"Tall, thin, light skinned, blonde hair pulled back in a ponytail."

"That's Lisa Baroni! The one I told you about in the hospital cafeteria," David said to Patrick.

"Well, we figured she was a fake and working with them in some capacity," Patrick replied.

"Baroni?" Pam said. "That's the name of that patient of yours who gave you the bead, isn't it?"

"Yeah. The woman is probably not his granddaughter. She used that name to get my confidence," David said, rubbing his face with his hands. "It's all a little overwhelming."

"Excuse, please, again," Adnan said. "This Banta. What he look like?"

"About six and a half feet, very black skin, muscular, no body hair, maybe thirty-five to fifty years old. Hard to tell," Pam said.

"How did you know about the body hair?" David asked, afraid of what the answer might be.

"They ran around in loin cloths, like a bunch of savages. Wore these strange headdresses. I wasn't raped, if that's what you're worried about. Listen, can we get going? I'm getting tired of walking around in this blanket, and I'd like to get some shoes."

"Did they speak English?" Adnan asked.

"Sometimes. Other times, they spoke in some language I'd never heard. Their English wasn't real good," she said, then looked apologetically toward Adnan.

"That's all right, milady. Me English is better at times," Adnan replied in a perfect British accent, sounding as though he'd schooled at Oxford.

Pam looked startled by the change. Patrick chuckled. "Come on. Let's go. He'll question you all night if you let him," Patrick said.

Gathering his coat, Patrick held the door for them, then lingered a second, turned, and said something to Adnan.

"What was that about?" David asked.

"Nothing, just a thought. Agent paranoia. Let's go," he said.

Adnan finished entering Pam's information in his computer and sent it to the central computers at the Department in Washington. The data wouldn't take long to assimilate, and a report should be ready upon his return later that evening. He gathered his small arsenal of offensive and defensive weaponry (two guns, extra ammo, a smoke grenade, an assortment of knives, and body armor, among other things) and secured each to his person, ready for immediate use. Hiding these under his coat, he headed out the door, minutes behind the others. Many times in the past, this delayed tail had been wasted effort. Adnan pushed aside the fear that prickled the back of his neck and hoped tonight would be another one of those times.

CHAPTER EIGHTEEN

Halfway to their apartment complex, David had a bad feeling. The bead hanging around his neck felt heavy and hot. The inky blackness of the night made even the street lights appear dim. He shuddered and looked to Patrick driving the car, seemingly lost in thought.

"Maybe we should go back to the hotel and do this in the morning," David said.

"What?" Pam nearly shouted. "Not a chance. I'm the one who's been manhandled and abused here. I want these guys put away, and the sooner the better, so suck it up, big guy. I kind of hope we run into them."

"You're just jumpy. Happens after being shot at," Patrick replied, but confidence was missing from his voice.

"Shot at!" Pam said. "Is that what happened to this back window? These bozos have guns now? Why didn't someone tell me?"

"You had other things on your mind when we picked you up," David replied.

"When did this happen?" Pam asked.

"Patrick picked me up after work, and some bum from the street fired a shotgun at us just before we heard the news you were ready at Police Headquarters."

"Some bum, huh? Some bum named Banta, I'll wager," she said, sitting back against the seat, then shifting sideways toward the door.

Patrick turned the car into the parking lot of David's apartment. He surveyed the grounds from within the car.

"I think it's best if we stick together," he said. "I'll go through the door first and you two follow. Keep your eyes open. If you see anything out of the ordinary, tell me, no matter how trivial. These guys haven't stayed on the loose this long by being stupid."

David helped Pam out of the backseat. The three climbed the outside staircase to his apartment. They walked by the attached unit when a noise from within made them all jump. Patrick took a deep breath, motioning them forward, pistol out and ready.

"Feels melodramatic," David whispered.

Patrick shushed him, reaching for the door handle. Apparently, management had repaired the door, for it was locked. David stepped forward with his key and turned the handle. Patrick elbowed him aside. He flipped on the light switch. The place was still a mess, but it looked as they had left it. Patrick placed them against the wall just inside the door. He cleared the apartment, then signaled for David to get what he needed.

Pam gasped as she walked by the bathroom, seeing the blood—her blood. She massaged the wound on her right arm.

"Let's get out of here. I'm sorry David, but your place gives me the creeps. I don't know if I can ever be comfortable here again."

David was surprised at how saddened her statement made him feel. Was she rejecting him, or just his apartment?

"Maybe we'll hang out at your place from now on, when this is all over, that is," he said. He hoped that hadn't sounded as lame as it felt. Quickly, he gathered the few things he needed for work.

Patrick said, "You do have a car here, don't you?"

"Yeah. It's in the far corner of the front parking lot."

"Take it when we leave. Right now, let's put your stuff in my car and drive to Pam's."

"We could walk," she said. "I'm in the building next door."

"Nope. If I could pull the car into your apartment, I'd do it. Let's go. Got everything you need?" Patrick asked David.

"Yeah, I think so. I agree with Pam. This place gives me the creeps. I might have to move, even though I've only got a few more months here."

Patrick led the way out while David locked up. The bead felt heavy, getting hotter. Patrick left the headlights off as they pulled out of David's lot and into Pam's.

"Same routine here. I'll lead. Ready?"

Pam and David nodded in response.

"I don't like this," David said. His tension had inexplicably doubled in the last minute.

"Oh, sure. You get your things and want to keep me barefoot and in these tattered rags. No thanks."

Pam lived on the ground floor; her door faced outward. Patrick led to the door and Pam unlocked it. Kicking open the door, he stepped through.

The butt of a shotgun smacked Patrick square on the side of his head. He crumpled to the ground. Pam and David sprang back, nearly falling over each other. In the doorway, Banta appeared, still wearing his street person disguise. He stepped over Patrick, lowering the gun at them.

A shot rang out from the parking lot. The butt of the shotgun splintered, flying from Banta's hands. David grabbed Pam and pulled her away from the door. Before Banta had time to react, a second shot caught him in the left shoulder, spinning him back into the apartment. He recovered his balance and raced away from the door, into the unit.

Pam and David hurried toward the car. Adnan nearly knocked them over, running full out toward his downed partner. He crouched low and sprang into the apartment, hurriedly glancing about, checking Patrick's neck for a pulse. Apparently satisfied, he rose and dashed into the room. Moments later, he reappeared, holstering his pistol.

"Escaped out the back." He motioned toward Patrick. "He's alive, but out cold. Give me a hand, will you," he said, all traces of accent gone.

David looked to Pam, already scrambling to help.

Adnan pulled out his phone and placed a call.

"We probably shouldn't move him," David said. "With such a blow to the head, he might have injured his neck."

"Ordinarily, I'd agree with you," Adnan said, phone at his ear. "But we need to get him out of this area—fast. I don't know where the perp went, or if he'll return. See my van over there?" he said, pointing to the back of the parking lot.

David nodded.

"In the back, there's lots of stuff. On the right wall is a stretcher and a neck collar. With your help, I think we can get him into the van and to a hospital."

The look on Adnan's face left little room for negotiation. David did as told. Within a few minutes, they had Patrick's unconscious body secure and loaded into the back of the van. While the two men did that, Pam hurriedly grabbed a few things from her apartment.

"Pam, take your car and either follow us to the hospital or go back to the hotel," Adnan said. "David, I'll need you to come with me."

"Sure. Let me grab my things out of Patrick's car."

"Here," Adnan said, throwing Patrick's keys to him. "Lock it when you're done. Hurry."

"David, I'm going to the hotel. Call me when you know any-thing about him," Pam said, motioning toward Patrick.

"You think it's all right for her to be alone?" David asked.

"They don't know about the hotel. Besides, there's some added security there you don't know about," Adnan said.

"You have a room key, right?" David asked her.

She nodded, getting into her car. Adnan had the van ready to go and David hopped in. The two vehicle caravan pulled out of the dark lot. Pam drove towards the hotel. Turning east, Adnan stepped on the gas.

"Where we headed?" David asked. He swiveled the captain's chair around so he could steady Patrick's head as they drove.

"We have these things planned out before arriving in an area. Methodist Hospital knows we're coming, and there won't be any wait or check-in process," Adnan replied.

"You know how to get there?" David asked, anxious to be helpful.

"*Turn—right—at next light*," said the pleasant recorded female voice from the dashboard.

"Should have known," David muttered, shaking his head.

Soon, they pulled into the emergency entrance. Several male attendants rushed to help cart Patrick into the hospital. Adnan talked with the nurse in charge and then returned to the van. Digging in the back, he pulled out a small briefcase. On his way back to the ER, he flipped the keys to David.

"Mind parking that for me?" he said, nodding toward the van. "I'll be in with Patrick. Don't touch anything except the gear shift and the ignition. Password's '*wahed*.'"

"What?"

"It's Arabic for 'one.' You'll figure it out. *Wahed*," he repeated.

David climbed into the driver's seat. He hadn't paid attention on the way. As he strapped himself into the front seat, he felt as if in the cockpit of a small plane: dials, instruments, gauges, buttons. Finding the ignition on the side of the steering column, he turned the key.

"*Hello. Who—are—you?*" the van asked.

"David Freeman," he replied, feeling a little silly.

"*Please say password—or exit vehicle—immediately*," the female voice said.

The sound of a ticking clock filled the cab.

"Wahed," he said, quietly.

The ticking got louder.

"*Repeat, please*," the angel of doom replied.

"*Wahed! Wahed!*" he screamed.

The ticking stopped.

"*Welcome aboard—David Freeman. Please drive me carefully*," the woman said in a more comforting tone.

David sat shaking in the front seat. What would've happened if he'd forgotten the password? Carefully, he stepped on the brake and shifted into drive. The van pulled forward. He parked it uneventfully.

Walking back from the parking garage, David reflected for a moment. Neither his apartment nor his workplace was safe. Could he go to work tomorrow? Would he endanger others at the hospital? What of Pam? Tomorrow was an operating day, and he couldn't remember the schedule. Was it something he needed to prepare for? He thought of Patrick. Hopefully, he'd be all right. David wavered, unsure what to do. Should he call his friend's parents in Nashville? How had things gotten so messy?

He found Adnan in the ER waiting room, working on his laptop.

"Any word on Patrick?" he asked.

"Nothing," Adnan replied, once again sounding foreign. "Doctor say he talk to me soon. Don't know."

"I'll go see what I can find out," David said. "Be right back."

Not recognizing the person behind the glass, he paused at the ER entrance and identified himself as Dr. Freeman. The clerk buzzed him in. He found Patrick in the CT scanner, still unconscious. A nurse with him monitored his vital signs. He confirmed with her that Patrick was okay, then ducked into the control room where the tech sat watching cross-sections of Patrick's brain show up on the screen. The tech looked up.

"You his doc?" he asked.

"Sort of. See anything yet?" David asked.

The tech pointed to a small dark patch just beneath the scull on the left side. "I'm no doctor, but that looks like a small epidural bleed to me."

David's heart sank. Bleeding inside the skull could cause pressure on the brain, resulting in loss of brain function or even death. "How much longer until he's out of the scanner?"

"Three or four minutes. Doesn't take very long with these new ones. Not like in the old days when—"

David missed the rest of the reverie as he ran back into the ER.

"Who's the neurosurgeon on call?" he asked the first nurse he ran into.

"I believe it's Dr. Miller," she answered. "In fact, I think he's down here, in room three."

David found Dr. Miller working on the chart of another patient. Miller was on the teaching staff at Methodist. As a medical student, David had done a rotation with him. Reintroducing himself, David quickly explained Patrick's situation.

"Has he been given any Mannitol or steroids yet?" Miller asked.

"I don't think so," David replied.

Miller quickly signed the chart he held, and headed with David to the scanner. The tech, with the help of a nurse, loaded Patrick onto a gurney.

Miller took a quick look at the scan and barked at the nurse. "Get me the protocol dose of Mannitol and Medrol—NOW! Has his neck been cleared?"

"He had some x-rays before coming over to the scanner," the tech responded.

Miller checked Patrick for pupil reaction and various reflexes. "Pull them up for me, will you?"

"It'd be better if we did that over in the ER. I've got another patient—"

The look Dr. Miller gave him shut off further talk and the tech quickly pulled up Patrick's neck x-rays on the digital monitor. Miller turned long enough to give them the once over.

"Good. Neck looks fine. Get this collar off him."

"What do you think?" David asked.

"Okay, so far. No sign of increased intracranial pressure yet, but we're going to have to watch him real close. The drugs should help prevent a pressure spike. He'll be in the ICU a few days. Any increase and I'll have to open his head."

David shuddered. Doctor or not, it was always different when you knew the patient. He helped Miller wheel the gurney back into the ER bay, then left them to find Adnan.

"How is he?" Adnan asked.

"I don't know," David said. "He bled into his head, but right now, he's okay. Doc says he'll be here for a few days and might need an operation."

"He'll be okay. His head very hard," Adnan said, with the faith of the ignorant. "We should return to hotel. I tell nurse where to call," he said, closing his laptop and gathering his things.

"Yeah, I guess you're right. Let me tell Dr. Miller where he can reach me."

Both men were on their guard as they walked through the lighted parking garage toward the van. It was close to midnight. David hesitated before getting in the passenger side.

"What would have happened without the password?"

Adnan chuckled. "Nothing. The van not start, that's all. Scary, huh?

"Yeah. Very funny. I about wet my pants."

"Sorry. No time to explain then. Have you called Pam?"

"No. I guess I'd better do that. Listen, can we go by my place and at least get my car? I still have to work in the morning."

Adnan agreed. David called the hotel and was put through to her room. No answer. Probably asleep or in the shower, he thought.

In front of David's apartment, Adnan cleared his car for signs of tampering, then followed him back to the hotel.

Pam wasn't in the room.

CHAPTER NINETEEN

Banta's shoulder burned like the bite of a viper. In the dark, he slowly drove to their new hideout, an old abandoned gas station. Anger and frustration over his failed attempts at the bead overshadowed the physical pain. Where had that shot come from? How many men did he fight now? He knew of David Freeman and the girl and this new man with the gun, but who was the fourth, the man who had shot him? How could he be sure Freeman still carried the bead? His attempt to wound the doctor and take him from the hospital had failed. He'd need to see him up close, alone somewhere. That would be more difficult now with these other people interfering.

Blood poured from his shoulder onto his clothing. He used pain to drive off the lightheadedness. His thoughts drifted to his home in Africa and his boyhood family. His oldest brother, Jarmangi, would jab him in this same shoulder when they played, sometimes hard enough to leave bruises. His mother scolded them for hitting each other. She'd suffered from the loss of Jarmangi and that he'd died without her at his side.

After Jarmangi's death, she quit her job. He often found her in their little house, sitting alone, rocking and talking to herself. He frequently skipped school to check on her. Always, she was the same: withdrawn, tearful, looking at him almost without recognition. That frightened him. He'd shake her from her thoughts, and she would rise from her chair, muttering to herself, totally unaware of his presence. Afraid to disturb her, he watched over her until she drifted to sleep. If only he could bring back Jarmangi, then she'd be all right. She'd love him and hug him and everything would be like it was.

She died the next year; not sick, not injured—just tired of living. He'd been out hunting instead of in school, and when he returned, he found her propped in her chair, her face peaceful and unworried for the first time since Jarmangi's death. Banta sat at her feet and talked to her, promising he'd make it right, somehow. Those minutes or hours he sat with her burned in his dreams. That time marked the end of innocence, his last hurrah at boyhood. With his mother and oldest brother gone, nothing mattered. That day began his search for a purpose he wouldn't find until nearly twenty years later when men from England returned four of the original beads to his country.

He'd worked long and hard to gather the resources and knowledge to mount a search for the missing twenty beads. He'd spent many years tracking them down and planning their recovery.

The American doctor had no right to wear one. Banta fingered the three beads at his neck, though to do so hurt his shoulder. He'd get that bead back, and he'd have the unrighteous head of the doctor. Jarmangi deserved no less.

Banta had left his men and Lisa to secure their new hideout. They had disposed of its previous squatter, who'd been reluctant to leave. As Banta pulled into the abandoned lot, he noticed light flickering through one of the dirty windows.

Cutting the engine, he jumped from the car and burst through the door of the building, blood streaking down his left arm. His two men prepared food over an open fire. Lisa sat in a corner but rushed to him as he entered.

"Cover window!" he ordered. "I can see you from street."

The men hurriedly did as told, using their bedding as curtains. Lisa examined his arm, her forehead wrinkled with concern. "You're hurt! How did this happen?" she asked. She pulled at his shirt. "Let me look."

Banta pushed her away, but felt faint from the effort. He dropped to a knee and lowered his head. With his right hand, he felt the wound on his shoulder. Two holes; the exit wound on the back of the shoulder being larger and more painful. He could move his shoulder, so the bullet had probably missed bone. He'd be fine as long as infection didn't set in.

One of his men approached, carrying their aid kit. He knelt beside Banta and poured something over the wounds. Banta ground his teeth, sitting hard on the floor, but said nothing. His comrade sprinkled powder from their supplies on the wounds, bound his shoulder, and leaned him against a wall. The second Zulu helped him out of his clothing and into his native loin cloth. They would honor their African origin, tonight, as they did every night, with native rituals. His wounds would not alter this.

Lisa handed him water and he drank greedily, feeling better.

"We need to plan carefully," he said. "It will be harder here in America, where people carry guns and know how to use them. We *will* have bead, but getting it will require stealth and surveillance."

The men listened and did not interrupt. Lisa could not contain herself.

"We need to get you to a doctor!" she said. "You've lost a lot of blood—"

"Quiet! No doctor and ..." He stopped mid-tirade. Lisa spoke the truth, though in a way different from what she intended. He did need a doctor. Perhaps this wound could be put to use. "Leave me now. We talk more in morning." He motioned to his men. "Prepare the altar."

The two Zulus dragged a footlocker into the middle of the room. They removed a large bag from within and closed the lid. Over the footlocker, they spread a woven blanket, elegantly decorated with symbols of Africa. One of them extinguished the cooking fire, and the other placed candles about the makeshift altar, then lit a bowl of dried leaf, filling the small room with pungent smoke. Banta and the others squatted, facing the trunk. Lisa huddled in a corner, as far away as the room would allow, burying her face in her hands.

The men made no sounds at first. As the drugged smoke filled their lungs, they began to sway and chant. Banta removed the beads from his neck and donned an elaborate feather head-dress. He placed the beads on the altar and fetched the bag taken from the trunk. Lisa whimpered from her perch in the corner. From the bag, Banta removed the dried, smoked heads of the three British subjects—previous owners of beads. He arranged the heads around the altar on top of the trunk. His chanting grew bolder and his actions more animated. His shoulder wound forgotten, he danced what had become his ritual. He honored his long lost brother, his dead mother, and his country of Africa. He rained curses on those who would defile them and keep the beads from their rightful place. In his right hand, he carried the heavy curved sword he'd taken from the doctor's apartment. It became an extension of him, whirling and cutting through the air in mock battle. The chanting of his men increased, as did the rhythm of his gyrations. He lifted each severed head by the hair and passed the sword underneath, ceremonially duplicating the decapitation. How much nicer this weapon felt: much more natural than the crude machete he'd used in England. He sensed it belonged to him and his people, like the beads.

Replacing each head on the altar, he discarded the sword, and took up the beads. Falling to his knees, he offered up the strand, holding them above his head. His men abruptly stopped chanting, and the room plunged into a deathly stillness. Not even Lisa dared disturb this morbid solitude.

The drug sharpened his vision, his hearing grew more acute. He could hear the flames of the candles and the smoking of the leaf. He slowly placed the beads back on the altar and swore the oath, as he had for many years. He'd retrieve the beads and return them to Africa, avenging his brother and restoring his mother's pride.

As he resumed his squatting position in front of the altar, the others took up a low rumbling chant. This went on until the smoldering leaf in the bowl died away. They then disassembled the altar and prepared bedrolls for the night.

No one noticed the two small, black heads with eyes as big as silver dollars peering through a corner of one of the dirty windows of the old gas station. The two boys made a game of spying on the homeless in the area, and one of their favorites had been the old man holed up here. They hadn't checked on him since last week and a lot had apparently changed. Too scared to move, they watched until the new inhabitants of the building rested quietly on the floor. Slowly, the boys backed away until safely on the asphalt surrounding the building. Then, they turned and ran with a burst of speed neither knew they had. Two blocks later, they slowed to catch their breath.

"Did you see that?" Jamal said. Breathing hard, he bent and supported his weight on his knees.

"What were those things he danced around the room with?" Tyrone asked, leaning against a wall and wiping his forehead.

"I think they was heads," Jamal said, looking up at his friend.

"Heads of what?"

"Heads of people. What do you mean, *heads of what*?"

"Really? You think those was people heads?" Tyrone asked.

"Did you smell that weed they was burning? That's some strong shit, man. No wonder they's dancing around with heads and swords and stuff."

"Think we should tell somebody?"

"Who? Who we gonna tell?" Jamal said. "And what we gonna tell 'em? That we saw some crazy brothers smoking weed and cutting off heads? I ain't sayin' nuttin' to nobody."

Jamal and Tyrone shuffled back to their tenement housing, each replaying the strange sights of the night in his head. They were scared; each knew the other was scared; each knew they'd be back the next night.

CHAPTER TWENTY

David paced about Pam's hotel room. With no signs of a struggle, Adnan wasn't worried.

"She probably stepped out for a few minutes," Adnan said. "She'll be back soon.

David looked at his watch. He needed sleep, but not until he knew Pam was safe.

Both men jumped at the sound of the card sliding into the door lock. Pam strolled in looking refreshed in her fluffy hotel bathrobe and slippers, a towel wrapped around her head.

"Where have you been?" David asked. "In light of recent events, I've been worried about you."

"You were?" She smiled. "Sorry. The idea of a sauna and hot-tub after my shower was irresistible. There's a great spa on the second floor." She fluffed her hair. "How's Patrick?"

"Don't know yet. Dr. Miller, a neurosurgeon, is watching him in the ICU. The CT showed a small intracranial bleed."

Pam stopped her drying. "He's going to be all right, isn't he?"

"I hope so, Pam." David sat on the side of the bed.

Adnan pecked away at his laptop. "Pam, you remember any more details of Banta? Anything that might help narrow down who he is?"

"Well, I've given you a physical description and we know he's from South Africa. What else do you mean?"

"I don't know. Give me your impressions—educated, mannered, intelligent—just anything."

"Well, I had the feeling he'd been in the military. Some of their interactions—I don't know—struck me as training rather than street knowledge."

Adnan turned back to his laptop. David and Pam prepared to head for their room. After another minute, Adnan turned the laptop toward them.

"That him?" the agent asked.

Pam gave a start. On the screen was a mug shot from what looked to be a Government ID.

"That's him! That's the face in the mirror!" She shuddered and looked away. "I'll never forget that face."

David walked to the computer. "Got anything else?"

"Well, if that's our guy, I have complete bio right here. Bad boy, prison record for multiple minor offenses, military training, loner, though he came from family with four sons. Here's picture of family at funeral of one of his brothers. Made papers back then. His oldest brother got shot here in States on Scouting trip."

"You mean like Boy Scouts?" David asked.

"Yeah. Looks as if he came here in '67 for Idaho Jamboree. Ruled accidental shooting. No one ever brought to trial."

"This whole bizarre episode started with a reference to Scouting. See what more you can find out about that Jamboree," David said, studying the computer image of Banta as a child with his family. "Can you blow up this image?"

"Sure," Adnan replied. "You want closer look at Banta Mangabe as child?"

"No," David said, staring closely at the screen. "I want to see his mother. Zero in on her, if you can."

After a few clicks on the keyboard, the mother's face filled the screen and the computer automatically enhanced the image.

"Holy cow! That's Gladys. Pam, come look at this. You know the scrub nurse who works with us at the VA? Gladys Vaughn? Does that not look like her, or what?"

"Looks sort of familiar. I don't know the OR crew real well," she said.

"That's scary. Hair's different and Gladys is a little heavier, but that's her," he said, pointing.

Adnan pulled up another screen with stories regarding the Jamboree. Prominent among them was the description of Jarmangi's shooting and the part he played in the events of the Jamboree. David read over Adnan's shoulder.

"So these beads originated in Africa, and Jarmangi Mangabe brought replicas to the Boy Scout gathering," David said. "You suppose that's what's behind all this?"

"Maybe in some off-wall way," Adnan replied. "This Banta's got to have screw loose to be going to all this trouble for few beads. Maybe his brother's death pushed him over edge."

"But that was nearly forty years ago. He was just a kid at the time."

"Guys, I'm exhausted," Pam said, yawning. "I'm going to bed."

David looked away from the screen. "Yeah, I guess I'd better do the same. Have to work tomorrow, you know."

Adnan's brow furrowed and his lips tightened. "About work. Hospital and apartment are places Banta knows he can find you. He'll assume you're not going to your apartment for while."

"I've got to go to work, Adnan. I can't—"

"I think I go work with you," Adnan said. "I blend in. Maybe I be medical student from Pakistan. You know, visiting on exchange program with your clinic."

"I don't know. The hospital rules are pretty strict. You can't just walk in and say you're a medical student. You'd need an ID badge, verifying papers, background checks—that sort of thing."

Adnan closed his computer. "You go to bed. I see you in morning."

Pam seconded that motion by grabbing his hand and dragging him toward the door. David shrugged to Adnan, who smiled back. They exchanged "goodnights" and Pam and David gathered their things before going next door.

Unlike Adnan's room with two single beds, this one had a large queen-size. Pam headed straight for the bathroom. David threw his belongings on the bed and started to put them in drawers. He sat quietly for a few minutes as Pam showered, fatigue washing over him.

The water in the bathroom stopped. She came back into the room carrying some bandage gauze. "Look at my arm and rewrap it for me, okay? I think it might be getting infected." She sat on the side of the bed, holding her right arm out for him to see. Her bathrobe opened to her waist, covering all parts, though just barely, wet hair hanging loosely to her shoulders.

David drew a deep breath and sat next to her. Taking her arm, he examined the healing wound, found no evidence of infection, and rewrapped it. He tried to remain objective, but couldn't. Her wound hurt him. Seeing her body torn made his skin feel peeled and his belly churn. There's a good reason doctors don't treat those they love. He held her arm a moment longer than necessary.

Pam smiled and pulled away. Making no effort to cinch up her robe, she rose and returned to the bathroom. The sound of the hairdryer shook David from his reverie. He needed a shower, but didn't want to disturb her routine. As if reading his mind, Pam turned off the dryer and leaned out of the bathroom. "You can take a shower, if you want. I won't attack you—not tonight, anyway. I'm exhausted."

David nodded, but decided to wait until she finished. The sexual tension hung thick in the room, but he didn't feel up to it either. Still, no sense tempting fate. He turned on the TV and flipped through the channels, then dialed the operator and left a wake-up call.

Pam entered the room. Ignoring him, she arranged her clothes for tomorrow. She'd made an attempt to hide some of her facial bruises with make-up. Some of the old bounce was back in her step, or so it seemed. Not even the oversized terry-cloth robe could hide her abundant sexuality.

David hurried into the bathroom, uncomfortable with the desire he felt. What had she experienced at the hands of the Zulus? She already kept so much inside concerning the death of her husband in Iraq. He wanted so much for her to let it out and him in—into the world she kept bottled up.

The room smelled of dried hair. A small pang of disappointment struck him when he finished and she wasn't there holding his towel just out of reach and taunting him. He brushed his teeth and, wrapping himself in one of the hotel robes, flipped off the light and opened the door. The outer room was dark, Pam already in bed.

He tip-toed to the empty side of the bed and put on his scrub pants. Normally, he slept nude, but that didn't seem right. Pam was either asleep or feigning such. She made no acknowledgement of his presence. Slipping between the sheets, he turned his back toward her and laid his head on the pillow.

Pam purred and turned toward him, throwing her bandaged right arm across his chest. She spooned up next to his back, snuggling in. He felt her breasts on his back. She nestled her top leg on his bottom one, pulling him closer. He made some attempt to respond, but she thwarted it.

"Just let me sleep tonight, David," she whispered. "I'll make it up to you later."

He smiled inwardly. "Goodnight, Pam." For a moment, he regretted having called for a wake-up.

CHAPTER
TWENTY-ONE

David awoke before the operator called. He slid out of bed, careful not to disturb Pam. Fifteen minutes later, he prepared to walk to the hospital, but couldn't leave without saying good-bye.

"Pam … Pam." He touched her shoulder. "Five-fifteen. Time to get up."

She groaned once, rolled over and smiled, but winced as she moved her jaw. "How'd you sleep, Doc?"

"Pretty well, thanks. I'm getting ready to leave. You gonna be all right?"

"Look at my arm before you go. See if it's okay."

She sat up in bed, clutching the sheet to her breast and holding out her right arm. The bed sheet almost covered her. She scooted over to give him room to sit beside her.

David sighed and acquiesced. Her laceration was mending well with no evidence of infection. He earlier worried about one of the extensor tendons to her wrist, but that appeared uninjured and functioned fine this morning. "Looks okay. Want me to rewrap it?"

"No. I'm gonna jump in the shower. You go to work. Maybe I'll see you there and we can decide about tonight."

David racked his brain. Had he forgotten something? What happens tonight? "Yeah—tonight," he said, stalling for time.

Pam laughed. "What I meant was, will we be staying here—at the hotel or at our apartments?"

"Oh, that. Well, I won't be at either. I'm on call tonight, so I'll be staying at the VA. Ask Adnan what he thinks would be best, and go with his advice."

"Wonder how Patrick's doing," she said.

"Want me to call real quick and find out?"

"Would you? I'll run to the bathroom while you call." With that, she threw aside the sheets and scurried by him. David tried to be a gentleman and look the other way, but wasn't quick enough. Pam turned before closing the door and caught him. "Unless you'd like to do something else?" she cooed.

He turned to dial the phone. She laughed again and closed the door. How did she do that? It's as if she had him on a string and pulled it for fun every now and then. The shower splashed on.

"Hello, operator? This is Dr. Freeman. ICU, please." A few seconds passed, enough for him to become distracted thinking of what he'd just witnessed. "Oh, yes. This is Dr. David Freeman. I'm calling to check on Patrick Dartson. Could I speak with his nurse, please?"

"That would be me," the friendly voice on the line said. "He had a good night. Regained consciousness several hours ago and has a splitting headache, but it looks like he's gonna be okay. Dr. Miller hasn't been in yet, but I imagine he'll send Mr. Dartson to the floor later today if he continues to improve."

"Thanks. That's a relief. Would you tell Patrick I called and that everyone is okay?"

"You're Dr. Freeman?"

"Yes ma'am. I'm one of the ortho residents and Patrick's room-mate in college. Just tell him I called, if you would. Thanks for all your help," he said, hanging up the phone.

Rapping on the bathroom door, he relayed that information to Pam, and then made to leave. Pam stuck her head out the door.

"Hurry home, honey," she said with sarcastic domesticity.

At least she had a sense of humor about it. He thought about popping in on Adnan. The door to the adjoining room stood open, and for a moment, a sense of dread filled him. Shock replaced this when Adnan stepped into the hall wearing a short white coat containing a stethoscope, reflex hammer, pen light, scissors, and all the other paraphernalia of a medical student.

On his lapel hung an ID badge identifying him as a Pakistani exchange student.

"How'd you get all that stuff?" David asked.

"Special delivery. We work very hard at department." He smiled and raised one eyebrow. "You like? I want very much to learn ways of American medicine." His voice ping-ponged comically, and David had to chuckle.

"Don't guess there's much chance I can talk you out of this, is there?"

"No. I work very hard, study very much for this opportunity. We go now?" Adnan waved his arm down the hall and bowed slightly for David to lead the way.

Walking to the hospital, they got to know each other better. Adnan, too, had checked on Patrick, and they talked of their mutual friend. David explained that today, he had two cases in the operating room, followed in the afternoon by general orthopedic clinic, where they saw post-operative patients and those with new complaints. Adnan absorbed information like a sponge, and the questions he asked were better than those of most medical students. David began to relax.

"You really think Banta might try for me in the hospital?"

"Did he not shoot at you outside VA?"

"Yeah, I guess he did. But there are always so many people around."

"Crowds can be used to advantage. I think this Banta is wise in ways of stealth and murder. We not underestimate him. Think of least likely place for him to be, and there you find him," Adnan said.

David found his team waiting for him in the hospital cafeteria, drinking coffee. He introduced Adnan to the medical students and Jim McCallum, who looked suspiciously at Adnan. They'd never had a medical exchange student, and it was late in the year to be getting one. David motioned it was time to go. The others grabbed their Styrofoam cups and followed him to the elevator.

This time of the morning was used for work with dressings, wound checks, and charting. The three sleepy medical students didn't ask much. Jim, however, must have been feeling professorial, as he peppered them with questions on anatomy and orthopedics.

"Adnan? How would this wrist fracture be handled in your country?" Jim asked, standing at the bedside of a patient.

"Yes. Thank you very much," Adnan replied, entertaining them with his accent. "In my country, which is very far backwards from America, we have very little things to do for this. The doctors in Pakistan work very hard using what they have to—" He droned on and on, prepared to talk all morning, saying nothing. David grinned. *So Adnan's a bullshit artist also.* Eventually, the group moved to the next patient, and though Adnan continued to talk, one by one, they started to ignore him and resume rounds. Jim didn't ask any more questions.

Floor work completed, they headed to the locker room to change for surgery.

"Uh oh," Adnan said, leaning in close to David.

"What?"

Adnan held open the left side of his lab coat so only David could see the large hand gun in the shoulder holster.

"Geeezz! You gonna wear that into surgery?"

Adnan sheepishly shrugged and nodded. David grabbed him by the arm and took him to a deserted corner of the locker room. "Here," he said, handing him a scrub jacket popular with the nurse anesthetists. "Put this on over your scrubs and your little friend there. We keep the ORs cold, and you can tell everyone you're not used to that. Try not to shoot anybody during the operation."

"Maybe I shoot other doctor if he asks more questions," Adnan said, glancing in Jim's direction.

"Don't think that'll happen. None of us are anxious to hear another monologue on Pakistani medicine."

The operations came off without a hitch. Adnan played the part of the interested medical student, even to the extent of being occasionally annoying. They broke for lunch before afternoon clinic. David led Adnan to a booth in one corner of the dining room. He hoped they could talk privately.

Pam appeared out of nowhere and slid in next to them. Her make-up covered most of her facial bruises. He bristled at the thought of someone striking her. She acted as though nothing had happened and even seemed upbeat. His anger melted into affection, and he saw her through changed eyes. Though they'd been a couple for more than three years, she still stirred emotions in him, perhaps more so now than ever before.

"Hi guys. Mind if I join you?" she asked.

"Please. Very much." Adnan stood and bowed slightly, hands together in front of his chest. Pam laughed out loud. "Keep it down, will you? He's supposed to be an exchange student from Pakistan," David said, scooting over to make more room for her.

Pam raised an eyebrow, looking to Adnan.

"Pleased to meet you," she said, setting down her tray and extending her neatly bandaged right arm.

"Yes. Very much. Me too." Adnan shook her hand and waited for her to sit before reclaiming his seat. David rolled his eyes.

"So, how do you find medicine in America?" she asked, grinning.

Adnan nodded his head and took a deep breath. David cut him off. "Please, no more," he said, holding up both hands. To change the subject, he said to Pam, "Your face looks good. The bruises are barely noticeable."

"I laid the make-up on pretty heavy this morning. Still, all the nurses on the floor asked about it. They're convinced you're a woman beater," she said casually, taking a bite of her salad.

"What? You're kidding, right?"

Adnan stayed in character, looking a combination of embarrassed, puzzled and amused. Pam nearly lost her bite of salad trying to contain her mirth. "What can I tell them? That I was abducted and beaten by a Zulu? Maybe I walked into a door? They're not going to believe anything I say, so I just told them it was none of their business."

"Great. My career is coming to an abrupt halt, I'm being shot at, and now I'm a woman beater."

His expression suddenly changed. The bead around his neck felt heavy again, like it had last night going to his apartment. He looked around the dining room, but saw nothing.

"What is it?" Adnan asked, sounding less Pakistani.

"I don't know. Probably nothing." David toyed with the bead through his scrubs. Adnan apparently picked up on his uneasiness and casually scanned the lunch area, continuing to eat.

Pam, seemingly oblivious to the sudden rise in tension, looked to Adnan. "Have you decided where we'll be staying tonight?"

Continuing his surveillance of the cafeteria, he answered her in a voice that left no room for discussion. "There will be no change."

"What is it?" she asked, suddenly aware. Neither man answered. "Come on, guys. You're scaring me."

"Oh, nothing. I guess I'm a little jumpy, that's all," David said, but continued to scan the area. "Adnan, we need to finish lunch and head to clinic."

The three chatted as the men wolfed down their food. Pam expressed the need to go back to her apartment for some things she'd forgotten, but Adnan nixed that idea. As the men got up to leave, she slid out of the booth, making a small space for David to get by. Their bodies squeezed together for an instant, enough for Pam to give him a familiar pat on the rump.

Five chairs with attached desks lined up in the center of the room for the providers of health care. In front of these sat five waiting room chairs for the patients as the nurses ushered them in and out. David occupied the middle chair with medical students on either side. The addition of Adnan caused them to be one chair short, and the staff pulled up an extra for him, minus the desk. David positioned Adnan close to his side, just behind the group, then signaled the nurse to bring in the first batch of patients. The controlled chaos of the government delivery of medical care began.

Clinic at the VA lacked doctor-patient warmth. Medical students and residents screened patients four or five at a time, ordering tests and x-rays, performing cursory exams, and discussing treatment plans, all in one large room. If they needed privacy or a bed, both patient and doctor went into one of the enclosed areas. This herded a lot of Vets through efficiently and provided many teaching opportunities. Usually, one of the attending orthopedists from Campbell's Clinic floated about the room providing help and instruction where necessary. Nurses constantly shuffled patients in and out. Clerical staff hurried to complete the mountain of required paperwork. The atmosphere resembled that of a busy bus terminal, with only half-hearted concerns to comply with government regulations mandating privacy.

The patient population of the VA fared only slightly better than that of the indigent clinics at the charity hospitals. Few had done well in life after their military service. Many were homeless, living on the street. Those who could afford it used private insurance and sought care elsewhere.

David supervised the administration of injections, prescriptions, braces and cast changes. A few needed surgery and were more closely examined and dates scheduled. These afternoons usually sped by in spite of the volume of patients. Midway through clinic, David turned to Adnan, motioning him closer.

"There's a drink machine down the hall and to the right. Would you mind getting me a can of something, whatever's available?" He reached into his back pocket, pulling out his wallet.

"No, no. Please. I get. It is my pleasure," Adnan replied, refusing to take the money. Glancing about the room, the agent hurried down the hall and out of sight around the corner.

A patient plopped down in the chair in front of David. He hadn't seen a nurse bring this one in, but no matter. Typical patient: black, old, dirty and down on his luck. He wore rags, and smelled of alcohol and sweat. Though downtrodden and slumped, he filled out the large, tattered coat draped over his shoulders. His head, topped with a faded baseball cap, hung down onto his chest. He did not acknowledge nor even seem aware of David sitting in front of him. The left side of his coat fell away from his body, revealing a gauze bandage on his left shoulder, only partially obscured by his unbuttoned shirt.

"Good afternoon sir," David said. "How can I help you today?"

He sat patiently, waiting for a response. Maybe the old man was hard of hearing. He leaned forward and spoke louder. "I'm Dr. Freeman. What can I do for you? Have you hurt your shoulder?"

The old man slowly raised his head off his chest. As his face began to appear from beneath the bill of the cap, David became uneasy. The bead around his neck seemed to catch fire. The old man's eyes caught his and burned with frightening intensity. David bolted back against his chair and sucked in a breath. The man's hand shot out and pressed against David's chest; the bead now searing the flesh of his breast bone. Moving his hand up to the doctor's chin, he turned David's head from side to side, apparently examining his neck. The dark lips parted slowly as he smiled and continued his icy stare.

David regained composure and brushed the man's hand away. "Who are you and what do you want with me? Is it the bead? I'll give it to you right now if you'll leave us alone." His heart beat rapidly and his throat felt dry.

"You and bead are one," Banta replied in broken English. "Can you not feel it?" He stood and leaned in close to David, their faces inches apart, his breath rancid. "I come for both of you soon."

By now, this had attracted the attention of others in the room. Banta turned and hurried into the crowded corridor, running into Adnan, causing him to spill some of the Pepsi he carried.

"So sorry. I not see—"

"Adnan!" David shouted. "That's him! That's the guy—the bead guy!"

Adnan looked to David and then immediately chased after the man, handing the drinks to a startled student. David sat frozen in his chair; the medical students, nurses, Jim, and the remaining patients staring at him.

"What was that about?" Jim asked.

"What—oh, nothing. Just some crazy old vet. Probably drunk."

"Then why did Adnan take after him?" Jim asked. "Something's screwy here. What's going on?"

David rose from his chair and motioned for Jim to follow him to a far corner of the room. "Remember when I asked you to cover for me? Something strange *is* going on and I'm in the middle of it, no fault of my own, mind you. The details are complicated and probably best left unsaid. Did you get a look at the guy who darted out of the room?"

Jim nodded.

"If you see him again, please tell me or Adnan immediately, okay?"

"Yeah, sure." Jim turned to look down the hall. "Who is this Adnan, anyway? I knew there was something not quite right about him."

"Never mind. He's an exchange student, that's all. Now, let's finish clinic and get out of here."

The two residents walked back to their seats. The commotion settled down and the medical students had numerous questions regarding their patients.

Moments later, Adnan returned and tried to sneak unnoticed to his seat. He leaned into David and spoke quietly. "I lost him, but saw him leave the parking lot. Got a make, model and license number. That should help. I've already called it in to our people. They'll contact me if they find anything."

David nodded and continued with his work. "He said he'd come for me, Adnan."

"Good. Maybe we'll come for him first." Adnan leaned back in his seat. "Sorry to spill Pepsi," he said loud enough for others to hear. "You want I get another?"

"No, but I would like you to call to the fourth floor nurse's station and see if Pam's there and okay. It's getting close to the end of her shift."

Adnan returned moments later, shaking his head. "Gone," he mouthed.

Shit.

CHAPTER
TWENTY-TWO

After clinic, David cornered Adnan, away from the others. "I have to stay here tonight and I'm worried about Pam. Would you mind going to the hotel and checking on her?"

"And leave you here alone? You think you can handle that guy if he come back?"

"How do we know he's not hassling Pam?" David asked. "He's done that before, you know."

Adnan's phone rang. After seeing the number, he walked away from David and talked quietly. He returned moments later, smiling. "The problem may have solved itself. That was Patrick. He says Dr. Miller will discharge him, as long as someone stays with him next few days. I pick him up and take to hotel. He can babysit Pam tonight."

"You think he'll be okay to do that?" David said. "He's probably still having some post-concussive symptoms."

"He sound good on phone. If he not up to it, we think of something else."

Unable to suggest anything better, David agreed. Adnan left and David prepared for evening rounds. Until now, he hadn't realized how secure he felt with Adnan around. Suddenly, he felt bare and vulnerable. As the evening wore on, he viewed everyone with suspicion and, as much as possible, tried to stay in crowds. When and how would this end?

Adnan picked up Patrick at the Methodist hospital and filled him in on Banta and the events at the clinic. Patrick seemed normal, occasionally rubbing his temples, though he denied having a headache.

"So what's our next move?" Patrick asked.

Adnan glanced up. This question alarmed him. Patrick always had ideas; some bad, others brilliant, but he always had a plan.

"You sure you feeling all right?"

"Drop it. I'm fine. Okay?" Patrick said. "Let's get back to the hotel and see if Pam's there. Have you tried her cell?"

"She doesn't have one anymore, remember?" he replied. "I thought I leave her in your care tonight. David has to stay at hospital. I'll either be with him or doing some reconnaissance on my own. We might have a lead if department comes up with info on car I saw leaving hospital today."

Patrick nodded and leaned back against the headrest, closing his eyes. He still appeared peaked. Adnan turned his attention back to the road. He'd have to trust his partner, though he wondered how much pressure Patrick had put on the doctors to discharge him.

He and Patrick found Pam at the hotel, again returning from the spa in a terrycloth robe, drying her hair.

"Patrick!" she said. "Good to see you. I was so worried. Are you all right?"

"I'm fine. Head hurts some, but I'm okay. Thanks. How are you doing with your wounds?"

"David's been taking care of my arm, and everything else seems to be healing." She followed the two men into their room. "What's the plan now?"

"Adnan and I have been discussing that. I think I'll hang with you this evening, and Adnan's going to look after the doc."

While Patrick and Pam talked, Adnan called David to let him know about Pam. He then checked his PC and found the information he looked for. "Good news. One of police units report seeing car matching description in rundown neighborhood south of city. Might be our guys. I check this out."

"You can't go alone," Patrick said. "You know the policy: no solo field work."

"What you suggest, then? We leave Pam here alone while you and I and your scrambled squash strike out into night? Or maybe we do nothing and pass up opportunity?"

Patrick sat on the bed, rubbing his eyes. "Okay. Just be careful, and report back to me often. In fact, why don't you wear a mic? Let me listen and follow along. How far away is this place?"

"Close enough for transmission. I do that, if make you feel better. I even wear earpiece so you can talk to me. I may not respond, though. I'm thinking about blending in and becoming street person for night. In clinic today, I got good idea how to look and act."

"Okay. I'll stay here with Pam and my PC." He dropped his hands away from his head. "Another angle occurred to me in the car. For over one hundred years, these beads have been connected in some fashion to the Boy Scout movement. Surely, someone there must have noticed something strange about them. I'll see what I can dig up."

Adnan felt better. This was the Patrick of old—always thinking. Adnan left the hotel room and retrieved a large suitcase from the van. He sent Pam back to her room to dress for dinner. Patrick helped him with his make-up and disguise. Thirty minutes later, just as they finished, Pam returned.

She pushed through the door and nearly bolted back into the hallway, eyes wide and frightened. "What the—" she exclaimed.

"Down, girl. It me—Adnan."

She lowered her hand from her mouth and stared more closely at him. "Adnan? Is that really you? That's fantastic! I'd have never known. You look like one of the city's finest bums."

Adnan looked her up and down. "And you look ravishing. I can see why David likes you."

She ignored the compliment. "How long are you going to be out, Adnan?"

"I don't know. I'd like to find their hideout and maybe get idea what they up to. No intervention tonight, not by myself," he said, more to Patrick than to Pam.

"Pam, give me a minute to clean up and change and I'll be right with you," Patrick said. "I'll come over to your room."

Pam left, and the two men made final additions to Adnan's street disguise. He already wore body armor, and Patrick helped him conceal his weapons and technical equipment. Then, Patrick cleaned up and changed clothes for his dinner date.

"Wish I were going with you," Patrick said.

"Now I know you not right. You rather be with me out on streets, instead of having fine meal with beautiful woman? I'm taking you back to hospital."

Patrick laughed. "You be careful. I'll have my earpiece on during dinner. Anything happens, I want to know about it—immediately."

"You will." Adnan left the room and took the back stairs out of the building, avoiding contact with the hotel's guests and staff.

———

For over an hour, he cruised the streets where the car had been reported, before seeing the vehicle pulled part way in behind an old gas station. He continued down the street until out of sight of the building and parked the van in the best lit area available. Securing the vehicle, he hurried into the darkness and emerged several blocks away as a street person down on his luck. He sank into the recessed doorway of a closed pawnshop and watched the sparse street activity for an hour, making no move toward his target. The occasional passing car and pedestrian paid him no mind. The warm and muggy night caused sweat to bead on his brow and stain his clothing, adding to the disguise.

A flicker of light from the abandoned gas station caught his eye. He adjusted his sitting position to see better. Thirty minutes passed with nothing out of the ordinary. He decided to check his equipment.

"What time is it?" he slurred into his jacket, scratching his head to cover his mouth movement.

"Ten-thirty. Anything?"

"Maybe."

"Keep me posted and stay safe," Patrick's voice said in his ear piece.

Sometime later, Adnan saw two small figures dash to the side of the building. He rose and drunkenly stumbled across the street until he could see behind the station. The two small boys crouched beneath one of the windows. Cupping a tiny set of night-vision binoculars in his right hand, Adnan slid down the wall, his knees curled in front, his hands supporting his weary head. He adjusted the range. The two boys came into focus, raising up to occasionally peer through the window into the abandoned building. Adnan scanned the window: it appeared covered with cloth from the inside. He searched the darkness for the getaway car and saw it to the left of the boys. Looked like the same one, though he couldn't be sure. Surveying the area, he decided the boys had only one way to flee undetected. Positioning himself in the middle of their escape route, he didn't have to wait long.

The boys apparently got an eyeful of whatever it was they were watching and slowly backed away from the building. When a safe distance away, they turned and hustled down the path, directly toward Adnan, whispering and poking each other. From his hiding place, Adnan let them pass and then stepped out from behind, collaring both.

"Don't make a sound," he said softly.

The two struggled and he dropped them both to the ground, kneeling between them and holding the fronts of their shirts.

"Who are you?" the smaller of the two whimpered. "We didn't do nuttin'."

"Quiet, Tyrone," the other said.

"So, you're Tyrone, and what might your name be?"

"He's Jamal. It was all his idea. I didn't wanna come back here. Honest."

"Be quiet, I said," Jamal barked.

"Well, Jamal and Tyrone. I ain't gonna rob or hurt you. I just want to know what you saw."

"What if we don't tell you?" Jamal asked.

Adnan gambled. "Then I take you right back down there and turn you over to those men you've been spying on."

"Oh, no. Please don't do that, mister," Tyrone cried. "They might cut off our heads, too."

"Tell you what. Why don't we take a walk away from here and you tell me all about it? If I think you're telling me the truth, there might even be some money in it for you. What do you say?"

The two frightened boys looked at each other and quickly agreed. Adnan raised them up, still holding on by the neck of their clothing and led them away from the gas station. Safely away, he sat them next to a large tree in the middle of a small park, deserted this time of night. He let his coat flap open purposely, briefly exposing his shoulder holster. Their eyes widened even further.

"You a cop or sump'in'?" Jamal asked.

"Maybe. Now, let's hear it and don't leave nuttin' out. I'll know if you do."

They couldn't talk fast enough. Adnan had to slow them down and make them tell it one at a time. They told him about the ritual they'd witnessed that night and the night before, including the smell of dope and the heads they thought were human.

"How many heads are there?" he asked.

"Three," Jamal said.

"I'll bet there's more in that trunk," Tyrone added, not to be outdone. "Probably full of heads."

"What did the leader hold up in front of the altar?"

"I don't know for sure. Sump'in' he had around his neck, maybe a necklace. I don't know," Jamal said.

"Yeah. That's right. It was a necklace," Tyrone said. "Looked like it had some beads on it."

"Lots of beads or just a few?" Adnan asked.

"Just a few, maybe three or four. Not like they went all the way around or anything," Jamal added.

"And you say there were only three men, right?"

"There was a woman too," Jamal said. "Over in the corner. White woman. I don't think she cared much for what they was doin'."

"The other men—all black?"

"Yeah. They was *real* black. Blacker than us. You're black too, ain't cha'?" Tyrone asked.

Adnan ignored the question. "Okay, I'm gonna let you two boys go, but if I ever catch you around here again, I'm gonna give you to those men as a peace offering. Understand?" he said, handing them each a five-dollar bill.

"Yes, sir. No, sir. Thank you, sir. We won't never be around here ever again, will we, Jamal?"

Before Jamal could answer, the two boys sprang to their feet and ran away as fast as they could.

Adnan rose from his squatting position and watched them scamper off. "Did you get all that?" he said into his coat.

"Sounds like we got our guys." Patrick said from the earpiece. "Think they'll be there for another night, at least?"

"Don't know. What you think I should do now?"

"Nothing without me. Come back to base. I've uncovered a few things and have a plan."

"You don't think I should try to confirm what the boys told us?"

"And risk getting caught or spooking them? No way. Head in."

"On my way."

Adnan worked back to the van, which sat surprisingly unmolested. He watched the van for a while to be sure no one hid in ambush, then got in and drove back to the hotel, being careful to avoid driving by the gas station. Over and over in his mind, he played the story the boys had told him. Apparently, this was all tied up in some tribal ritual. Zealots probably. It would take a religious experience or death to bring this to conclusion.

He wondered what ingenious plan Patrick had cooked up. He worried about David working at the hospital, but felt better knowing he'd left the three Zulus at their hideout, probably in a drugged stupor. Were there other bands like this one? What would Banta's next move be? Too many questions, too few answers. He needed sleep.

CHAPTER TWENTY-THREE

The following morning, Patrick was up first and found a note from Pam stuck under his door. His head still ached, but less than before. Occasionally his vision blurred, but only fleetingly, and he kept it to himself.

"Adnan. Get up, man. We've got work to do."

His partner had few flaws, one of them being the inability, or unwillingness, to function immediately after awakening. Adnan rolled over in bed and mumbled something unintelligible.

"Come on. Get up." Patrick turned on the TV and shuffled into the bathroom to start the shower. The hotel supplied the rooms with automatic coffeemakers, and the night before, he'd prepared a pot. The aroma filled the room, overpowering that of two bachelors. He poured a cup while the shower water heated.

"As I started to tell you last night before you crashed and cranked up the cacophony of snorts and snores, I spent some time on the phone yesterday with Scotland Yard. They've been tight-lipped about these murders, but I figured we had information they didn't, and maybe they'd be willing to swap. They don't trust us. Not so much you and me, but our press. They're afraid our media will get a hold of this and turn it into a circus, like they do everything else."

Adnan struggled awake, but looked none too happy about it. He sat up, rubbing his eyes. "Sorry to fall asleep last night, but I was beat." He grinned. "Out in humid air for hours acting like bum is tough work."

That was the cue his partner was now truly awake—the sense of humor. "I'm gonna take a shower," Patrick said. "Why don't you order room service for both of us? I'll just be a minute."

Adnan ordered breakfast, and stumbled into the bathroom. He brushed his teeth and washed off the rest of the make-up from last night, then he poured himself a cup of coffee and turned on the news, offering Patrick the bathroom.

"Anything happen in the world while we slept?" Patrick said, emerging from the bathroom, drying his hair.

"No. Just usual drivel: media making something of nothing to fill thirty-minute time slot. Once, I'd like turn on news and hear something like, 'Today, nothing of importance happened, so we show *Bugs Bunny* cartoons to brighten your day.' Fat chance."

"What makes you think they'd want to cheer you up? More likely, they'd show pictures of roadkill, lamenting the existence of man and his evil machines. The first network that figures out how to report the news and leave you with the feeling of being proud to be an American will clean up."

"Okay, my turn in shower. Adnan smell like—"

"Yeah. I know. You smell like goat. What'd you order for breakfast?"

"Everything. I clean up, then we talk. You sign for breakfast."

"Very clever," Patrick said. "You spend lavishly, and I get the blame. Hurry up."

Room service arrived ten minutes later, with several trays of food. Adnan wasn't joking. He did order everything. Patrick started in on the eggs and French toast, and waited on his partner. The food made his head feel better. He turned off the TV and sat at the small desk with his laptop, reviewing information he found yesterday. Adnan stayed in the bathroom with the door shut until dry and partially dressed—Americanized in many ways, but still bashful about nudity.

"You need to read these reports the Brits sent," Patrick said. "I had to tell them what Pam learned to get this stuff. They actually seemed grateful. I don't think they have any clue yet about the identity of the killers."

"You tell me. I eat now," Adnan said, sitting down in front of the buffet of food and eating like his plane was going down. It amazed him Adnan could eat so much and remain thin. Probably had some strange Middle-Eastern tapeworm.

"As you know, our initial information said the victims were slain in their beds or at home. Turns out, that's not the case. That's what the Brits released to the media. The three men were actually abducted, taken to a deserted site, and ritualistically beheaded, probably in some ceremony performed by the killers. The heads were never found."

"That fits with what boys saw last night. They said men danced some sort of rite, apparently centered on beads," Adnan said through a mouthful of food.

"This changes things. They're not going to kill David outright and then make off with the bead. They'll try to abduct him, or lure him to some site where they then can separate him from his noggin. That explains why they abducted Pam and didn't kill her. They intend to use her as bait. Banta must be one sick dude."

"This will not have peaceful ending," Adnan said.

"Speaking of that, shouldn't you be at the hospital, learning things and protecting our mark?"

"I make excuse yesterday and say I spend early morning with other doctors at different hospital. They not expect me early."

Patrick turned to his computer and typed a message for David's beeper. Adnan continued to eat while his partner finished dressing. Soon the phone rang.

"Everything okay at the VA?" Patrick asked. "Have you seen Pam? She left here more than an hour ago."

"All's quiet here," David said. "I saw Pam earlier as we made rounds. What's the plan?"

"Adnan will be there shortly, and he'll stick close to you, maybe closer than before."

"Why? You find out something I should know? Something going to happen?"

"Nothing definite. Just be on your toes and call me on my cell if anything suspicious occurs."

Patrick disconnected and turned to Adnan. "Go over with me, once again, everything you learned about Banta. It looks to me like he's on a religious crusade and we're going to have to eliminate him to stop all this."

Adnan recited what he'd dug up through his research, adding one more piece of information. "You remember David say Banta's mother looks like scrub nurse at VA? Well, he no joking. I saw her yesterday. She look very much like her."

"Pull up that image on your PC and let me look," Patrick said. "This might be useful."

Adnan shoved half a donut into his mouth and rose from the bed, retrieving his computer. Seconds later, the grainy likeness of Mama Manjabe filled the screen.

"And you say the nurse looks like this."

"Yes. Very much," Adnan replied. "Scary."

"Zoom in on her teeth. Looks like she's missing a few."

Adnan manipulated the image. The picture was not high quality, but there appeared to be some gaps in the dentition.

"Why would she be smiling?" Patrick wondered aloud. "Wasn't this the family photo taken after the funeral of the brother? You'd think everyone would be somber."

"Remember, this taken over forty years ago. My guess is picture taking and cameras not commonplace in South Africa at that time. The photographer probably instructed family to smile, and they might have done so out of fear, certainly not from joy."

"You're pretty clever, when you put your mind to it. I'll bet you're right. Does this scrub nurse have teeth?"

"Don't know. Only saw her for short time with surgical mask off."

"Try to get a better look today. Think we can find more pictures of Banta's mom?"

"I doubt it, but I try later. What you thinking?"

Patrick ignored the question. "How far away is their hideout? Can you drive me by there on your way to the hospital?"

"It is not on way, but not far. I drive you, if you want."

"Finish your gorging and let's go. This room is driving me nuts," he said, rubbing his forehead.

"Are there buildings across from this gas station," Patrick asked as they headed south on Danny Thomas Boulevard. Dawn was barely breaking and morning traffic sparse.

"Yes. Some are abandoned, but there are few small businesses. I got to know outside of pawnshop well last night," Adnan replied.

"What kind of magnetic stickers you got for the van?"

"Oh, we can be plumbers, carpenters, electrical repairmen—"

"That'll do. Pull over before we get close and let's turn into electricians, out to check wiring. You got coveralls back there too, right?"

Adnan glanced at him, looking disgusted he would even have to ask.

Patrick laughed. "Okay. Just checking."

Adnan pulled off the road behind a small strip mall, yet to open for the day. Soon, they emerged into traffic as "Hanson's Electric." Adnan slowed as they approached the hide-out. Without being obvious, Patrick absorbed what details he could of the gas station.

"Is that your pawnshop?" Patrick said, indicating the barred window to their left. Adnan nodded. "Pull in front of it. I think they need some additional surveillance cameras. Seems bums have been sleeping in their doorway."

Adnan smiled, catching on to Patrick's plan. With the van parked to obscure observation from the gas station, the two men installed a tiny video camera high on one of the bars and aimed it toward their target. As they made final adjustments and checked the aim with their van computer, two small boys approached.

"What's cha doin'?" the larger of the two asked.

With Patrick in the van, Adnan worked on the camera and had his back to the boys. He turned slowly, his voice growing louder and more threatening as he did. "I thought I told you never to come here again," he boomed in as deep a voice as he could manage.

The two boys froze, eyes bugging out of their heads. In a flash, they turned and disappeared down the street.

"Were those your two informants?" Patrick asked, stepping out of the van.

"One and same. I hope they won't be trouble. I wish they stay away, for few more days, at least."

"I think you scared them good. They about turned white. Finish securing that, and let's drive off and test it."

Adnan drove. Patrick changed out of the coveralls and then checked the computer images. Though grainy, the gas station was easily seen from the high perch on which they'd mounted the camera, unobstructed by street traffic.

"That'll hopefully tell us when Banta's at home," Patrick said.

"I drop you off at hotel, then I go to hospital. What you do today?" Adnan asked.

"I need to talk with Scotland Yard this morning before it gets too late over there. There's something they're not telling us—something about the beads. If we knew Banta and his merry men were the only group on this crusade, we could end it here and now, but I'm not sure they are. I don't want to start a war and make things worse. For right now, I'm afraid we have to play defense and wait for them to make the next move. How's your Zulu?"

"My what? Zulu? You got to be joking?"

"Brush up on it when you have a chance. We may need it."

Adnan pulled into the hotel parking lot. Patrick removed the "Hanson's Electric" signage from the van while Adnan quickly changed into his medical-student disguise. Backing out of the lot, Adnan leaned out the window, addressing his partner. "You sure you know what you're doing?"

"Have I ever let you down?" Patrick replied.

He watched as the van pulled away. His plan had to work. Two people's lives depended on it.

CHAPTER
TWENTY-FOUR

Banta's left shoulder ached terrifically. Overnight, he developed fever and chills. The front of his shoulder was swollen, red, and tender to touch. All night, Lisa sat with him, trying to keep him comfortable.

"Your wound is infected, Banta. Please, let me take you to a doctor," she begged.

"No doctors! They might know me now," Banta replied, his teeth chattering, sweat beading on his forehead. "How could wound be infected? Bullet went right through."

"You were wearing street clothes and the bullet might have dragged some filaments of cloth into the wound," she said, her voice cracking. "I've seen that before, in the mission where I worked in South Africa. Until the wound is washed out, you're going to get sicker. You might die."

Banta did not respond. A new round of chills hit him, causing him to shake even more violently. Lisa ran into the front room of the hideout. The other men waited there, eating bread and drinking hot tea, as was their custom in the morning.

"Banta's sick!" she said, pointing to where he lay. "Needs doctor—now! You understand? Sick—infection—shoulder. Needs doctor." She knew their English was poor, but they understood some things. Finally, she mustered her courage and went to the one closest and grabbed him by the arm, dragging him away from his meal. As they entered the separate area serving as Banta's room, the putrefying smell hit her. Staying with him all night, she hadn't noticed the odor, but upon reentering the room, the stench was overwhelming. The Zulu warrior made a face and stopped in the doorway. Banta was on his bedroll, shivering uncontrollably.

"See?" she said. "Needs doctor." She made a cutting motion across her own shoulder to help him understand. He nodded and returned to his companion. She could hear them talking in their native tongue. They returned and one said, "We take. You show us place. Go doctor. Come."

The two warriors hurriedly changed into their rags. Lisa dressed Banta in his street-person clothes and the three carried him to the car. Lisa got behind the wheel and drove to the city hospital where indigent care was rendered. They pulled in front of the emergency entrance. She slammed on the brakes and cut the engine. Darting from the car, she ran to get help. Soon, orderlies had Banta on a gurney, wheeling him into the ER. The staff got him out of his clothes and into a hospital gown. Banta was too weak to resist.

Lisa explained to the staff, she and her companions were here on a mission trip from Africa, and the man had no insurance or next of kin to be notified. The nurse checking them in had heard it all before. She asked how he got in this condition. Lisa explained they were robbed while on their way to one of the churches. He'd been shot trying to protect her.

"Yeah, sure," the nurse said. "Usually, they're sitting on the toilet, reading their Bible and 'some dude' breaks in and shoots for no reason. Can't you come up with something better than that? You know, we have to report all shootings?"

"Oh please, don't do that yet. Wait until he's better and he can tell you himself what happened. His friends here don't speak good English, but his is passable."

The old, obese black nurse looked up from her papers. She turned to Lisa and must have seen something she liked, or at least pitied.

"Okay. It's Sunday. I guess we can wait until tomorrow before calling the cops. Normally, there's one stationed here at all times, but sometimes, they're a little slow getting in on weekends. Don't think they'd appreciate a call from me this morning, anyway.

Have a seat in the waiting room. The doctor will be with your friend in a minute."

"Can't I wait with him? In his state, he might not be able to communicate well."

The nurse acquiesced and led her back to the bay housing Banta. The ER wasn't busy that morning and the staff hovered over him, starting an IV, drawing blood, and taking his vital signs.

"Temp's one hundred and four," said the tech. "B.P.'s eighty. Pulse one-ten. He's septic. Better call the doctor right away."

Another tech left the area and moments later returned with a tired looking surgical intern.

"What's wrong with this gentleman?" The young doctor yawned, looking at his watch. "My replacement will be here in thirty minutes, you know. Couldn't this have waited that long?"

"Gunshot to the left shoulder," the tech said. "Looks to be several days old and pussed out. He's septic, I think."

The intern removed the hospital gown from Banta's left arm. Foul smelling fluid oozed from the entrance wound. He rolled Banta to his right side, enough to see the exit wound. Banta grunted through clenched teeth.

"Get some X-rays of the shoulder and chest. Draw blood cultures. Call ortho." Looking to Lisa, "Has he had anything to eat today?"

She shook her head.

"He needs to have this opened and washed out in the OR. Probably be here a few days for IV antibiotics. Does he have any other medical conditions I need to know about?"

Again, she shook her head.

Turning to the head nurse, the intern said, "Get him ready for surgery. I'll be in the call room if ortho has any questions." He left the area, pulling the curtain behind him.

The nurse looked to Lisa. "Don't mind him. He's young, and this does get old after a while. Your man will be all right. I know the ortho resident here today, and he's a good one. He'll get your man taken care of."

Lisa looked about anxiously. "I have to find his friends and tell them what's happening. I'll be right back," she said, hurrying from the cubicle.

She found the two Zulus in the waiting area and, as best she could, explained the situation. She told them to wait there and she'd be back when they had a room for Banta. It was unclear to her if they understood, but they nodded and didn't look in any hurry to leave.

Back in the ER, she found the ortho resident examining Banta. "Are you with him?" he asked.

She nodded, and he stuck out his right hand.

"I'm Dr. Ganz, the senior orthopedic resident. We need to take him to surgery right now and explore this wound. It's full of pus and making him sick. Does he understand English? Can he sign his permit?"

The staff began preparing Banta for surgery. "You're welcome to stay until the OR crew comes for him. The nurse will tell you where to wait and what room he'll be going to after surgery. Shouldn't take too long. I expect he'll be okay once we wash this out. Any questions?"

"How long will he have to stay here?" she asked.

"A few days, until we get the infection under control. He'll have a drain in his wound for two or three days to keep the infection from reforming. After that, he may need therapy to get his arm working again. Anything else?"

Lisa shook her head. Dr. Ganz left the ER.

Banta grabbed her arm with his right hand. "After surgery, you take me from here—quickly," he said through chattering teeth. Sweat rolled off his body and his skin felt cool and clammy.

"No, Banta. You need medicine and rest to fight the infection and—"

"You listen to me," he said, more forcefully, rising up on the gurney. "They will know I'm here. Soon, police will come. You take me from here as soon as you can, understand?"

Nodding weakly, Lisa submitted to his will. Banta relaxed onto the stretcher, breathing labored. Soon, orderlies from surgery wearing scrubs, surgical caps, and shoe covers took him away. Lisa watched until he was out of sight, then found her way back to the waiting room. She acknowledged the two men, though she chose a seat away from them, facing the blaring TV in the corner.

She must have fallen asleep, because the next thing she knew, a nurse was shaking her shoulder. "Ma'am? We have a room for your friend. If you'd like to wait up there, you might be more comfortable."

Lisa looked around and saw no sign of the other two Zulus. This worried her, but there was nothing she could do about it at the moment. She followed the nurse out to the corridor and took the elevator to the second floor and the room assigned to Banta. He wasn't back from surgery yet. There was still no sign of his friends. She told the nurse about the other men and that their English was poor. The nurse assured her she'd watch for them and direct them to the room as soon as they showed up.

Again, she must have fallen asleep, as it seemed just minutes later, the recovery room nurses wheeled Banta into the room. Though still not out from under the effects of anesthesia, his color already looked better. He breathed easier. Lisa watched anxiously as the orderlies transferred him to the hospital bed. Dr. Ganz entered the room as they finished the transfer.

"He'll be all right now. There was some debris in the wound and lots of infection, but nothing critical was injured. Most importantly, the bone was not involved. Nonetheless, he'll need two to three days of IV antibiotics to treat the infection. We'll check on him later," he said, writing something in the chart and turning to leave.

Lisa stopped him. "Doctor, will he need prescriptions for anti-biotics and pain medicine when he goes home? If so, could I get that from you now? I may need to raise money to get them filled."

He granted her request and filled out the prescriptions, then left.

Banta stirred and moaned in bed, trying to get up. Lisa rushed to his side and prevented him from doing so, one of the few times she'd dared touch him against his will. He was too weak and drugged to resist, and lay back down. "We must leave," he muttered.

"I know, I know. And we will. But first, you must rest and get something to eat, then I promise I will take you from here." She knew there was no way he'd stay in this bed for three days of antibiotics. She only hoped the oral drugs would do the trick.

His men entered the room. Banta seemed to come out from under the drug effects rapidly. He and the men spoke in their native tongue. One of them removed something from under his clothing and passed it to Banta, who hid it under the sheets. Apparently, he gave them orders, for they then hurried away. The floor nurse entered, asking if he'd like something for pain. Banta declined forcefully. She took his vital signs and left. Lisa sat next to the bed, and soon both were asleep.

Later that evening, Banta tried to get up, and passed out. Lisa and the nursing staff helped him back to bed. The next morn-ing, he was still too weak to go to the bathroom unassisted. The orthopedic team made rounds and changed his dressing. Lisa watched and asked questions about removing the drain.

"It's really easy," Dr. Ganz explained. "This piece of rubber is held in place with one suture. All we'll do tomorrow is clip that stitch and the drain will slide right out. He won't even feel it." They redressed the wound, which looked much better. His tem-perature had remained normal overnight.

"When will this weakness pass?" she asked.

"Probably this morning, after breakfast. That's a normal thing after having a bad infection. May take him a few days to get his normal strength back. Today is Monday. I think he'll be strong enough to leave by Wednesday morning. We'll be by again tomorrow morning to look at the wound. Have a good day," he said, leaving the room.

When they were alone, Banta spoke. "We leave today, as soon as I can stand."

Lisa could only hang her head.

Out in the hall, the ortho team proceeded to the next room. The junior resident turned to Ganz. "I don't buy his story, do you?"

"No. The cops will be by sometime today, and I suspect we'll see one sitting outside his door when we make rounds tomorrow. Don't think he'll be going anywhere today. Probably some drug deal or robbery gone bad. Come on, let's finish rounds. We've got a busy day in the OR."

"He's definitely not from here. South Africa's my guess."

"Maybe he's part of that Mardi Gras contingent some guy brought over," Dr. Ganz said. "Remember? The annual Zulu float wasn't going to happen after hurricane Katrina. Some rich guy flew twenty Zulus to New Orleans, just for the occasion."

"Yeah. That's right. Funny. That's the second time in a week Zulus have come up."

Ganz stared at him. "When was the first?"

"Jim McCallum over at the VA said something about a Zulu bead some patient gave David Freeman. Weird things have been happening over there ever since."

"We'll ask David about it tonight at the pathology conference. Maybe he'll want to see this guy," Ganz said.

CHAPTER
TWENTY-FIVE

David and Pam had Sunday off. Waking up in a hotel room had lost its allure. She and David ate breakfast with Patrick and Adnan in the hotel restaurant and discussed plans for the immediate future. Patrick gave in on letting them go back to their apartments, but only with security measures, including video surveillance and some means of protecting themselves. Both David and Pam felt comfortable with firearms, so after they'd finished eating, the agents outfitted them with appropriate pistols. He gave Pam a Colt Detective Special revolver with .38 hollow-point ammunition. David got the larger Colt Anaconda with a four inch barrel and .44 magnum loads.

"You sure you can handle a gun that large?" Patrick asked. "It's got a hell of a kick and is accurate only at close range."

David nodded as he turned the weapon over in his hands. "It's been a while since I've fired anything, but as a kid, I shot lots of different handguns. Dad was a collector."

"Since you two insist on staying in your apartments, this morning we're going to the police range and test your shooting skills. I'll feel a lot better knowing you're armed."

They checked out of the hotel and Patrick took them to the range while Adnan installed security equipment in their apartments. The local police accommodated Patrick after a check of his credentials. That morning, they had the range to themselves.

"Let's do this one at a time," Patrick said. "Pam, we'll start with you. We'll wear hearing protection for now, but before we leave, I want you to shoot a few rounds unprotected. If you have to use these at home, I doubt you'll have time to put on ear muffs. I don't want the explosion to startle you."

He set up Pam in one of the stalls, and using the electric controls, moved the target to about ten feet away. He demonstrated the proper two-handed stance, or modified Weaver position.

"Are you right- or left-eyed?" Patrick asked.

"What?" she said, looking at him as if he were out of his mind.

Patrick stepped away from her and made a tube with his right hand. Holding up his left index finger several inches behind the tube, he said to Pam, "Open both eyes and focus on my index finger through the tunnel formed by my right hand. Make sure the finger is right in the middle. Got it?"

She nodded.

"Now, without moving, close one eye at a time and tell me which eye still sees the finger in the middle."

"My right eye," she said, grinning.

"So you're right-eyed. You should really keep both eyes open when shooting, but that's hard for some people to do. We'll try it both ways. You'll shoot with your right hand and use your left for support. That way, you can sight down your right arm. Ready?"

She nodded. David stood to the side doing the same exercise to determine his dominant eye.

"Aim for the largest part of the body. Don't try anything fancy and shoot at a leg or something. That's movie stuff. One of the rules of firearms is to never point a gun at anything or anyone you don't intend to destroy or kill. There are no such things as warning shots or wounding shots, only hits and misses. So aim for the center of the chest."

Pam brought the gun to eye level, arms out straight, and smoothed six shots into the dead center circle of the target. She then rolled open the cylinder and set the empty gun on the shelf before them, removing her earmuffs and shaking out her hair.

The men stood mute behind her, staring at the perfectly struck target.

"Something you want to tell me?" Patrick said, breaking the silence.

"I've been in a war zone, but not as a combatant," she said. "Still, you'd think an ex-military nurse could shoot better than that." Her shooting was better than her acting, and a thin smile creased her lips. In response to the continued stares from the men she confessed, "Okay, so I've had some training."

Patrick nonchalantly reloaded Pam's gun. "Put your protection back on," he said quietly not looking up as he clicked the loaded cylinder into place.

Pam had barely complied when his arm shot up and fired off six shots so rapidly, it sounded like an automatic weapon. A ragged hole perhaps three times the size of a bullet appeared in the middle of the face of Pam's target.

"Okay, your turn," he said to David, who a moment ago had acted bored and nonchalant, now stood mouth agape, staring at Pam and Patrick. "Let me have your gun," Patrick said.

David, still staring disbelievingly at the woman he loved, pointed the gun down range, opened the cylinder and handed it to Patrick.

"Very good. Safe pass. Let's start with just one live round in the cylinder."

"How come?" David asked, turning his attention to Patrick.

"You'll see." Patrick loaded the pistol with one .44 magnum hollow-point and five empty casings he got from the collection barrel next to them, spun and closed the cylinder, and handed the weapon to David. "Now, aim and shoot. You won't know when it will fire. Makes you concentrate on the target."

David assumed his shooting stance, aimed the pistol and braced for the recoil as he pulled the trigger. The hammer fell on a blank cylinder, but David jerked anyway. He looked sheepishly at Patrick. Pam gazed down range and appeared not to notice.

"Hard to do, isn't it?" the agent said. "Try again."

David repeated the process. Again, there was no shot, but his reaction improved.

"Keep firing until you hit the live one."

The next fall of the hammer produced a loud explosion, even through the ear protection. The gun jerked violently in David's hand, but he controlled it well, bringing the pistol rapidly down and centered on the target. He'd missed the chest, but did hit the left shoulder of the outlined body.

"That hurt," David said. "Strained my wrist."

"It's a big gun," Patrick said, consoling his friend. "I'll get you a smaller one if you like."

"No, let me try this a few more times."

"Nice thing about these .44s is that you don't have to be very accurate. That shoulder shot you just made would knock an attacker on his butt, and at that range might take his arm completely off."

He handed a box of .44 magnum shells to David. Opening the cylinder, David ejected the casings and loaded the weapon with live rounds. He turned back to the target. Each shot inched closer to center. After twelve shots, David set the unloaded gun on the counter in front of him.

"I've got to rest my hand for a minute. That thing kicks like a showgirl."

Patrick laughed. "It's not my intention to make you an expert marksman. I do want to be sure you're safe with it and can hit a Zulu at close range, if necessary." Patrick slipped a live round in the next-to-fire chamber. "Okay, David. Try it with the ear protection off."

David took aim and fired once. The explosion was deafening and painful. He set the gun on the counter. "Geez! That hurt," he shouted, his ears ringing.

Pam had covered her ears with her hands and worked her jaw open as if to accommodate a drop in pressure.

"The ringing will stop after a while," Patrick said. "I think that's enough for one day." He checked the guns to make sure they were unloaded and then packed them in their carrying cases. "Pam, yours is small enough to carry in your purse, but if you do, please keep your purse with you at all times or lock it up somewhere. And one of these days, I'd like to know where you learned to shoot like that." He glanced up from what he was doing and squinted at her. "David, we're going to have to rig you a shoulder harness. The safest thing would be for Adnan or me to be with you if you're out and about, in which case you wouldn't need to wear it at all. I'm more concerned about the times you're alone in your apartment."

"Maybe I should keep an eye on him, so he won't be alone, that is," Pam said, smiling.

"That's one option," Patrick said. "Not a bad one either." He looked to David and grinned.

"Are you two in cahoots?" David asked.

They all laughed and left the police range. Patrick took them back to the hotel, where they got in their cars and drove to their apartments.

Adnan had already worked on David's place and was finishing with Pam's as they arrived. He gave them a brief overview of what he installed.

"I put no video, only audio, in bath and bedroom."

Pam looked skeptical.

"Really. Scout's honor," he said, raising his right hand in the Scout salute.

She chuckled. "Okay. If you say so."

Adnan left them. David and Pam got together for dinner, but spent the rest of the day, and night, alone, picking up the pieces of their disrupted lives. They knew this was not over.

CHAPTER
TWENTY-SIX

Sunday night and Monday morning passed uneventfully, giving David false hopes things would get back to normal. Early in the morning, he checked with Patrick who assured him that Adnan, posing as the new medical student from Pakistan, would still be with him. Before leaving, David tried on the shoulder rig and slid the .44 magnum into the holster. It felt heavy and bulky, but with Adnan at his side, it wouldn't be necessary. He looked for a hiding place in his apartment. Finding none that satisfied him, he decided to start driving to work instead of biking. He'd keep the gun in his car. This seemed a good compromise.

He didn't like the feeling of having to constantly look over his shoulder. The short walk to his car in the early morning darkness worked on his nerves. He slid into the driver's seat, locked the door and glanced about. He thought back to the incident of being attacked in the car with a club. His windows wouldn't hold up as well as Patrick's. He put the gun in the compartment between the two front seats but couldn't decide on the best position. It wouldn't lie flat, so he rested it on its barrel and handle with the hammer sticking up. He practiced pulling it out of the compartment. This was silly. If he had to get at it that fast, it was probably too late anyway.

The trip to the hospital proved uneventful. He thought about calling Pam, but she'd still be asleep at this hour. Parking in the employee's lot under a bright security light, he glanced about, then grabbed his backpack, exited and locked the car.

Though nothing happened throughout the day, David's nerves stretched thin. Every stranger he passed in the hall, every patient in clinic, even the employees he didn't recognize caused anxiety.

He wondered if this affected his abilities as a doctor. Late that afternoon, after he'd seen the last patient in clinic, he sat back in his chair and let out a long breath, as if he'd been holding it for some time. Jim McCallum approached him.

"What's eating you, man? You've been on pins and needles all day."

"Nothing you need to worry about," David replied. "It's that unresolved issue from last week."

"You mean the thing with the bead?"

David reached to his chest and felt the bead through his scrubs. It had become a part of him; he'd almost forgotten he wore it.

Adnan returned from the bathroom and approached the two men. "We go to Monday night meeting now?"

Adnan looked fresh and raring to go, but David felt exhausted and said, "What's say we grab dinner from the cafeteria first, then head for the meeting?"

"The meeting. Is long way away?"

"Yeah. It's at the main office of Campbell's Clinic. If we leave around 6:30, we should get there in plenty of time, depending on traffic. You need a ride Jim?"

"No, I'm on call tonight, so I'll take my car in case I get summoned away. Thanks, though."

After dinner, David drove Adnan to the meeting. "We were so busy during the day, I didn't get a chance to talk to you," David said. "What do you think is going on? How come nothing happened today?"

"I don't know. Worries me," Adnan replied. "Either they given up and gone back to Dark Continent, which I doubt, or they planning something. I rather them act impulsively than with careful planning." He paused. "I wonder how bad I hurt one of them with shots at Pam's place. I know I hit the shotgun. We found splintered stock and blood at scene. Second shot, I think, hit him in shoulder."

"The guy I saw in clinic last week had a dressing on his left shoulder."

"That's right. It would be left shoulder, judging from how he spun away. I wonder if it slow him up much."

"So you think we'll see more of him?" David asked.

"A wounded lion is dangerous. He might start taking this personally."

They drove for a few minutes in silence. "You know, you don't have to go to this meeting," David said. "It can sometimes be boring, going over orthopedic tumors and pathology slides."

"No. I very interested," Adnan said, switching from feigned terrorist-English to Pakistani-English. "I learn much that help me when I return to Pakistan."

David laughed and relaxed. He wondered if part of Adnan's genius included being able to put his charges' minds at ease.

———

The staff of the clinic assembled in the large conference room for the weekly Monday night "prayer meeting," as the residents referred to it—the only time during the week when all the professors and residents commingled. David sat next to two other residents with whom he'd started training.

"Fred. Karen. How goes it?"

Karen smiled and shrugged. Fred Ganz replied, "Hey, fellow short-timer. Things are fine at the Med. How's it going at the VA?"

"Nothing new and exciting, orthopedically."

"Hear anything from Nashville?"

"No news is good at this point. I've already signed, you know."

"Yeah, I know. I'm jealous," Ganz said. "While you're up there with all the music stars, I'll be right here taking care of stabbings and gunshots. Should have never accepted this job. Speaking of that, I've got a pussed-out GSW in the hospital right now you might be interested in."

Adnan sat up straighter and leaned toward David and Fred.

"Some black dude. Doesn't speak English very well. I think he's from Africa."

Adnan interrupted. "Left shoulder gunshot wound? Maybe two or three days old? Big muscular guy?"

"That's him. How'd you know?" Fred asked, glancing at David and Adnan, who looked at each other.

"He still at the Med?" David asked. "What room?"

"Second floor, front hall. Don't remember the room number?"

"He give you name?" Adnan asked.

"Yeah. It was something weird like Bantu or Banya or something."

"Banta, perhaps?" David asked.

"Yeah, I think that's right. You know this guy?"

David looked to Adnan, who already prepared to leave.

"Come, we go now. I call Patrick. He maybe get there before us," Adnan said.

"You need me to come with you?" Fred asked. He was a big man, played linebacker for Tennessee as an undergrad, and never passed up an opportunity to *rumble*, as he called it.

"No thanks, Fred," David said, hurrying after Adnan. "In fact, it's best if you don't get involved. Please explain my absence to the staff. Tell them I have an emergency."

The two of them hurried to the car. Adnan called Patrick on his cell phone. He made the connection as they pulled out of the lot.

"Hey. It's me," Adnan said. "Banta's at the city hospital, the Med, second floor, front hall. Gunshot wound to the left shoulder. Looks like I hit him. We're on our way, but it will take us about twenty minutes. You can get there faster."

He paused and listened. "Okay. See you there."

"What'd he say?" David asked, pushing his car over the speed limit.

"He's going ahead to make sure the target is still there. If so, he'll wait for us to arrive before making contact."

"So what do we do if we find him—Banta, I mean?"

"We hold him, call the locals, swear out a warrant, and have him deported or locked up—at least that's the way it'll appear officially."

"And unofficially?" David asked.

"He'll be out of your hair, one way or another. You bring your weapon?"

"Here between the seats. I didn't bring my holster, though. Think I'll need it—the gun?"

"Never know. It'll fit in the pocket of your lab coat. Take it along. But don't touch it unless to save someone's life. Leave the offensive stuff to me and Patrick."

David wove through traffic, thinking how'd he get into this? Playing cops and robbers instead of doctor. Adnan talked on the phone, describing their situation to a third party, giving times, locations, and estimates of people involved. Probably someone at the Department of Homeland Security. Minutes later, Adnan's phone rang.

"Patrick? You there already?" He paused and listened. "We're two minutes away. Don't go anywhere near that room until we arrive … Yeah … Bye."

"He's there?" David asked.

"He's on the second floor at the nursing station. Hasn't gone to the room yet. The nurse says the patient's in the room and hasn't been discharged. As far as they know, he's had only one visitor—a woman."

"Probably Lisa. What now?"

"Let's just get there first," Adnan said. He checked his weapon and racked the slide, chambering a round. After engaging the safety, he holstered it beneath his white lab coat and put on an earpiece. "Patrick? … Yeah, hear you fine … We're pulling into the lot. Be up in thirty seconds. Out."

"You guys really talk like that? Roger, Wilco, and Out... all that stuff?"

Adnan ignored him and continued his preparations, checking and adjusting things by feel in the dim light of the parking lot. They hurried into the hospital. *Please let this be the end of it.*

The two men ran up the stairs to the second floor. Patrick paced in front of the nurses' station. "I've kept watch down the hall," Patrick said. "No one's come or gone. There are no connecting doors. The windows are the only unknown. It'd be possible to get out through them, but not on the spur of the moment."

"How you want to handle this?" Adnan asked.

"I'm glad you two showed up in medical garb. You and David go in with the chart. Pretend to be the night staff, at least until we see if it's our guy. David, hold the chart in front of your face. Banta will recognize you otherwise. I'll be right outside the door. Say the word and I'll be right behind you."

"You think he's armed?" said Adnan.

"The staff here says he isn't, but they weren't really watching for that sort of thing. Someone could have easily brought him a weapon. You got cuffs?"

Adnan raised the back of his lab coat to reveal several items on his tool belt, one being cuffs. He addressed David. "You go in first. I'll be behind you, gun drawn. I can easily hide it, if necessary. First sign of trouble, you step to the right, away from me. Patrick and I will take it from there." He nodded to Patrick. "Ready?"

"Guess so." David grabbed the chart. His heart pounded rapidly against his chest wall. He felt nothing from the bead and this struck him as odd, though he didn't know why.

They stopped outside the patient's room. David took a deep breath and knocked as he opened the door. The lights were out, the patient apparently asleep beneath his covers. David flipped on the light.

"Sorry to disturb you," he said, approaching the bed. Adnan held him back and stepped in front. He grabbed the linen near the foot of the bed with his left hand, pistol drawn in his right. David put his hand in the pocket of his lab coat and held the grip of his .44.

Adnan yanked back the sheets. Several pillows lined up to look like a body. He shouted to Patrick, who stepped rapidly into the room, gun drawn, and immediately assessed the situation. Patrick swung into the bathroom and Adnan dropped to the floor, clearing the underside of the bed.

"Shit!" Patrick said.

"Guess he's gone, huh?" David felt relieved.

"Not necessarily. He's just not here in this room. And he might know we are. Not a good situation. He might be across the hall, at the nurses' station, in the parking lot—who knows? Maybe he's flown the coop, but we can't assume that."

"What now?" David asked.

"You wait here. Adnan and I will clear the hallway."

The two agents stepped quickly into the hall, back to back, nearly knocking over an old, black orderly in the process. David had done his last rotation here at the Med and knew most of the staff. He didn't recognize the orderly, but those types came and went. Still…

Patrick called for David and the three quickly exited the hospital, checked the cars, and left to rendezvous later at the hotel. David took Adnan back to the VA to retrieve his van.

David stopped by Pam's apartment before going to meet Patrick. She'd had no problems at work or home. He filled her in on what they thought had happened at the Med.

"So, he's running around with a fresh surgical wound and a partially treated infection," she said.

"Looks that way. Listen, I've got to meet with Patrick and Adnan and find out what our next move is." He stopped abruptly in the doorway, clutching his chest. The bead felt heavy, strange. He stepped back into the apartment, slamming the door.

"He's out there," he whispered.

"Yeah. I know. You told me he left the hospital."

"No. I mean he's out *there*, outside."

"You saw him?" she said, going to the window.

"No. Don't. Stay away from the window. You have your gun?"

"David, you're scaring me. What's going on?"

"I know this sounds crazy, but I've been near this guy three times. I could tell each time," he said, still clutching his chest. "I can feel him out there."

"Probably just an anxiety attack, don't you think?"

"Pam, I'm serious. Get your gun. I'm going to call Patrick." He still wore his lab coat and his .44 magnum was in the pocket. He set it on the table while he dialed the phone.

"Patrick, listen. He's here, outside Pam's place somewhere. Don't ask me how I know. I just do ... Okay ... Yeah ... We'll be right here. Hurry, please," he said, putting the phone on the table without cutting the connection. He felt as though he was having a heart attack.

"Pam?" he called out. She returned from the bedroom, clutching her .38.

"Patrick's on the way and said for us to—"

The door to her apartment crashed open. Shoved through the door came the woman David knew as Lisa Baroni. Behind her stood Banta with one of his men. Banta held Lisa by the hair with a large knife at her throat. He motioned for his man to pick up the .44 magnum on the table. Pam raised her gun and pointed it in the general direction of the intruders.

"How good shot you are?" Banta said. "Can you hit me and miss her? Put down your gun. *Now! Do it!*"

Pam looked to David.

"Better do as he says. They've got my gun, a knife, and a hostage." He turned his head toward her and whispered, "Stall."

Pam hesitated. David knew what she'd been through with these men and he was afraid she might act impulsively. "Pam, please. Do as they say. I'll stay with you."

"David. These men are animals. They'll kill all of us."

Banta jerked Lisa's head back and drew blood by skimming the knife across her throat. Lisa gasped and cried out, "Please do as he says. He'll kill me!"

Pam drew a breath and swung the barrel of the gun to the other man standing a little behind and to the side of Banta. The explosion of the two gunshots shook the walls of the small apartment. They caught the man full in the chest and blew him back out the open door. Banta shoved Lisa into Pam, at the same time backhanding David across the face. Lisa hugged Pam, pulling them both to the floor. David fell back against the wall. Banta sprang to the two women, stood on Pam's bandaged wrist holding the gun, and put the knife to her throat.

"You brave—and foolish. Release gun."

When she did not do so immediately, he increased the pressure on both her wounded gun arm and her throat. She gasped and relaxed her grip. He took the gun, opened the cylinder, closed it again, and stepped away.

"Get up," he said to Lisa. "Check Daya and get him into car. You two. Lay face down, hands behind you." Neither moved. Banta took a menacing step toward Pam, gun in one hand, knife in the other.

"All right, all right. Leave her alone," David said. "We'll do what you say." He sat on the floor and rolled prone, putting his hands behind him. Pam scooted next to him and did the same. Banta bound them and connected their tied hands with another length of cord.

"Now, get up. We go for ride."

"Is it the bead you want? You can have it. It's around my neck. Just take it and leave us alone."

"It's not that easy, David," Pam said.

"What? How do you know?"

"I'll tell you later. Let's try to get up."

Still stalling for time, David and Pam struggled to stand while being linked together, back to back. Banta lost patience and jerked them to their feet, forcing them out the door. Lisa wrestled to put Daya into the car, leaving a trail of blood.

"Where are you taking us?" David asked loud enough to be heard over the open cell phone on the table.

Banta shoved them out the door and moments later, into the back seat. He loaded Daya in with them. Lisa climbed behind the wheel and Banta slid up front into the passenger side, keeping his gun on them.

Lisa backed the car out of the lot and sped down the road. David and Pam had to sit sideways, their backs to each other. Daya lay across their twisted laps, frothing up blood with every breath.

"He's dying back here, you know," David said.

"His blood not on my hands," Banta said. Then to Lisa, "Drive to camp. Then pick up Shinto at hospital."

"Who's at the hospital?" David asked.

Banta smiled. David recalled the black orderly they'd run down coming out of the hospital room. At the time, he'd thought there was something odd about that man. He leaned forward to take the weight of the bead off his chest.

"That hurts my hands, David," Pam said.

"I'm sorry, Pam. This bead is killing me."

"Is that how you knew they were out there?" she whispered close to his ear.

"Yeah," he said, letting out a deep sigh.

"Lisa told me there'd be a connection between the wearer and the bead," Pam said, her voice soft, covered by the sound of the engine. "She and I had a long talk the last time I was in this predicament."

"Did she tell you how to break the connection?"

"She said it couldn't be broken as long as the bearer lived. The full power of the bead only returned once the bearer died—or was killed."

Daya took a final breath and ceased moving. His head rolled in their laps, eyes open and staring, blood running from his mouth. David looked at Daya and saw himself.

CHAPTER
TWENTY-SEVEN

Patrick and Adnan arrived too late. The door to Pam's apartment hung open and a two inch wide trail of blood led from the door to the parking lot. David's .44 magnum lay on the asphalt, fully loaded. Checking the apartment gave no clues, except for the live cell phone on the table.

"We know from their conversation David and Pam were still alive when they left," Patrick said, turning off David's phone. "Banta gave instructions to Lisa after the gunshot, so this blood must belong to someone else, maybe one of Banta's men."

"How good a shot is Pam?"

"Good enough. Judging from the amount of blood, unless they went straight to a hospital, that guy's a goner."

"You think they went to their hideout—the gas station?" Adnan asked.

"Probably. They have no reason to think we know about that."

Adnan retrieved his laptop from the van and opened it on the small table in the apartment. He pulled up the picture of the service station generated by the small camera mounted in front of the pawn shop. Lighting was poor, but good enough to make out the grainy images of people coming and going.

"No activity yet. They should be getting there soon, though," he told Patrick. "I watch. You search apartment again."

"Police will be on their way," Patrick said, resuming his search. "That gunshot must've attracted attention from the neighbors. I'm surprised none are nosing around already."

Finding nothing of interest, he joined Adnan at the computer. It wasn't long before their efforts were rewarded. A car pulled up beside the gas station. Four people got out, two of them walking clumsily. They appeared to circle behind the garage. One returned and dragged something bulky from the car.

"Okay," Patrick said. "That should be Banta, Lisa, David, and Pam. I assume that load being dragged out is the body of Pam's victim."

"What now?" Adnan asked. "Time for showdown?"

"That's one option. Could be bloody, though. Let's get out of here before we have to talk to the cops. I've got an idea, but it'll require some quick planning and a little luck."

They grabbed David's cell phone and left the apartment, being careful to erase all signs of having been at the scene. Adnan drove and Patrick talked as they made their way to the hotel.

"There's something about these beads no one understands," Patrick said. "The higher-ups in the Scouting Organization have known this for a long time, but until recently, kept it to themselves."

"The Boy Scouts?" Adnan interrupted.

"Yeah. Apparently, Lord Baden-Powell knew something was special about these beads after he retrieved them from the battlefield, over one-hundred years ago. He locked them away in a trunk for thirty years. Couldn't bring himself to destroy them or toss them out, maybe because he was afraid they'd be discovered or fall into the wrong hands. He divided and scattered them all over the world by giving them to the early Scoutmasters. Today's Scouting leaders think he assumed this would dissipate the beads' power."

"Wait a minute. Power? Beads?"

"I know," Patrick said. "It sounds crazy, but listen: The four beads donated by Baden-Powell to the Scouting museum in Gilwell Park, England were returned to the Zulus in the late 80s, I believe. A secret movement started within the Zulu nation to recover all of the originals. The British think this Banta guy is either spearheading the movement or is one of the key figures in the retrieval effort."

"So, other 'Bantas' might be out there?"

"It's possible. We can take out *this* Banta easily enough, but who's to say another won't take his place?"

"I know this sounds obvious, but why don't we give him bead and be done with it?" Adnan asked.

"That brings me to the second strange part of the equation. Apparently, the holders of the beads are reluctant to part with them, even under threats of violence. In addition, the Zulus feel it's necessary to decapitate the bearers. Only then can the bead necklace be made whole and its power fully restored."

"How many beads are there?" Adnan asked.

"Twenty-four, according to the Scouts, and that jives with the strange memo we saw in Cisneros's office. Baden-Powell gave them to nineteen different men in 1919. I assume he kept five for himself. As I said, four of these were returned to the Zulus. We think Banta has three of the remaining twenty and David has another. That means sixteen more are unaccounted for. I have a feeling the international leaders of the Scouts know where they are, but aren't talking, possibly out of fear for the owners."

"So if we wipe out Banta, there's no guarantee this is going to stop. Another Zulu might pick up where he left off," Adnan said, shaking his head.

"That's right."

Adnan parked the car, and both men exited the vehicle, heading into the hotel. They hurried to their room, where Patrick continued his thoughts.

"We can easily solve today's problem with overwhelming force and with a high probability of rescuing David and Pam. I've got another idea, however, and it might go a long way towards solving future problems."

"Oh, boy. Here we go," Adnan said, flopping onto the bed.

"No, wait. Hear me out. We can always resort to Plan B and shoot everybody if we have to."

"This had better be good—and fast. I don't think we have much time."

"Suppose Banta is the leader of this movement and we can convince him to give up the quest. If he has a change of heart, maybe David and the others, whoever they are, can live in peace. We should at least learn from him if there are other searchers. He also might know where to find the other bead bearers."

"How we do that? You want to capture and brainwash him?"

"I'm not sure our techniques work on the Zulu brain," Patrick said. "We have to work within Banta's world—think like he thinks—get his mojo working for us."

"A religious conversion, maybe with Pat Robertson or Jimmy Swaggert?"

"Don't be silly," Patrick said. "I want his mother to talk him out of this."

"Banta's mother's dead. She died a long time ago."

"Thank goodness for that. She'll be more help to us from the spirit world than if she were alive."

"You need sleep or counseling or both. That rap on head shook something loose. You sure you feeling okay?"

Patrick ignored him and continued with his plan. "The British think the beheading ceremony is long and involved, and involves hallucinogenic drugs. They calculate the three previous murders took place at the same time of day—sunset. That means it's too late for the ceremony today. Also, Banta's still weak from his shoulder wound. Plus, they have a dead body to deal with. I'm guessing we have twenty-four hours."

"What if you're wrong?"

"Then we go in tonight, guns blazing. One of us will need to closely monitor their hideout and be ready to intervene should Banta decide tonight is the night. If the beheading ceremony is tomorrow evening, the other will need to make preparations for my idea."

"And I guess you've already figured out who's doing what?"

"I'll need to do the monitoring, and you'll need to put the pieces of my plan together," Patrick said. "You'll understand after I explain."

"Why I not surprised?"

Patrick laid out his idea and set up a time table. Adnan voiced his skepticism, but could think of nothing better. The two split up to carry out their parts.

CHAPTER
TWENTY-EIGHT

Lisa needed to pick up Banta's remaining warrior, the orderly at the hospital. Before she left, though, she helped Banta securely tie Pam and David to each other, seated back to back around a vertical pipe. She then coaxed Banta to lie on his pallet and take medication of some kind; David guessed antibiotics and perhaps something for pain. She checked and changed his dressing. David could see Banta losing blood.

The effort in Pam's apartment must've taken a lot out of the wounded Zulu, for he made no objection to Lisa's ministrations. Banta gave Pam's .38 to Lisa and laid a double barreled shotgun across his own chest. Lisa helped him prop his head so he could watch the prisoners. She hesitated at the door, but Banta barked and waved her away with the shotgun. As she left, she turned to look at them, her face showing worry and fear.

After Lisa had gone, Banta said, "Do not underestimate me. You will not escape. I let you escape once. It will not happen again."

"What do you mean, you *let* me escape?" Pam asked.

"I do not need you. I need him," Banta said, pointing the gun at David. "I arrange for you to befriend my woman. Then I use her as hostage to capture both of you."

"That's crap," Pam snapped back. "I suppose you also arranged to get shot."

Banta chuckled. "No. All good plans have setbacks. But I can still use you to bargain for time."

"What does that mean?" David asked.

"You, doctor, are not long for this world. After you gone, I may need woman for bargaining."

Banta settled into his bedding, and after a few minutes, appeared to become more comfortable. The pain medicine seemed to be taking effect. Several minutes later, Banta's head sank into his chest, his breathing deep and unlabored.

"I think he's asleep," Pam whispered, her mouth as close to David's ear as she could manage.

"Don't know. Might be playing possum," David replied, equally as quiet.

"What do we do now?"

"Not much we can do at the moment. There are two wild cards that might get us out of this. One is Patrick and Adnan. The other is Lisa. She's a strange one. A little unbalanced, I think."

"Yeah. Banta's got a real psychological hold on her. She could have come with me last time I escaped, but didn't want to. But she didn't alert them to my running, either."

"Maybe she knew you were supposed to get away."

"Don't think so. She broke down and cried, baring her soul to me. I don't think she's had anyone to talk to for a long time. The other men abuse her. Banta's her port in the storm, even though he roughs her up occasionally."

"Do you really think they mean to kill me? Why haven't they done it already?"

"My guess is there's some kind of ritual involved," Pam said.

"Great. That's a comforting thought. Nothing quick and easy, huh?"

Pam pulled against her restraints, trying to work her hands free. Her struggles tightened the bindings on David's wrists.

"That hurts, Pam. If you think you can get loose, keep it up. But if you can't, my hands are going numb."

"Sorry, David. We can't just sit here and do nothing. Soon, Lisa will be back with the other guy. And I think he's the one who wanted to get frisky with me last time. Maybe if we try to slide up this pole and stand."

"Worth a try."

David and Pam worked together to shimmy up the pole into a standing position, arms bound, back to back. They got as far as a crouch when a metallic click from Banta's direction stopped them. Both turned their heads slowly. Banta had not moved, other than to close the breech of the shotgun and shake his sagging head from side to side, waving the gun in their direction. They slid down the pole.

"Guess we're gonna need help," David whispered.

Pam leaned her head back onto his shoulder.

Patrick parked his car around the corner, two blocks from the gas station. Quietly and carefully, he worked his way as close as he dared, watching the building through his night-vision goggles. He tested his earpiece and advised Adnan of his position. The Zulus' car was gone. He saw no movement through the back window. A small light flickered from within. Were they still there? Did they leave while he was in transit?

He needed to get closer, but was undecided about the best way to approach. A noise from behind startled him, and he rolled into cover among some overgrown bushes.

"This is a bad idea, man," a child's voice said. "They told us to stay away, and they wasn't kiddin'. Let's get outta here."

"Be quiet, will you," another responded. "It don't look like nobody's home, anyway. Maybe they left some good stuff in there. If you don't wanna split it with me, go on. I'll keep it all to myself."

With his night-vision goggles, Patrick made out the figures of the two small boys. He let them pass, then stepped out of the bushes, behind them.

"Pssst."

The boys froze in their tracks.

"Don't move and don't make a sound," Patrick said. "Aren't you Jamal and Tyrone?" he said softly.

"I told you we'd get caught," Tyrone squeaked in a high-pitched panic. "It was his idea, mister. I didn't wanna come. Honest."

"It's okay," Patrick said. "Just be quiet. Come back here to me. I can use your help."

They slowly looked to each other, apparently uncertain whether to bolt or obey.

"Come on. I won't hurt you. Might be some money in it for you."

"How much?" Jamal said.

"Don't be greedy." Patrick stepped out of the shadows and put the short-barreled shotgun over his shoulder. The boys took a step backwards at the sight of the armed man, then inched their way toward him. "Sit down," Patrick said. They did as told, and he squatted in front of them.

"What are you doing back here? Thought my partner told you not to be messing around this place anymore."

"We thought they might be gone. Bums don't usually stay in one place too long. Sometimes, they leave stuff," Jamal said.

"A few days back, you spied on them and saw some strange things, didn't you?"

They nodded.

"Now, real quiet like, tell me what you saw, and don't leave anything out."

They quickly ran through the events of that evening, describing Banta's dance with the large knife, the human heads and the heavy stench of drugged smoke emanating from the room.

"Didn't you tell my partner, the guy doing the dancing had a necklace?"

"Oh, yeah. I forgot. After he was done jump'n around, he took this necklace over his head and put it on the bench where they had candles and smoke and stuff."

"What'd they do after that?"

"I don't know. That's when we bugged out."

"How'd you get down there? What's the best way?"

"Well, mister, when we went last time, there was a car there and we kind of hid behind it until we got close to the building."

As if cued, a car pulled onto the gravel beside and partway behind the building. Two people got out and entered the back door.

"That's the bit—the woman," Jamal said. "I remember her from before."

"Is that the window where you watched?" Patrick asked, pointing to the small window at the back of the building.

"Yeah. You can see real good from there. Only you gots to be extra careful so's they don't see you. You know, kinda duckin' down every now 'n then," Jamal said, obviously feeling better about the situation, and trying to be helpful.

"Thanks a lot, guys. Here's five bucks for each you. I catch you here again, I'm taking you down to the station. Understand?"

"I did more talkin' than him. Why'd he get the same as me?" Jamal asked, looking at his five-dollar bill.

"Scram," Patrick said, lowering his night-vision goggles and his shotgun.

The two vanished in a heartbeat, disappearing into the night. Patrick silently worked his way down the slight incline to the gas station.

Inside, Lisa rushed to Banta, who raised his head and tried to sit up. Shinto, the other Zulu, took the shotgun from Banta and stalked over to inspect the prisoners. He smiled at Pam and said something not in English. Then, he stared at the body against the far wall. He glanced at Banta and Lisa and hurried to the corpse, pulling aside the covering blanket. Falling to his knees, he dropped the shotgun and wailed, hugging the body as he chanted, tears streaming down his face.

Banta glared at Pam. "They were brothers. You may yet have price to pay."

Shinto rose to his feet and exchanged words with Banta. He turned, scowling at Pam and crept toward her.

Pam cried out, "What's he doing? What'd you tell him?"

"I told him truth: You shot his brother in cold blood."

Pam struggled against her bonds. Shinto stooped and backhanded her across the face, shouting. He reared back for a harder blow, when Lisa grabbed him. Banta rose unsteadily and separated the two. He stood in front of the prisoners and said something, apparently easing Shinto's mind. Shinto's scowl turned to an evil smile and he nodded his head toward Pam.

"I don't know what he just said, but I'll bet I won't like it," Pam told David.

"Hang in there," David said. "We'll get out of this."

The Zulus prepared for the nightly ritual. Shinto did most of the set up, arranging the altar, lighting the candle and fires for the dried leaf. Shinto and Banta changed into native costumes. Shinto undressed his brother's body and wrapped the loin cloth around the corpse's waist. The room filled with smoke. Lisa huddled in the corner. Banta sat before the altar and began a low chant. Shinto soon joined him. They rocked and swayed, eyes closed, arms resting on their crossed legs.

"Eengonyama Gonyama! Invooboo!
Ya-boh! Ya-boh! Invooboo!"

David watched, fascinated and terrified. Would he and Pam be included in this ritual? Was tonight the night?

Banta's chanting became louder and more frenzied. He opened his eyes, glaring at the prisoners, staring straight through them. His right hand slapped to his left shoulder, ripping off the bandage, the drain dangling from the wound. Banta grasped the rubber Penrose tubing and yanked it from his shoulder, snapping the suture holding it. Blood oozed from the wound. The big Zulu grew more excited.

"You getting high?" David whispered to Pam.

"Yeah. My head's spinning. What *is* that stuff?" Pam asked.

"Don't know, but it's pretty strong. Try to breathe shallowly."

Banta stood, retrieving the sack Shinto removed from the footlocker. From it, he lifted the blackened heads and set them on the makeshift altar.

Pam gasped. "Are those what I think they are?"

"'Fraid so. They look dried out to me." David felt his throat constricting, either from fear or smoke or both.

Banta snatched up one of the heads by the hair and danced around the room, waving the large scimitar, the one he'd stolen from above David's bed. Holding the head with his injured left arm, he made cutting motions, calling out each time the knife passed through the imaginary neck. He stalked to their corner of the room, pushing the head into their faces while performing the ritual decapitation. Pam closed her eyes and turned away, uttering a small cry. David watched in fascinated horror. His head could become part of this ceremony. The effects of the drug blurred his vision, scrambling his thoughts. He shook his head, trying to clear it. Banta bent beside him and placed the large sword at his throat, slowly drawing it across, making a shallow incision in the skin. David held his breath, the pain dulled by the drugged smoke. Banta stood, licking the blood from the ancient weapon, and wiped the blade across his bare chest.

Time stood still. Banta finished his dance and replaced the head next to its mates on the altar. He again sat before the burning candles and slowed his chanting. Minutes, perhaps hours, passed before the two warriors rose and put their relics away, preparing for sleep.

When Banta and Shinto ceased stirring, Pam nudged David. "You all right?"

"I've got a new neckline, but I think it's shallow. I can't feel much bleeding."

"Oh, David. What's going to happen?" she sobbed.

"Nothing, I think, until tomorrow night. But we've had a preview of coming attractions. Doesn't look good."

"I know this is silly, but I have to pee."

"Just go. It doesn't make any difference now."

Lisa must have overheard them; she approached and squatted before them. "I can help you to the bathroom. I don't dare release your bonds to each other, but I can loosen you from the pole for a moment. Please don't make any noise or try to escape."

With that, she undid the bindings from the pole and took them to a toilet in the back room. She looked over her shoulder. Banta and Shinto had not budged.

"How do we do this, with our hands tied together behind us?" Pam asked.

Lisa reached down to Pam's jeans and undid them. She then slid down her prisoner's panties. "Sit," she said. "David, you'll have to squat or kneel."

Pam sat sideways on the toilet and David squirmed to allow her room. He had to squat, leaning away from her. His hands burned.

Pam relieved herself. "Okay. I'm done," she said.

The two captives stood, and Pam turned to face Lisa. Grabbing some tissue, Lisa wiped Pam dry, lingering longer than necessary and looking up at Pam during the process, her face a mixture of sorrow and loneliness. She finished and pulled Pam's panties and jeans back into position.

"I hate to bring this up, but I'd probably better go too," David said.

"I've done this before in my work in the missions," Lisa said.

She turned them and unzipped his fly, reached into his pants and brought him out, aiming him toward the toilet.

"I don't think I can go with you holding me," he said.

She let go and stood back as he relieved himself. Once done, they turned so Lisa could arrange his clothing. All three weaved from the lingering effects of the drug. Lisa guided them back to the pole and began to secure them.

"You don't have to do this," Pam said, pressing her advantage. "I'll help you, if you'll let me."

Lisa hesitated, but continued tying the knots. "No. He would punish me severely. I cannot," she said, tears welling in her eyes.

"Lisa, look at me," Pam said. "I'll be your friend. Help us. We can get you away from this."

Lisa avoided her eyes and did not reply. She returned to her corner where she curled up and soon cried herself to sleep.

"That was not the *ménage a trios* I've always heard about," Pam said, trying to make light of their predicament. "Think we'll remember any of this in the morning?"

"I doubt it. My head's still swimming," he said.

"Mine too. I guess we should try to rest."

"Good luck. You're right. We'll need as much rest as we can get for tomorrow."

They squirmed, getting as comfortable as possible and napped in short intervals throughout the night.

———————

It had taken all of Patrick's will power and training to watch the events of the night unfold through that small window. Several times, he'd leveled his weapon at Banta's chest, and nearly pulled the trigger. With all the smoke in the room and dirt on the window, he couldn't be sure he wouldn't hit David or Pam. If Adnan had been with him, he'd have ended it right there. Too risky alone. Everyone was alive and okay, for the moment. This might still work. He needed that big Zulu alive, drugged, and scared out of his mind.

From his carefully prepared bag of equipment, Patrick removed a small explosive charge and attached it to the window frame, out of sight. He also rigged a small video camera to transmit images of the room. Then, he backed away from the building, attached a homing device to the underside of Banta's car, and made his way back to his vehicle.

CHAPTER
TWENTY-NINE

When Patrick was well away from the hideout, he contacted Adnan. Speaking into his mouth-piece as he hurried toward his car, he brought his partner up to date. "Did you hear all that with your little buddies, Jamal and Tyrone?" he asked.

"Sounds like their story not change much," Adnan said.

"Well, I got to see it firsthand. Apparently, I was right. This is a nightly ritual. Nothing was done with David or Pam tonight, but I'll bet it's their turn on center stage tomorrow at sunset. Made any progress on your end?"

"Surprisingly so. You not be happy with what I give in return, but that price of doing business. I think we good to go for tomorrow."

"Great. I'm not going very far from the scene. I'll find a secure place for the car, then monitor the activities of the hideout on my dashboard computer. Can you pick up the signal at the hotel?"

"It not greatest, but I think I can tell if something starts going down," Adnan said.

"Good. We'll both need sleep. I'll keep the volume up on my headset. If anything happens, I can get to them quickly. I've mounted some C-4 on the window at the service station. I can blow it from here, if necessary, to give David and Pam time. If you see anything on your end, make sure I'm awake and aware."

"Right. Between two of us, I think that's good as we can do. You still not hot on idea of going in right now and ending this?"

"That's just it. We could never be sure it's ended. Is this the only group of Zulus after David?" He paused. "Tomorrow night will arrive soon enough. Get some shut-eye, if you can."

Patrick pulled the car into a parking garage and paid for the night. He then backed it against the wall, pointing the front end directly at the exit gate. He could drive straight through it and be at the gas station in less than thirty seconds, if he had to. He hoped he wouldn't have to.

The night passed fitfully for all.

Tuesday morning, David jolted awake, momentarily confused by his surroundings. He felt as though he had a hangover, and his mouth was dry. He tried to talk, but no sound would come from his throat. Pam moved and grabbed his hands with hers, squeezing gently. She also had trouble talking. Lisa tended to Banta, dressing his wound and giving him more pills. Shinto was gone. When Lisa finished with Banta, she brought water to the two captives and held it to their lips, helping them drink.

"Thank you, Lisa," Pam said, clearing her throat. "Any chance we could clean up and maybe get something to eat?"

Saying nothing, Lisa turned and tore off some bread from their stores, feeding it to them. She followed this with more water. She seemed to enjoy taking care of the room full of people, all dependent on her. Banta rose from his pallet and made his way into the bathroom, taking a towel with him. The sound of running water covered their conversation.

"Lisa, why do you do this?" Pam asked. "It would be so easy to get help. I'll testify in your behalf. You are as much a prisoner as we are. Please help us."

"It's out of my hands now," Lisa said. "Banta has sent Shinto out for supplies—for tonight. There'll be the—the ceremony and the retrieval of the bead. Then, the smoking preservation. Afterwards, we will leave for our next destination. I'll do what I can to see no harm comes to you," she said to Pam.

"What about me?" David asked.

"I'm sorry. Your fate is sealed. There can be no other way. The power of the beads must be restored, and when they are all collected, returned to their land of origin."

"Are there other teams looking for the missing beads?" David asked.

Lisa did not answer.

Banta returned from the bathroom and addressed Lisa. "Take them and clean them. They must be pure for tonight. Dress them in these," he said, throwing to Lisa two brightly colored, folded pieces of cloth he'd retrieved from the footlocker. "You may untie them once you are in bathroom. There is no way out but through door. I wait here." He looked straight at Pam and David. "If you try escape, I wound you—severely. You live long enough for ceremony this night."

Turning back to Lisa, he said, "I tie them after your preparations complete. Do woman first. Send her out before you prepare 'Bearer.' As always, leave bead in place."

Lisa knelt to untie them. They struggled to their feet.

"I can't feel my hands," Pam said.

"Neither can I," David said. "The feeling will come back soon after we're untied. The pain will be excruciating, so be ready."

Lisa led them into the small bathroom. After untying them, she sat David on the toilet to make room to work on Pam.

Pam's hands were useless, and Lisa undressed her. David looked away. Lisa moistened a cloth and washed all of Pam's body. After drying her, she walked from the bathroom, closing the door. Pam was left naked and shivering.

"My hands are starting to ache and tingle, David."

"So are mine. As the circulation improves and the nerves wake up, they're going to really hurt, though it'll go away in a few minutes. Might help us if we continue to act like they're useless."

Lisa reentered, carrying a small bottle. She removed the cap and poured some of the flowery scented oil onto her palms. She began anointing Pam's body, starting with her hair and face. Few men and no women had ever taken such liberties with her body as Lisa did in the next few minutes

She kept her cool during this abusive treatment.

"It's not too late for you to help us," she gasped, as Lisa massaged her in places and ways meant only for lovers.

"Shhh, now," Lisa said softly, as she might to a troubled infant. "I'll take care of you." She finished and stood away from Pam, inspecting her, looking for spots she might have missed. Finding none, she unfolded the cloth Banta had given her. She passed Pam's head through a hole in the center of the garment. There were more holes for the arms. The colorful poncho hung to her knees. Lisa opened the door.

"Go. You are ready," Lisa said.

"Ready for what?" Pam asked. "Please, think about this, Lisa. I can help you."

"Go."

Pam stepped into the hall and walked to the other room. Banta signaled for her to come to him by the pole. He held a length of rope.

"Oh, please don't tie my hands," she said. "They're painful and useless as it is." Were this not true, she'd try to take this big bastard down right now. Though he towered over her, she'd bested larger. The moves from her previous training and life were right there at her numb fingertips.

He turned her, grabbing her arms. She sobbed aloud. Banta hesitated, and then looped the rope around her elbows, crossed it in the back and looped the other end around the pole and then around her neck. The loose end he tied again to the rope at her elbows. Struggles tightened the cord around her neck.

Pam stood for a moment, her back to the pole. Her body ached and felt no better after her makeshift bath. She knew she should feel violated, but instead felt only sorrow and pity for the woman who'd molested her. What a sad and lonely life. Lisa had probably not talked to or been with anyone other than these Zulus for months, if not years. Her connection to Lisa was stronger now, and she hoped to use this to their advantage, though she wasn't sure how.

Minutes later, David walked into the room, wearing a similar poncho. His, however, was darkly stained about the neck with deep, irregular streaks. At first, Pam thought this was just a bad pattern. She gasped when she recognized the dried, old blood—lots of it.

Pam watched as Banta tied David in a similar fashion, but without looping his neck, the significance of this not lost on her. Instead, he passed the rope around David's elbows at his back, encircled the pole, and ended back around his waist.

Banta and Lisa walked outside, leaving David and Pam standing back to back, tied to the pole.

"At least we smell better," he said. "She didn't spend as much time with me. I thought I was to be the guest of honor."

"She raped me, David."

"What? You didn't say anything!"

"What were we going to do? It was strange—nonviolent, almost loving. Did you hear how she talked to me? Like a child—her child. I think I can use this to our advantage."

"I hope you're right." He paused. "Wonder what Patrick and Adnan are doing this morning? You know, it occurred to me: what if they got called back to Washington on official business? We'd be stuck alone in this."

"Don't give up hope," she said.

"I'm not, but I'm thinking…we might have to save ourselves. The best chance will be tonight when they're drugged up. Somehow we'll have to keep our wits about us. Lisa has your .38, doesn't she?"

"I don't know. I'm thinking that's what Banta will give her, if he needs her armed."

"It's going to come down to the wire, but if they'll free you from me sometime during the—ceremony, maybe you can get it from her. How are your hands doing?"

"Better. The feeling has returned and they hurt pretty bad, but I can move my fingers."

"Sorry. Me, too. Don't let them see you moving them, though. Complain about the pain and loss of function throughout the day. Make them think they're useless."

"David, if I'm going to work this bond between me and Lisa, it might mean I'll have to do some distasteful things."

"I'm sorry, Pam." He tilted his head back against hers. "You're the bravest woman I've ever known."

"Desperate people do desperate things."

"If we ever get out of this—"

"Don't say any more," she said. "We'll get out. If you start saying things like that, I'll hold you to them."

He chuckled. "Gallows humor."

A car pulled in behind the building, stirring the gravel under its tires.

In his car in the parking garage, Patrick sat up in the front seat, shaking off his sleepiness. Checking the monitor, he watched the events of the morning unfolding at the gas station. David and Pam were led from the room, then brought back wearing different, baggy clothing. He lost Banta and Lisa as they left the building. He checked in with Adnan.

"Anything on your end?" he asked.

"Nope. Quiet night. How about you?"

"Same. Actually got some sleep, though not much."

"What now?" Adnan asked.

"We, you, need to rehearse for tonight. This has got to look real. Incorporate the C-4 charge into the event. That'll create the confusion we need at the right time to get them safely out."

"I think this is nutty but brilliant. I haven't thought of way to let the two of them in on this. Have you?"

"No. We'll have to trust they can sort it out," Patrick said. "I'll stay close to them today, so I can't help you."

"I know. Keep in touch. Out."

Patrick, accustomed to stakeouts, had everything possible to make it tolerable in the car—everything, that is, except hot coffee and a bathroom. Pulling the car from the garage, he drove to a convenience store down the road. He thought of how David and Pam must be feeling and wished there were a way to reassure them, to let them know he was close and watching. He hoped he was making the right call about tonight. So much would depend on timing.

Banta and Lisa walked the short distance to the corner store. She'd dressed him in his street-person clothes. Hers were starting to look ragged. They'd need the conveniences of a hotel, soon, maybe tonight after—she didn't like to think about it. Necessary as it was, but still… She liked Pam. The woman acted nice and understood her. Maybe she could talk Pam into coming with them. No, that wasn't going to happen. Maybe she should go with Pam and get help, like she suggested. What would happen to Banta, then? She couldn't leave him. Not now. Not until they had all the beads. Life would be better and more normal, once this quest ended. They would return to South Africa. Banta would be a hero and a leader. She'd be his queen. Maybe they could still have children. She'd been pregnant before. Couldn't be sure which of the three was the father. She'd lost that baby, but next time would be different. Maybe if they weren't traveling so much.

Banta looked weak, his gait not as spirited. His shoulders slumped. Usually, when they went for food, she had trouble keeping up with him. Today, she had to slow her gait so as not to get ahead.

They entered the store and began collecting supplies needed for the day. Banta walked the aisles, she thought as much for exercise as for the purpose at hand. The store was nearly deserted that time of morning; only one other customer, a man, browsed the merchandise. Lisa watched the stranger for a moment, then turned back to help Banta. As the two men rounded the corner, they nearly collided. The white man looked startled and hurried off. Banta glared at him, a look of concern crossing his face. He turned and followed the man, who quickly paid for his purchases and left. Banta followed him out of the store and watched him get into his car and drive off.

"What? What is it?" Lisa asked, as he reentered the store.

"I've seen that man before. Don't remember. My head's still cloudy." He turned to her. "No more pain medicine. I know you gave me some. Is too dangerous. I must have clear head. No more. Understand?"

Lisa was worried. "Maybe you're mistaken. Maybe you've seen him here before, in the store, I mean."

He shook his head. "I will remember soon. I have bad feeling. We hurry and go now, back to camp."

———————

That was close, Patrick thought. He'd been stupid. Should have driven farther from the site for what he needed. Of course the Zulus would use the closest store. He should have thought of that. He didn't think Banta recognized him. Nothing to do now but wait and see.

CHAPTER THIRTY

Shinto stirred from his sleep and quickly searched the gas station, apparently looking for the rest of his team. Not finding them, he turned his attention to the two captives.

"You make this?" he said, pointing to the covered body of his dead brother.

Pam shook her head rapidly. "It wasn't my fault. We were being threatened. It was self defense."

David grasped her hand from behind. The bonds at their elbows allowed enough motion for them to touch, if they angled toward each other. "His English is poor, Pam. Save your breath."

"This one scares me more than Banta," she said.

"I know. Try not to antagonize him. Banta and Lisa should be back soon."

"Quiet!" Shinto yelled. Turning from them, he crouched beside his brother's body and began reciting what sounded like a prayer. He uncovered the body and tried to arrange it differently. The limbs had stiffened overnight and gave way grudgingly. This didn't help his temperament and he became more agitated. Apparently unable to accomplish what he wanted, he threw the blanket back over the body and whipped around, glaring at Pam. He closed in on her face, jabbering in his native tongue. Pam moved her head. Shinto grabbed her hair, twisting her towards him. With his other hand, he slapped her. Pam cried out.

"Leave her alone!" David shouted, striking out with his feet, ineffectively.

Shinto walked to David's side and leered at him, curiously at first; then, he threw his head back in maniacal laughter. Continuing to ramble in Zulu, he lifted David's chin and drew a finger across his neck, along the scratch made by Banta the night before.

"You—be like him—tonight," Shinto said, pointing to his dead brother. He laughed again, and then his countenance darkened. He crossed the room and withdrew the razor sharp scimitar, David's great-grandfather's, from the footlocker. Returning to his captives, he put the blade beneath their chins, and one at a time, raised their heads. Again, he babbled something and began the slow dance Banta had performed the night before. Spinning, he thrust the blade to David's chest.

"You—Banta."

Circling to Pam, he tipped her head back with the weapon and held it to her throat.

"You—Shinto."

As the pressure of the blade increased against Pam's throat, David could hear her breathing becoming more rapid and shallow. She felt for and squeezed his hand.

"Hey!" David yelled, not knowing what else to do.

Shinto's head jerked towards him. Still holding the ancient weapon below Pam's chin, the Zulu backhanded him across the mouth. The movement pulled the blade slightly and broke the skin at Pam's throat. She screamed.

The back door to the hideout burst open and Banta rushed at Shinto, who remained frozen in place, a look of hatred and madness on his face. Banta grabbed Shinto's knife arm, pulling him away. The two faced each other across the room, shouting and gesturing. Shinto threw the sword to the ground and stalked from the room.

Lisa hurried to the tied captives. Pam cried softly. David watched as she turned Pam's head, examining the wound. Apparently satisfied it was minor, she left and returned from the bathroom with a damp cloth. She cleaned Pam's throat and applied an ointment. He could hear Pam slow her breathing.

"He'll kill me, Lisa," she said. "You have to help me."

"He won't hurt you. I'll see to that. Would you like something to drink? I brought some juice from the store."

"Yes, please. And give some to David."

"Are you okay?" David asked when Lisa was out of earshot.

"Shaken *and* stirred," she said, her voice trembling. "But I'm okay. I thought it was all over for a minute. We're going to have to keep Lisa close by. That Shinto is nuttier than Banta."

Lisa brought orange juice and helped them drink. Again, she checked Pam's neck.

"Banta may not like this—I might have to clean you again," Lisa said, frowning with her mouth, but not her eyes.

Pam squeezed David's hand. "I'd like that, Lisa," she said, grinning up at her.

Lisa smiled and left to talk with Banta, who was now checking the footlocker and moving things around.

"Are you nuts?" David whispered.

"David, our only chance is through her. I have to play it."

"I don't know, Pam. There must be another way."

Well, think of it quick. Time's running short here. I don't like this either."

"Let's hope Patrick and Adnan come through."

———

At the hotel, Adnan returned from the bathroom to his computer. He saw Banta's accomplice on the monitor, dancing about the room with the heavy sword. Then, the Zulu moved towards David and Pam. Oh, God! He's going to hurt them. Quickly, he called Patrick.

"Glad you called. I just had a close en—"

"Patrick! One of them's back at the hideout and going nuts with that sword thing. I think he might hurt them—or worse."

"On my way. If you think harm is inevitable, let me know and I'll blow the charge. Be there in less than a minute."

Patrick was already in his car and jerked the wheel hard, stepping on the gas. The car fishtailed, spinning onto the road. Two pedestrians stopped to watch. Fortunately, the neighborhood was quiet this time of morning. Within seconds, he was speeding toward the hideout.

"Hold up, man," Adnan said. "Banta just arrived and has things under control again."

"Anyone hurt?"

"I don't think so. David and Pam are at the edge of the screen, but they appear to be all right."

Patrick eased the car past the gas station. Trying not to appear obvious, he glanced out the car window. One of the Zulus was leaving the building. Patrick continued down the street, watching in his mirrors as long as possible. Maybe he should storm the hideout now. Maybe this was too risky. He'd have to stay closer to the gas station, perhaps even out of his car. That made the chance of discovery higher, but this last episode scared him. He counted on Banta being in control at all times. Two errors. He couldn't afford another. Pam and David couldn't either.

Banta looked tired. The encounter with Shinto had evidently taken more strength from him. He wavered near his bedding and sank to his knees. Lisa hurried to his side, helping him lie down. His brow glistened with sweat, his breathing rapid. She felt his forehead.

"You're burning up," she said, undressing his shoulder. The wound festered, red and swollen. David could see from where he sat the red streaks extending up Banta's shoulder and around his arm.

"That wound looks bad," he said. "My guess is pus has collected deep in the shoulder. Unless he has it drained again, and soon, he's gonna get real sick."

"He's right, Banta," Lisa said. "We should take you back to the hospital."

"No! No hospitals," Banta yelled. "You treat me here. After ceremony tonight, we go, if necessary. You open wound now. Do it."

"I can't," she protested. "Not here. I don't have the instruments or any medicine to numb the pain."

"Use knife," Banta said. "Be quick."

Lisa whimpered, but gave up arguing. She gathered a few medical supplies from their footlocker and prepped his shoulder with alcohol, spilling some onto his bedding. He reached out and grabbed her wrist.

"Enough! Open wound. Now!"

Lisa poured more alcohol over the smaller knife blade. Her hands trembled as the point hovered just millimeters from his skin. Lowering it gently, she worked the tip between the edges of the wound. Banta grunted, but did not move. The muscles of his jaw tightened. Lisa wiggled the blade from side to side, wishing it through the skin. The small scar over the wound gave, and a gush of foul smelling green and yellow pus flowed from his shoulder. Lisa gagged and dropped the knife, shifting her head and backing away. She turned back toward him as Banta reached across his chest and squeezed the muscle of the injured shoulder. He grimaced, but continued to apply pressure. More pus spurted out. The room reeked of putrification.

"Pseudomonas," David said, under his breath. "That's not good."

"How long can he hold out like this?" Pam asked.

"He'll get better temporarily, now that the pus has been drained. If he doesn't have that washed out and get some IV antibiotics, it will re-accumulate soon and get worse."

"He needs medical attention, Lisa," Pam said. "He'll die without it."

"You are nurse," Banta said, through gritted teeth. "You treat. Woman. Untie nurse. Keep doctor tied. If she tries escape, kill her."

Pam looked to Lisa, who was obviously uneasy about this. She crossed again to the footlocker and removed Pam's .38, holding it unsteadily. With the gun in her right hand, she knelt by Pam and tried to undo the bonds. The knot held tight and this proved impossible one-handed. Laying the pistol well out of reach, she returned and using both hands, undid the rope. Pam eased away from the pole, rubbing her wrists. Looking to David, she wiggled her fingers, out of sight of the others. David shook his head, almost imperceptibly.

"My fingers are numb," Pam said. "I don't think I can use them."

"Tell woman what to do," Banta groaned, his breathing more rapid and shallow.

"We'll need to heat water to wash the wound," Pam said. "Then, it should be packed open so more pus doesn't collect. Do you have some gauze?"

"Yes," Lisa said. "We bought dressing supplies at the store this morning. Just gauze and tape."

"That'll have to do. How about something to heat water in?"

"Well, Shinto should have gotten a small charcoal grill," Lisa said. "It and the charcoal are probably still in the car. I guess we could use that. These cups are metal and we could heat water in them."

"What'd he get the grill for?" David asked.

Lisa looked away. "It's part of the ceremony, to dry and preserve the—heads."

"Oh," he said.

Shinto had disappeared. Lisa brought supplies in from the car and set up the grill. Soon, she had a small fire going and water boiling. Holding the cup with a cloth around her hands, she set it aside until it cooled enough to handle. Pam coached Lisa through the next part.

"First, moisten the gauze with the water. You'll have to hold the edges of the wound open while you pour the water into it with your other hand. Follow this with some of the alcohol. That will hurt quite a bit, but it's the best we can do. After that, poke one end of the gauze into the wound, before you let go of the edges. Then, dress it."

"I don't know," Lisa said, shaking her head.

"Come on. You can do it. I'll help you." Pam rested one of her hands clumsily on Lisa's shoulder.

Lisa looked up at her, a hint of a smile on her lips. She leaned into Pam and rested her head momentarily on Pam's chest. Pam looked over at David, who nodded toward the .38 resting on the floor, five feet away. She answered him with a wink.

Lisa went to Banta's side. She gathered the water, alcohol, and dressings close by. "This will hurt," she said, opening the wound edges with her left hand.

Banta hummed something from his chants. Sweat poured off his forehead. He darted his eyes about the room, focusing on nothing; his head twisted side to side. As the water hit his exposed muscle, he groaned and hummed louder. The alcohol that followed caused him to cry out in pain, though he didn't move his shoulder or try to escape the cause of his torment.

David wondered that Banta remained conscious. The pain must've felt like a hot poker shoved into his shoulder. How could he stand it? If he lost consciousness, Pam would have a chance at the gun.

"Now tuck the gauze into the wound," Pam said. "Hurry. I don't think he can stand much more of this."

Lisa did as told and then dressed the wound. In the excitement, Pam had worked away from the two of them and inched toward the pistol. She was about to reach for it, when Shinto burst into the room. He saw Pam close to the gun and leaped at her, knocking her to the ground. He kicked the gun out of the way, far from her grasp.

"What are you doing, you fool?" Lisa cried. "She was helping me."

"She get gun," Shinto said, pointing to the weapon, now lying ten feet away.

Pam pushed away from Shinto, backing towards David, and away from the gun. "No, Lisa," she said. "I was helping you, you know that."

Banta said something to Shinto, who picked up the gun and put it back in the footlocker."Clean knife," he said to Lisa. "Then clean bedding and room. Clean nurse and tie to doctor. We have much to do in preparation for tonight. I must rest. Will need strength for ceremony."

"Let me give you some medicine first," Lisa said.

"No pain pills. Only infection," he said.

"Of course," she replied. David watched as she dumped two pills from one bottle and, with some hesitation, one pill from another into her hand. These, she gave to Banta, then began cleaning up the mess.

Shinto stood guard, scowling, watching Lisa and the two prisoners.

When Lisa finished with Banta, she guided Pam into the bathroom, away from the other men. "Now, I must do as Banta has instructed me and clean you in preparation."

"You've made a mess of yourself in this process," Pam said. "I think you got some of that pus in your hair. Looks like there's some on your neck and shoulders too."

Lisa brought her hands to her face and looked into the mirror. She made a small noise of disgust as she saw the spots Pam alluded to. She closed the bathroom door and hurriedly stripped off her blouse, leaving herself naked above the waist. Old scars mixed with new bruises across her thin, ribbed torso; her small breasts hanging as sad tributes to her emaciated state. Bending over the sink, she washed the two small areas of contamination and used the wet blouse to clean her hair. Satisfied, she began undressing Pam.

"It's probably just my neck that needs cleaning," Pam said.

"Shhh. I'll take care of you and get you ready."

Pam pretended to help by fumbling with the poncho, but due to the feigned uselessness of her hands, only got in the way. Lisa brushed her hands aside. Soon Pam, once again, stood naked before her captor. Lisa used the small wash rag to bathe her.

Pam took a chance.

"You're getting that all over your pants, Lisa."

Lisa looked down and saw the few small water marks on her slacks. She raised her head and looked into Pam's eyes. Pam smiled back at her. Slowly, Lisa wiggled out of the rest of her garments. Pam noted the multiple scars of abuse across her buttocks and thighs. When she turned, there were similar marks on her back.

Again, Lisa approached, this time much closer as she cleaned Pam, their bodies frequently touching. Pam closed her eyes and prepared for the abuse she knew was inevitable. As Lisa took liberties with her body, Pam pressed her advantage.

"Help me get away, Lisa. Help me and I'll help you. Do this before they hurt David. This doesn't have to end badly."

She flinched as Lisa worked from behind, running her hands the length of her torso, pressing their bodies tightly together. Pam's every instinct was to pull away, but she resisted the urge, instead, leaned back into Lisa.

Lisa moaned from behind and paused in her cleaning motions. She turned Pam, wrapped her arms around her, and hugged her tightly.

Pam gritted her teeth and raised her arms behind Lisa, returning the hug. Lisa began to weep and kissed Pam's neck, then her chin, and finally, her mouth. Pam didn't respond, but didn't resist either. Their only hope was this bond between the two of them.

Lisa pulled her head back, looking lovingly at Pam.

"Help me, Lisa," Pam whispered. "Please, help me."

This time, Pam leaned forward, kissing Lisa full on the mouth. Lisa moaned louder than before and rubbed her body into Pam's, hands exploring. Pam choked back her revulsion and tried to put her mind somewhere else.

Suddenly, the bathroom door flew open. Shinto stood in the doorway, staring at the two naked women. He grabbed Pam and pulled her from the bathroom. She snatched her poncho before being thrown into the hall. Shinto stepped into the bathroom, closing the door behind him. Pam hurriedly covered herself. She heard Lisa's quiet cries as Shinto had his way with her. She looked into the other room. Banta sat propped against the wall, cradling his shotgun. He shook his head and motioned her from the bathroom. She went to David, but stayed far enough away to not incite Banta.

Lisa's torment lasted a long time. David and Pam sat helpless under the watchful, though drugged eyes, of Banta.

Shinto came out first, scowling, but looking pleased with himself. He tied Pam to the pole and to David. Lisa came out a few minutes later, dressed in her partially wet clothing, a new bruise developing on her left check, her lower lip swollen and split. She whimpered and went to Banta's side, not looking at Pam or David. She checked his shoulder and then lay at his side, head in his lap. Banta placed a hand on her head. Both of them looked at Pam, each with a different expression. Pam looked only at Lisa, with genuine sorrow and sympathy for the woman. She hoped their bond remained and was strong enough. Tonight would be the test.

CHAPTER
THIRTY-ONE

Patrick decided to check with his British counterparts one more time. He wanted to end it, right now—take out the Zulus and rescue David and Pam. He wished it wasn't so important to find out what Banta knew. He dialed his secure satellite phone. After a few checks, he was put through to the agent in charge of the British investigation and brought him up to speed.

"Any evidence there's more than just this one group of Zulus?" Patrick asked.

"Well, since the murders," agent Livingston replied, "we've done a thorough background check on known visitors to the Kingdom from South Africa and neighboring areas. Most are here on legitimate business. A few, we're not sure about. We haven't been able to locate these."

"Have you had any further incidents since we last talked?"

"No, we haven't. I wouldn't take any great comfort in that, however. The three known murders happened weeks apart. We're still on high alert and actively hunting those we think may have mischief on their minds."

Mischief. I wonder what they consider serious crime. "What I'm asking is, if we take out the group here, will there be others right behind them?"

"Can't tell you, mate. It's possible."

"Call me if you find out anything. It's important. I'm putting two people's lives at risk here."

"Righto. Anything further?"

"No. Thanks for your help," Patrick said, cutting the connection.

That hadn't made him feel any better. He'd have to stick near to the hideout. Any more close calls and he'd end this thing right now. He parked the car away from the gas station. After checking with Adnan, he grabbed his gear and retraced his steps to the hideout, selecting a secluded spot for his surveillance outpost. While daylight lasted, he'd watch from here via the video monitor. Darkness would allow him to move in closer.

The hours passed slowly for him and, he thought, even slower for the two captives. He watched each one by remotely adjusting the aim of the camera. Banta rested easily, and appeared to have recovered some of his strength. Shinto paced, occasionally stopping to do something with the dead body. By now, the corpse would be getting ripe. Lisa tended house and stayed away from Shinto. She gave Pam and David food and drink. Shinto supervised trips to the bathroom. The two captives seemed to fear Shinto, not hesitating to obey his hand directions.

Occasionally, Banta slept. Shinto and Lisa busied themselves in and out of the building, probably setting up for tonight. During these moments, David and Pam looked over their shoulders and talked. Patrick aimed his directional microphone to pick up their voices.

"They'll have to separate us—during the ceremony, I mean," David said. "Surely, they won't have us tied to each other then."

"I agree. While the men are doing their thing, I'll try to get to Lisa and work on her sympathies."

"I wonder where Patrick and Adnan are."

Patrick grimaced, wishing he could think of some way to contact them without blowing his cover.

"You know they're working as hard as they can. Maybe they'll find us—before it's too late, I mean," she said.

"Pam, if you're able, try to escape. Save yourself first, then call Patrick."

"I thought about that," she said. "If I can get to the gun—that might be our best chance."

"They're going to be drugged, Pam. You won't be able to reason with them. If you take that approach, you'll have to shoot first and talk later. You'll have to kill them. Can you do that?"

Sure she can, Patrick thought.

"Apparently, I already have," she said, inclining her head toward the body against the far wall.

"I mean, you won't be able to threaten them with the gun. You'll have to shoot them in cold blood, maybe from behind and with no warning."

"David, each of these men has hurt me and made me fear for my life."

Their conversation stopped. Patrick panned the room. Banta was up and motioning their way, effectively cutting off further conversation.

Hours passed. It looked as though Pam spent the rest of the afternoon trying to catch Lisa's eye. David seemed lost in thought.

Storm clouds gathered as evening approached. Patrick returned to his car for rain gear. To stay busy and feel he was doing something, he spent the rest of the afternoon reconnoitering the area surrounding the gas station. That kept him closer to those in his charge. Adnan assured him things were ready for tonight.

The skies darkened. Patrick pulled up the local weather map on his computer. Memphis was in for one of those early spring thunder-boomers. Would that help or hurt? Might interfere with Adnan's pyrotechnic display, but it would also be another distraction in the scene they hoped to create.

Something else gnawed at him. He couldn't quite put his finger on it. This feeling had grown after his phone conversation with agent Livingston. Why hadn't they pressed him harder for information? Their investigation was ongoing, yet Livingston had no apparent interest in what was happening here across the pond.

His earpiece crackled. "Heads up, Patrick. Looks like the act's beginning."

"Thanks. I'm ready. Is this rain going to hurt you?"

"Rain, no problem. High winds—maybe." Adnan said, a hint of concern penetrating his accent.

"Anything goes wrong, we take the hostiles down."

"That better plan anyway," Adnan said. "I'm going to set up. Keep me informed. I won't be watching video screen full time."

"Right. Good luck."

Lightning streaked across the skies, followed by claps of thunder. Wind gusted, blowing litter and leaves into the air. The temperature dropped. He'd seen this before. This would not be just a pleasant spring shower.

As the room darkened, the image on the monitor faded. Heavy clouds ushered in the night. He watched Banta rise from his bedding, speak to Shinto, then disappear into the bathroom. Shinto grinned, then poured more charcoal onto the smoldering grill. Retrieving a bag from the footlocker, he prepared the body. The legs of the corpse would not flex fully at the hips, and Shinto began throwing things about the room. He dressed the mottled body in a loin cloth and propped it in a corner, half sitting, half standing, then completed the preparation with a headdress and face paint. Apparently satisfied, Shinto dressed himself in a similar fashion. What was he going to do with that dead body?

Patrick slipped out of his street clothes. Underneath, he wore a skin tight, black bodysuit and light body armor. Pulling on a dark head cover, he closed the laptop, gathered his gear and quietly made his way under cover of darkness to the window at the back of the hideout.

Lisa huddled in her corner, facing away and paying no mind to the captives. Pam focused on Lisa, cocking her head to try to catch her eye. Words weren't spoken, but Lisa must have felt her stare, for she turned slowly to meet her eyes. Pam crinkled her eyebrows and put on a pouting frown, pleading passionately with facial expression. This must have touched Lisa, for she returned the visual embrace.

Good. At least they're communicating, he thought.

A clap of thunder made them all jump. Large raindrops beat down on the roof, slowly at first, then faster. Wind whipped the rain against the window.

Banta returned from the bathroom, dressed in a loin cloth and a large ceremonial headdress of feathers and jewels. He seemed to have grown; his presence dominated the room.

Banta inspected Shinto, then turned to the body in the corner. Apparently pleased, he nodded to Shinto, and the two dragged the footlocker to the center of the room. Banta reverently spread the colorful African quilt over the piece of luggage, converting it to an altar. He lit the candles, throwing a cast of flickering shadows on the old walls. The thunderstorm roared, like background music in a bad movie.

Shinto gathered a handful of dried leaf from their supply, and kneeling in front of the altar, placed it in the small, carved, wooden bowl. The butane lighter he used to ignite the leaf looked modern and out of place. Wispy tendrils of smoke rose into the air, dissipating rapidly as the violent storm penetrated the room.

The temperature dropped. The nearly naked Zulus seemed unbothered. Lisa huddled smaller in her corner. Banta gestured slowly with his right arm over the burning leaf. Shinto added more to the bowl, and blew on the embers. The smoke thickened. Flickering candlelight played on the smoke, painting rapidly vanishing figures about the room. The Zulus squatted closer to the altar, breathing deeply, humming, eyes partially closed.

It's now or never, Pam, he thought.

"Help me." He saw her mouth, making no sound.

Lisa shook her head violently and buried her face in her hands, the sounds of her weeping muffled by the storm. She appeared to grow smaller in her corner. Pam stared at Lisa, apparently not wanting to miss the moment when she might again glance up.

Patrick peered through the corner of the window. Lightning cracked across the sky, backlighting the trees. Another bolt quickly followed. David's gaze drifted from the Zulus and up to the ceiling. He appeared to mouth a prayer, then jerked his head toward the window and continued to stare.

Patrick held his finger to his mouth. Another burst of lightning lit up the room. The relief on David's face made Patrick's heart jump to his throat. David tried to speak to Pam, but Patrick cut him off with a shake of the head. Her energies were focused on Lisa, and for the moment, he wanted it that way.

The only light in the room came from candles. Minutes passed. The Zulus calmed, but their chanting grew louder. The drafts in the building blew the smoke away from Pam and David. They'd probably not feel the effects of the drug.

"Let ceremony begin," Banta's voice boomed over the storm.

"What ceremony?" Pam cried out. "You can't do this!"

Banta pointed the scimitar at her. "Quiet ... or you die, too."

"What do you want from us?" she screamed.

"What I want? I want my brother." Banta stalked closer to them. "He take beads to America. He come back dead. What I want? I want beads that were taken from my country. I want lives of those who take them, just as they took Jarmangi's life. I know where beads are. Tonight, I take one more."

Pam shook her head violently. "But you can't—"

Banta stepped toward her, arm drawn back for the strike.

"Wait! Don't!" David yelled.

Banta paused and snapped his head toward David.

"Pam." David leaned into her, holding her with the intensity of his gaze. "You've got to trust me on this one. It'll be all right. Don't provoke him."

"But David—"

"Pam, please," David said. "Trust me."

Pam hung her head. Patrick's mic picked up the sob that escaped her lips.

Apparently satisfied the disturbance was quelled, Banta turned and resumed squatting beside Shinto. After inhaling more smoke, he rose and retrieved the cloth bag previously removed from the footlocker. Reaching inside, he pulled out the dried, preserved heads of his victims, one at a time, placing them on the altar. He removed his own headdress, bowed, and using both hands, removed the bead necklace from the bag and placed it around his neck. Again, he donned his feathered crown. Chanting in his native tongue, he grasped the large scimitar with both hands, and slowly began to dance, the movement of his left arm hindered little by its wound.

"Eengonyama! Gonyama! Invooboo!
Ya-boh! Ya-boh! Invooboo!"

Patrick watched in fascinated horror as Banta knelt beside the corpse in the corner of the room. He cradled it in his arms, rocking back and forth, wails of anguish emitting from his throat. Laying the body as flat as it would go on the ground, he covered it with a blanket and appeared to say burial rites or prayers. He looked toward the heavens during these ministrations.

Banta swung his head towards Pam and David, pointing with his long knife. Dancing, gyrating, twisting to the center of the room, he picked up one of the smoked heads. Gesturing and singing, he passed the blade beneath it in another ceremonial decapitation, raising the head high in victory. His movements were slow and rhythmic, controlled, feet planted, upper body swaying.

Thunder boomed outside. Rain pummeled the back wall and window, the roar of the storm drowning the mantra of the Zulu warrior. Outside, Patrick huddled closer to the wall.

"Get ready," he vocalized into his microphone.

Twice more, Banta repeated this mock battle, using the other heads. Between each scene, he paused to suck in more of the drugged smoke. Shinto hunkered beside the altar, eyes half-open, adding his voice to the chants as Banta's energy grew.

Obviously frightened, Lisa shook, jumping with each clap of thunder. She looked to Pam as if wanting to rush to her side, but didn't dare. Patrick's admiration for Pam grew as he watched her visually plead with Lisa. He again motioned for David to sit tight.

Banta spun toward them, thrusting his knife, chanting, working himself into a frenzy. He drew the knife across his own chest, raising a line of blood. His yells grew louder between pulses of the storm. Kneeling before the altar, he stroked the bead necklace hanging at his chest, then rose and turned to the captives, brandishing his knife. His breathing slowed and calm seemed to settle over him. Menacingly, he crept toward them.

Pam pulled at her bonds and David stared wide-eyed at the window. *Any time now*, he seemed to be saying to Patrick. Lisa cried out in anguish. Banta slithered toward them, eyes wild, flickering, mouth moving but emitting no sound. He grabbed David by the hair and pulled his head forward. David cried out.

"Now!" Patrick said into his throat mike.

A clap of thunder—an explosion blasted the front door from its hinges. Wind and leaves filled the doorway. A figure appeared out of nowhere, light radiating from its body, shining on its face.

Banta spun, apparently stunned by the intrusion. Quickly recovering, he moved toward the door, sword raised over his head—and froze, eyes wide, mouth open.

In the doorway stood his mother dressed in her death robes, arms reaching out to him. Light from her body lit up her face. The rain drenched her and the winds whipped her clothing, her hair bound in cloth, her face, pale and gaunt, eyes dark and sunken. She smiled at him, her right front tooth broken off, as it had been in life.

"*Banta*," she cried out in a smooth, amplified and altered voice.

Banta shook his head, looking about the room. Shinto had crept away from the altar and toward the wall against which the shotgun leaned. Pam and Lisa stared at the scene unfolding before them. David raised his head slowly as if scared it might roll off, and did a double take at the apparition. He turned again to look in Patrick's direction. The storm outside raged.

"*Banta*," the specter again called, arms beckoning, voice booming.

Banta took a step toward the apparition, weapon raised overhead. The woman extended her arm, palm toward him, fingers up. Her smile changed to an angry grimace. With her other hand, she pointed at the wall to her right behind which Patrick knelt. Upon seeing this, Patrick dropped to the ground, covered his head and pushed the small button in the palm on his left hand. An explosion, muffled by a clap of thunder, blew a hole in the wall above him. The window and wall crumbled inward. Lisa screamed and as Patrick peeked over the rubble, he saw her scurry from the debris, huddling near Pam.

"*Iziqu*," the figure in the doorway boomed, pointing to the beads about Banta's neck.

From his concealed spot behind the rubble, Patrick leveled his weapon at the big Zulu. Banta froze in place, staring at the ghost of his mother, her face aglow with light emanating from her body. He turned toward David.

"*No!*" shouted the apparition.

Banta turned back. His mother's long, covered arm again pointed to the beads around his neck. "*Iziqu!*" The wind whipped her robe about her body. She remained rock steady in the doorway. How was Adnan making the dress of that hologram move with the wind? Patrick looked closer. Wait! That was no hologram!

"Adnan!" he barked into his throat mike. "What the hell is she doing here?"

"Later, man. Little busy at the moment," Adnan's voice said into his earpiece.

Banta weaved on his feet, his warrior expression now replaced with one of a scolded child. He looked back and forth from the captives to the specter of his mother. She nodded and smiled. He stumbled toward her, moving as if in a trance.

Patrick's attention turned to Shinto, who had shouldered the shotgun. Patrick swung and fired. The poor lighting hid the strands of the taser gun. The leads imbedded in Shinto's chest and he fell to the ground, twitching and jerking, the shotgun falling harmlessly away.

Banta gave a start and looked to his mother. Her finger pointed at Shinto; her eyes narrowed, mouth pulled tight. She spun her head toward Banta and without changing expression, moved her pointing finger back to the beads about his neck.

Satisfied Shinto was neutralized, Patrick evaluated the others. Lisa huddled closer to Pam. Pam leaned her head to Lisa's ear and said something.

The wind roared. Lisa looked from Banta to the figure in the door. Her hands went to the knot binding Pam to David and the pole. Within seconds, Patrick saw Pam shake the bindings loose and free her hands. Before moving, she stared at Banta, who appeared dazed, distracted; the wind buffeted his headdress and tore at his loin cloth.

Pam turned to get at David's bindings. Lisa saw what she was doing.

"No!" she said, grabbing Pam's hands. "You promised to help *me*!" The sound of her voice was barely discernable over the intensity of the wind and constant clattering of tree limbs and debris on the building. Pam glanced at Banta, who paid them no mind. Putting her mouth close to Lisa's ear, she spoke barely loud enough for Patrick to pick up on his directional mic. "Trust me, Lisa, like I trusted you. You and I … we're closer now." Lisa hesitated, but let go.

Pam's hands shook as she fumbled to untie David. The two of them, followed closely by Lisa, edged away from the pole and toward the opening in the wall created by the explosion. Banta held onto the three-bead necklace with his left hand, still clutching the large knife with his right. He walked as though confused, his drugged eyes darting, movements unsure.

The apparition shouted something in what Patrick took to be Zulu, pointing to the beads and beckoning with the fingers of her other hand. He did recognize the name of Banta's older brother, *Jarmangi*, included in the commands.

Banta looked startled, stopping a few feet in front of the ghost. Whatever Adnan had instructed her to say in Zulu had the desired effect. He replaced the taser with a more serious handgun. Banta could still turn on the captives.

"That's Gladys! My scrub nurse!" David said to Pam.

The roaring wind bore down on them, increasing in intensity. Cracks of breaking tree limbs and squeals of twisting wood punctuated the howling of the storm. Debris pounded the walls.

Without removing them from his neck, Banta held the beads out to his mother. She turned her hand to accept them.

Lightning flashed outside the gas station. Something must have caught Banta's eye, for he leaned to see behind the figure in the doorway. Again lightning streaked across the sky. Patrick ducked around the corner to see what had distracted the Zulu. Three small black heads looked out from behind the large hickory tree in front of the door, eyes wide and frightened.

"*Brothers!*" Banta exclaimed loudly, grabbing the outstretched arm of the woman, steadying himself. He stepped out of the building, toward the boys, pushing past the figure of his mother. His headdress flew off. Turning to watch it, he froze in place, staring.

Gladys reached for the beads, but Banta brushed her hand away. He shook his head, as if confused.

"I think I've been spotted," Patrick heard Adnan's voice in his earpiece.

"Take him down," Patrick subvocalized into his own mic. "The one inside has recovered and is up. Plan B."

Watching over the sights of his gun, Patrick saw Adnan spring to his feet, pulling Gladys away with one arm and leveling his pistol at Banta. In his black body suit, Adnan was nearly invisible.

Banta ducked inside, swinging his sword toward the two captives and Lisa. Shinto was on his feet, fumbling with the shotgun.

Adnan burst into the room. Patrick fired two shots into Shinto, knocking him into the wall.

"No!" Lisa screamed, leaping in front of Banta.

Adnan fired twice. Something slammed him in the back as he shot, hurling him to the floor.

Lisa crumpled into Banta's chest, arms encircling him, holding herself up. Blood streaked his chest as she lost her grip and slid down his torso, looking up into his face. He pushed her away, and clutching his sword, dashed through the doorway, into the night. Patrick raced around the corner to head him off and the two collided, tumbling hard in a tangle of arms and legs. Banta recovered first and leapt away into the storm.

"Adnan! Are you hurt?" Patrick scrambled back into the remains of the building.

David dragged Adnan from under the splintered tree limb while Pam knelt, cradling Lisa's torso.

"You okay?" Patrick yelled above the wind.

"Yeah, sure," Adnan replied, glancing toward the women.

Patrick checked Shinto's body. Two centered chest shots left little doubt Shinto was dead, but he checked for vital signs anyway. He jerked loose the taser barbs and returned to his partner. Rain pelted them through the torn roof. Wind whipped leaves and bits of trash around the room.

"I had the shot, Patrick. That blow in the back threw me off," he said, staring at Pam and Lisa. "Go after Banta. I'll cover here."

Patrick nodded but checked to be sure Pam and David were okay. Banta could wait.

Gladys stood against the wall inside the doorway; the battery operated light still shining up onto her face. Adnan reached behind her and clicked off her light.

David put one hand on her shoulder, shielding his face from the blowing grit with the other. "How'd you get involved in this?" he shouted over the noise.

"Last year, you saved my grandbaby's life at the city hospital," she replied. "Bet you don't even know who I's talking about, do you?"

"You can catch up later," Patrick said. "Why don't you help those two ladies right now?"

Gladys had risked her life for him, and Patrick could see the emotion in the doctor's eyes. David lingered a moment, holding her gaze long enough to let her know he appreciated what she'd done, then turned to help Pam. He nearly stepped on one of the heads from the toppled altar, and jumped sideways.

Patrick turned from David and Gladys and knelt by Pam. Lisa looked up into Pam's eyes, her breath coming in short gasps, blood frothing around her lips, a dark patch from her chest wounds expanding across her blouse.

"I'm … sorry," she said.

"Quiet. Try not to talk." Pam held Lisa's head, stroking her hair. "We'll get help. Save your strength."

"Forgive … " Lisa mouthed, and breathed no more.

Patrick bowed his head. Gladys came up behind David and placed her hand on his shoulder. They watched as Pam continued to rock the body, tears mixing with the rain streaming down her face. The storm raged, but they took no notice, lost in this room full of death.

CHAPTER THIRTY-TWO

Patrick pushed into the wind, shielding his eyes from the driving rain, hoping to catch a glimpse of the fleeing Banta, now probably long gone. Uprooted trees and downed limbs blocked his path. He stopped a few yards from the hideout, glancing left and right. Movement behind the large oak caught his eye. Weapon out and held with both hands, he marched toward the tree and flicked on the flashlight attached to the frame of his handgun. Taking a deep breath, he spun to the tree's far side, leading with the barrel of his gun.

Sheltered in the exposed roots of the massive tree were the three small black boys, whimpering in terror. One looked up at him. The others covered their heads with their hands and tried to push farther into the mud.

"Don't shoot, mister. We didn't do nothin'," one of them said.

"Tyrone?" Patrick asked, pulling off his black head covering.

"Honest, mister. Our friend, Lester, wanted to see what this was all about. We was gonna leave, but then we gots caught in the storm. We tried to run, but the wind knocks us over. Jamal here—"

"Settle down, Tyrone. You're not in trouble. Are any of you hurt?"

Three little heads shook in unison.

"Did you see someone run by here a few minutes ago?"

Jamal raised his head, keeping his arm over his forehead to ward off the wind and rain. He pointed up the slope toward an abandoned lot.

"He didn't get far, mister, 'til one of you all got him."

"What? What do you mean?" Patrick asked, looking in the direction the boy pointed.

"Up there, near the fence. That's where that other man dressed all in black left him. Wasn't much of a fight, from what I could see in the lightning and all."

"Stay put! I'll be right back." Patrick raised his weapon and headed in the direction the boy indicated.

The noise of the storm covered his approach. Keeping the cloak of trees between him and his suspected target, he slowly made his way up the small rise. The crumpled body of the Zulu warrior lay on its side near the wire fence separating the lots. Wary of a trap, Patrick nudged the body with his foot, keeping his pistol trained, its light scanning the downed Zulu. The body rolled to its back, revealing the garroted throat and bulging, dead eyes of Banta. His right hand still clutched the scimitar, his left hand empty. The head rolled with the body, then took an extra turn, showing the tenuous attachments that remained. No necklace.

Fitting end. Patrick shivered at the gruesome sight. Choking back his revulsion, he knelt closer, looking for the bead necklace. He had to brush aside some leaves clinging to the gore about the wound, but there was no sign of it. His thoughts turned to who might be the murderer. The storm made tracking the new killer impossible.

Patrick worked his way back down to the boys. "Come with me. Let's get you behind some walls at least. I have some people with me who will help you get home." He ushered them into the hideout, where they found the others huddled around the body of Lisa.

Adnan looked up as he approached.

"Any luck?" he asked.

"Sort of. I'll tell you later. Everyone here okay?"

The storm abated and conversation became easier. Gladys turned and spotted the three young boys, soaking wet and shivering, and rushed to check them over.

"Tyrone? Jamal?" said Adnan.

"You know these boys?" Gladys asked, continuing her ministrations to the frightened youngsters. She looked his way, scolding him with her eyes.

"Yeah. They keep turning up in this area." He paused as he made his way through the rubble. "Wait a minute! You don't think I knew they were here, do you? I'd never involve kids in something like this."

"Well, they sure had some kind of effect on that Banta," she said, not sounding entirely convinced of his innocence. "He saw them and made for them like they was kin. That's when he spotted you."

"Listen up, people," Patrick called out above the wind. "Technically, this is a crime scene. We're going to have to leave the bodies where they are until the local authorities are satisfied. Adnan, you and Gladys take the boys home in the van. David, Pam—come with me. Let's get out of this weather. Adnan, join me back at the hotel as soon as you can."

"It seems wrong to just leave her here," Pam said, not moving from her seat on the ground, still cradling Lisa's body.

"Come on," David said, kneeling by her and putting his arm around her shoulders. "She's free now. Her body will be okay here. We'll cover her with the quilt from the footlocker."

Patrick started to object, but thought better of it and let them do what they needed. David helped Pam to her feet, and the two of them covered Lisa's body. Though the threat of the storm seemed to have diminished, they were still in the middle of dangerous weather. David hesitated, then hoisted his great-grandfather's weapon. Patrick nodded consent. The three made their way through the debris to Patrick's car, parked around the corner.

Patrick opened the back door for the two of them, rummaged in the trunk, found a blanket and threw it into the back seat, then got behind the wheel. For a few minutes, they drove in silence. The car heater warmed them. Pam rested her head on David's shoulder.

"Did you find Banta?" David asked, breaking the silence.

"Oh yeah. He won't be bothering you anymore, though I can't take credit for that."

"What do you mean?"

"Someone got to him before I did. Canceled his return flight."

"You had other people there?"

"It wasn't one of us. Looked very professional though." Glancing into the rear view mirror and hoping to change the subject, he asked, "Pam? Are you okay?"

"I'll be fine," she said, pulling closer into David, cutting off further conversation.

"Listen," Patrick continued. "I'm sorry about how things worked out. The idea was to startle them, take them alive, and taking advantage of their drugged state, find out if there were other teams searching for the beads. Didn't plan on all that interference from Mother Nature. We had you under surveillance the whole time, so you were never in any real danger," he exaggerated. "I'm just sorry I didn't have a way to let you in on it earlier. The waiting was hard, I'm sure."

"Hard?" David shouted.

As they warmed and drove out of the rundown neighborhood into more familiar surroundings, Patrick could tell his friend was starting to get angry.

"Oh, it was hard, all right," David said. "I was reasonably certain I was going to lose my head." Taking a deep breath, he calmed down. "Still, thanks for getting us out of that mess. I know you risked your own lives as well. Speaking of that, who came up with that idea of using Gladys as a stand-in for Banta's mother? And how did you get her to go along with it?"

"Actually, you gave me the idea when you commented on their resemblance. Adnan didn't go for it at first, but he went along and provided all the details and pyrotechnics. She wasn't supposed to be there in person. When she heard you were in bad trouble, I guess she was game for anything. You must have really made an impression on her."

"She's a good lady," David said. "Guess I never appreciated how good."

Patrick dropped them off at their apartments and returned to his hotel. Adnan followed close behind. The two agents cleaned up and debriefed each other, putting together the details for their final report to the Department.

"Okay. Spill it. Why'd you involve Gladys?"

"Screw-up with holographic equipment," Adnan said. "I was getting ready to call you when she volunteered. Damn near bit my head off when I refused. Something about David and grandson."

"Pretty risky. If she'd gotten hurt—" Patrick shook his head and continued packing.

"So, who you think killed Banta?" Adnan asked.

"There's only one other group with the wherewithal and the interest to attempt such a thing, and that's the Brits. I don't understand why, though. And why would whoever it was, make off with the beads? I don't think this is over yet."

"What makes you think it wasn't another group of Zulus?" Adnan asked.

"Why would they work against each other?" Patrick paused. "Unless there's another unrelated group after the same thing. That would make this complicated, wouldn't it?"

"Have you told David and Pam?" Adnan asked. "He still has bead, right?"

"Yeah. He still has it. I didn't relay my concerns to them, although they know the identity of Banta's killer is still a mystery."

"What we do now?"

"We probably should do some old fashioned police work and comb the area looking for clues—after this storm passes, that is. Doubt we'll find anything. Might need to talk with those boys again. You know where to find them, right? They're the only ones who've actually seen anything."

"They pretty scared right now. And I imagine their butts are little sore. Their mothers were steamed." Adnan continued to clean and put away his gear. "I've called this in to locals. They understand it federal scene, but they help us keep area roped off until we go over the grounds. They also take care of bodies and try locate family. They pretty busy at the moment with all the calls coming in from storm."

"It doesn't add up," Patrick said under his breath. "There's another piece to this puzzle we aren't aware of. And I don't think we'll like it."

David and Pam split to their separate apartments to clean up. The interior of David's place was a mess. He showered and changed into sweats and called Pam. When she didn't answer the phone right away, his stomach twisted into a knot. Finally, she picked up.

"Pam, my place is still messed up and—"

"Sure. Come on over," she said. "I'm glad I didn't have to call you. I'm going to need some company for a while—maybe a long while. You still applying for the job?"

He smiled inwardly. This banter felt normal.

"Depends on the fringe benefits," he smirked into the phone.

"Honey, these fringes will loosen your hinges," she said, giggling and putting on her best *sister* act.

David laughed out loud. He gathered the few things he needed for the morning and glanced once more around his place. What would he tell them at work? How was he going to explain his absence? Would this affect his job offer in Nashville? Was any of this going to make the papers?

He reached through his sweatshirt and groped for the bead. It felt normal now; not heavy or hot. What was it Mr. Baroni had called it? *Helpful?* Was this the end of it all? Did Patrick know more than he was telling? He thought again of his possible connection through his great-grandfather.

As he switched off the light and pulled the door closed, he pushed these thoughts from his mind. For the moment, he'd rest and take comfort in the arms of the strongest woman on the planet. What were her true feelings toward him now? He knew better than to try to figure that out tonight. Would everything be clearer tomorrow in the light of day?

The storm passed, though the sky hung dark and starless. A broken tree limb settled in the bushes of the landscaping as he walked by, causing him to leap and cry out. How long would this jumpiness last?

He knocked on her door.

"Come on in. It's open," she called out from somewhere in the apartment. He entered and heard the shower running. Closing the door and dropping his backpack, he looked around the room again. A lot had happened here also, but Pam had somehow chased away the demons. The room felt warm and inviting.

"I'll be out in a minute. Make yourself at home," she shouted over the noise of the running water.

He stopped and smiled. Kicking off his shoes, he tip-toed noiselessly to the bathroom and quietly opened the door. He pulled her towel from the rack by the shower and stood in the hallway, out of sight. *Turn about's fair play.*

EPILOGUE

NYERI, KENYA, 1937

Baden-Powell and wife, Olave, unpacked their bags for the last time. Paxtu would be their final home. Named after Pax Hill, their home in England, paxtu is the Swahili word for "complete." He'd lived two lives, one in the military and the other as a Scout. Now, like a skinny, old bull elephant near death, he returned to the dark of the jungle. Paxtu was hidden from the world, purposely built away from people, amidst the wilds of Africa he'd come to love. At eighty years of age, his health was failing him.

Earlier that same year, he bid good-bye to Scouting at the Fifth World Jamboree in Vogelenzang near Bloemendaal, Holland. He sat next to Queen Wilhelmina of the Netherlands in the Royal Box. Twenty-six thousand Scouts representing countries all over the world paraded past them, taking over an hour and a half. The Queen delivered her address and a spontaneous chant of *"B-P, B-P, B-P!"* arose from the mass of boys.

The frail old founder of the Scouting movement took the stage for the last time.

"The time has come for me to say good-bye. You know that many of us will never meet again in this world. I am in my eighty-first year and am nearing the end of my life. Most of you are at the beginning, and I want your lives to be happy and successful. You can make them so by doing your best to carry out the Scout Law all your days, whatever your station and wherever this life takes you.

"I want you all to preserve the badge of the Jamboree on your uniform. It will be a reminder of the happy times you have had here in camp; it will remind you to take the twelve points of the Scout Law as your guide in life; and it will remind you of the many friends to whom you have held out the hand of friendship and so helped through good will to bring about God's reign of peace among men. Now, good-bye. God Bless you all!"

Fighting the tears, he waved his broad-brimmed Scout hat high above his head. The boys cheered endlessly for their founder, until finally he left the stage.

Now settling into their new home, Baden-Powell sorted through boxes containing the memories of his life. Many had been obtained here on the Dark Continent, during the Boer War. Bringing them home, he felt a sense of peace.

In the bottom of his trunk lay the dried leather pouch containing the remaining bead; the one he'd kept and not passed out to other Scouting leaders or the museum. He hesitated before removing it. Nineteen had been unstrung and given to the first Scoutmasters. He recalled that day—the mixed emotions of separating the beads, the unintended brotherhood he created, the mystic feel of the moment when he addressed each man and gave him a bead. He'd sent them into history with a talisman of his past.

Twenty years had passed since that day. The men stayed in touch, some with personal visits, most through mail correspondence. Their lives had taken odd turns. Some ended violently in World War I. Others reported feelings bordering on paranoia. A few preceded him in death with sketchy newspaper accounts of mysterious, brutal endings.

Shortly before he left England for Africa, the widow of one of the Scoutmasters sought him out. She broke down in his arms, telling him how much he meant to her late husband. Disturbing to him was her account of the man's obsession with the bead he wore faithfully about his neck. Sometimes it seemed to drag him down, she told him. She couldn't bring herself to talk of the details of his death, but curiously, she lamented the fact the bead was lost in the process.

B.P. held the tattered pouch containing the remaining bead. He reverently placed it about his own neck; the heaviness in his chest, which he attributed to the infirmities of age, now a constant companion.

Months earlier, at the Fifth World Jamboree, the leader of the fifty Egyptian Scouts had sought an audience with him. The two swapped stories of Scouting and their travels. B-P was embarrassed by the fawning behavior of the younger man, but he'd grown used to it in his meetings with others on the world stage of Scouting. He recalled the startled expression on the Egyptian's face when he pulled the bead from his shirt and recounted the tale he'd told countless times before. The man asked to see the trinket. B-P remembered the feeling of reluctance he had as he passed over the bead.

The man's hands trembled as he examined it more closely. He asked for a magnifying glass, which B-P was happy to provide him, demonstrating his preparedness. The Egyptian mumbled to himself as he turned the bead over and over in his hand, exploring each surface. B-P had done this many times, marveling at the nearly invisible carvings, unique to each.

With a strange combination of what appeared to B-P as fear and reluctance, the man passed the bead back. Dropping all formality, he took B-P by the arm, leading him away from others. Finding two chairs around a corner in the hotel, he offered one to B-P and pulled the other close and in front. Their knees touched as the man leaned closer, sweat collecting on his forehead, though the hotel air was cool. B-P recalled the smell of fear about the man, and the uncertainty in his eyes.

"Egypt is land of antiquities," the Arab Scoutmaster began. "The cradle of civilization. Throughout history, armies have attacked and overrun her: ancient Greeks, Romans, Napoleon and the French. Grave robbers and archeologists have looted our country of treasures. All are precious to us, but some date back before history. Some, we believe, come from the beginning of man. These found their way into collections of ancient pharaohs. These are not items of curiosity, but may have come directly from God."

He paused, removing his neckerchief and wiping his brow. He glanced about the room, tapping his feet on the wood floor and rubbing his hands on his pants.

"Calm yourself, man," B-P said. "How does this relate to me?"

"My family dates back thousands of years. My father and uncles work high in the Ministry of Antiquities. I know of secret things that would mean my death if told."

B-P feared the man might pass out. "Can I get you some water?" he asked.

"No," the Arab said. "I will be all right. Give me a minute."

The man took some deep breaths and visibly worked to settle his nerves. After some moments, he resumed his tale.

"The items of which I speak are not kept in museums. They are not out for public display, but are hidden in the desert and closely watched by bands of dedicated men. Some of these relics are spoken of in your Bible, and are sought by explorers. They will never be found. Only once has an army stumbled upon one of these treasurers and removed it from our soil. The thieves had no idea what they were doing. All of the men protecting the relic were killed. For years, we've hunted for this treasure, mostly throughout Europe. We did not think to look amongst the tribes of southern Africa."

He paused as a small group of people filed past. When they were again alone, the man resumed his tale, this time in a whisper.

"That bead you wear is a relic from the beginning of time. It has passed through the hands of many pharaohs. The beads were a favorite of the Queen of Sheba. We believe each bead holds a special charm, a spell, which works to bring it back with the others—among other things," he said, his low voice trailing off.

"Are you sure this is the bead?" B-P asked. "There must be thousands just like it all over the world."

"No. None have carvings like this." He paused again. "Have you tried to destroy one of them?"

"No, of course not," B-P answered.

"The bead you wear cannot be destroyed. Replicas will rot or burn or break under pressure."

Baden-Powell fingered the bead and studied it carefully.

"If what you say is true, what should I do with it? Should I return it to someone in your country?" he said, frowning and putting the necklace back over his head and safely into his shirt. This bead was a part of him and Scouting now. He did not relish the idea of losing it based on some childish tale.

"I am sorry, sir. There is nothing to be done at this point. Those who seek the beads will find them and return them to their sacred place of hiding."

"How will I know these people?"

"You will not. They are as secret as the beads. They often use what is termed in your country a 'blind.'"

"And what, pray tell, is that?" B-P was starting to get annoyed. Olave would be wondering where he'd gotten off to. He didn't need complications like this at the end of his life.

"A 'blind' is someone who does your work for you without knowing it. Once the 'blind' has collected all he can, our people will do what they have to do."

"And what's that?" B.P. asked.

"I have said too much. You are a great man, and it has been my pleasure to talk with you. I am sorry."

"Now just a minute," B-P said, rising from his chair and looking around the small alcove in which they'd been sitting. "You can't just—"

The man vanished. B-P looked up and down the hallway. He started to search, when he was pulled in another direction by someone wanting his attention.

That had been months ago. Nothing out of the ordinary had happened since then. Still, he wondered about the beads. Hesitatingly, he removed the one bead from around his neck and replaced it in the tattered pouch. Slowly, he lowered it into his trunk and buried it beneath some old clothing. Closing the lid, he stood over the footlocker. He fought the feeling of unrest that worked to consume him. They resided in Kenya now, safe from the rest of the world. Here, he and Olave would live out the rest of their lives in peace.

Four years later, on January 8, 1941, Baden-Powell died peacefully in his sleep with his wife, Olave, and long-time physician friend, Dr. D. Ernest Freeman at his side. He is buried in Africa, near his home in Nyeri, Kenya.

AUTHOR'S NOTE:

FACT VS. FICTION

The Zulu beads are real: recovered during the Boer War by Lord Baden-Powell. His finding them on the body of Chief Dinizulu is fiction, though photographs exist of the Chief wearing similar beads. That twenty-four were different from the other beads is fiction. Dinizulu is historic.

Lord Baden-Powell is historic. Known as the "Hero of Mafeking" for his lengthy defense of this small village in South Africa during the Boer War, he later returned to England and started the Scouting movement. His awarding of a Zulu bead to each of his original Scoutmasters is historic and is the origin of the "Wood Badge," a high achievement for Scoutmasters. His burial in Nyeri, Kenya, is historic.

The 1967 World Scouting Jamboree in Idaho is historic, as are the speakers: Vice-President Hubert H. Humphrey, Lady Olave Baden-Powell, and R.T. Lund. Zulu Scouts did present duplicates of the original beads as described. The shooting death of a Scout is fiction.

The ceremony returning four of the original beads to the Zulu people in 1987 is historic. Chief Minister Mangosuthu Buthelezi and Princess Mahoho, daughter of Chief Dinizulu are historic. Banta Manjabe is fiction.

The U.S. Department of Homeland Security is real, but agents with unlimited authority are my creations. All other characters and powers attributed to the beads are fiction. Any similarities to real people, other than as described above, are unintentional.

Replicas of the beads can be seen at the Scouting museum in Gilwell Park, near Chingford, England. The originals, excepting the one kept by Baden-Powell, were given to the first Scoutmasters and the Scouting museum. Since that time, replicas have been used. Four of the original beads were returned to the Zulus. The exact whereabouts of the other beads given to the original Scoutmasters, and their current owners, remain unknown.

For further information and photos of Baden-Powell and the beads, visit: http://www.pauldparsons.com

---

In Washington D.C., things are back to normal for Homeland Security agents Patrick and Adnan, until a dangerously beautiful woman interrupts their dinner, abruptly asking for the wooden bead. Suddenly, Patrick and Adnan are back on the case.

All roads lead to London as the mystery continues in *London Beads:* Book Two of the *Beads* Series.

For more information and a preview of the upcoming book, visit http://www.pauldparsons.com